Through the Flames of Desire

By
Brit Leigh

All rights reserved. Text Copyright © 2024 Brit Leigh.

No part of this publication may be reproduced, transmitted, or stored in an information retrieval system in any form or by any means, graphic, electronic, or mechanical, including photocopying, taping, and recording, without prior written permission from the author.

PUBLISHER'S NOTE

This is a work of fiction. Names, characters, places, and incidents either are the product of the author's imagination and experiences or are used fictitiously, and any resemblance to actual persons, living or dead, events, or locales is entirely coincidental.

Through the Flames of Desire

Chapter 1
Lexi
Chapter 2
Wash
Chapter 3
Lexi
Chapter 4
Lexi
Chapter 5
Arsonist
Chapter 6
Wash
Chapter 7
Lexi
Chapter 8
Arsonist
Chapter 9
Lexi
Chapter 10
Wash
Chapter 11
Lexi
Chapter 12

Wash

Chapter 13

Lexi

Chapter 14

Wash

Chapter 15

Lexi

Chapter 16

Lexi

Chapter 17

Arsonist

Chapter 18

Lexi

Chapter 19

Wash

Chapter 20

Wash

Chapter 21

Wash

Chapter 22

Lexi

Chapter 23

Wash

Chapter 24

Lexi

Chapter 25

Wash

Chapter 26

Arsonist

Chapter 27

Lexi

Chapter 28

Wash

Chapter 29

Lexi

Chapter 30

Wash

Chapter 31

Lexi

Chapter 32

Lexi

Chapter 33

Lexi

Chapter 34

Wash

Chapter 35

Lexi
Chapter 36
Lexi
Epilogue
Wash

Chapter 1
Lexi

I nervously bounce my leg up and down as I wait for the man of my dreams to walk into the diner. I haven't seen him since I was fifteen. It's been six years since I've seen the impeccable handsome Washington Spencer, or as he likes to go by Wash. I never thought I'd see him again. If I had pictured myself seeing him, well, it wouldn't be in the state I'm currently in. My life is in shambles. I'm twenty-one and homeless. Life went to hell after my brother, Jesse, died.

Jesse, the golden older brother who single-handedly acted like a father to me since our dad split shortly after I was born. Jesse was eleven when I was born. I was not planned at all. Dad had wanted Mom to get rid of me, but she refused. So in a classic dickhead manner, Dad left us. Jesse stepped up, helping my mom raise me while she slowly descended into her inevitable downfall.

My brother was an amazing person, and I hate that he isn't here. Six years ago, he was killed in a police chase gone wrong. Jesse was a good cop, and he saved someone, but in the process, he got himself killed. Mom damn near lost it. Jesse was only twenty-six. Still, he was just a rookie cop making a name for himself. He had plans to become a detective. His best friend, Wash, was always there for us. Wash came from a wealthy family, hence the pretentious name he got stuck with. Like my brother, Wash decided to serve the city he loved so much. However, Wash became a firefighter while Jesse became a cop. Both had big ambitions and dreams to take their careers to the top. They were two best friends, starry-eyed with the future. Then Jesse died, and it all went to shit. My mom moved us away, which meant I lost Wash. I know it's silly to have a crush on your brother's best friend, but I totally did. Wash was there for me when Jesse died. I relied on him. I would crash on his couch because my mom would drink so badly I didn't feel safe around her. Wash intervened and made my mom seek rehab. The three months I lived with Wash were amazing. I was clothed, fed, had a warm bed, and the company of the guy I swore I was going to marry one day.

I was naive to think I'd live in some fairytale where I'd be able to stay with Wash forever. To my dismay, my mother made a full recovery. In her revelations of recovery, she decided to move us from my childhood home because it was too painful for her. Wash let her take me and promised he would always be there for me. He told me I could reach out to him if I needed him, and well, I need him. I doubt he meant for me to reach out to him when I was an adult, but I'm up shit's creek right now.

My fantastic mother has relapsed more times than I can fucking count. In and out of programs and rehabs, promises she will do better, and loads of I'm a mistake thrown in. In her drunken state on several occasions, she's told me she wished I was the child that died, not Jesse. I can't live up to him and the hero he was. He had to step up and help provide for us because of me. It was my fault our dad left. Jesse would never outright say that to my face, but I could see it in his face sometimes. I knew he wasn't living a regular teenage and young adult life because of me. It was something I picked up on the older I got. I could see it. The weight of taking care of an alcoholic mother and younger sister weighed on Jesse. Still, he loved me, and I him.

This time during my mother's relapse, she got behind the wheel of a car and killed someone. She's in prison. It's been about a year since she got locked up. I've been struggling. I can't afford rent anymore on my own. My sleazy landlord had offered to give me a discount if I spread my legs for him, which I will not do because I will not stoop down to my mom's level. I'm not a virgin, but it wasn't my choice. One of my mother's shithead boyfriends decided I was his to play with. The bastard raped me and took my virginity. I haven't been with a guy since then, mainly because I have a distinct lack of trust in men, thanks to the losers my mom dated. Larry wasn't the first to touch me, but he was the only one who raped me. Still, over the years of being hit on, sexually assaulted, and raped twice by the same man, let's just say I've lost my sense of self-worth. Oh, let's not forget the verbal abuse from my mom that I'm the mistake that sent her life off the rails. I'm the reason Jesse died, too, not really, though. I had nothing to do with the police chase he was in, but Mom sure as hell thinks it's my fault. I was at school when he got killed. I have no idea how, in her insane mind, she justifies his death as my fault, but apparently, everything is my fault, so why not that too?

Wash walks in, and I quickly try to pick my mouth off the table. I don't know how it's possible, but he got hotter. His warm chocolate brown hair is styled on the short side with just enough length to run my fingers through and slightly faded on the sides. His bright blue eyes twinkle with life that I haven't felt in forever. His muscles peak out of his black t-shirt with a Firehouse ninety-one logo on it. I notice underneath it says Lieutenant under the station number. I guess he finally started working his way up the ranks. His dark wash jeans and black sneakers complete his look. I can see a tattoo peeking from under his sleeves as it pops against his porcelain skin. Damn it, why does he have to be even better looking than I remember?

Standing up, I wave to him. It's clear he is looking for me, and I doubt he expects me to pick a corner booth in the way back. He smiles once he sees me waving. Damn it, it's perfect. It's the smile that movie stars have, and it makes me want to kiss that stupid smile off his face. No kissing or touching, I remind myself. He's never gonna look at me in that way, no matter how grown up I might be now. To him, I'll always be Jesse's little sister.

"Lexi Martin, damn, you aren't little anymore." He says as he comes over, and for a minute, I think I see a flash of desire in his features, but it's gone so fast I'm not sure if I imagined it or not.

"No, not so little anymore." I agree. I'm not.

At fifteen, I wasn't fully developed, but by eighteen, my breasts had grown to a nice C cup that almost reached a D cup. Honestly depends on the bra, but either way, I'll take it. I know I'm on the thinner side from not really eating much these days. Still, I have nice curves that will surely fill out better when I put the weight back on. I know with proper meals, I'll gain it back just fine. My dark chocolate brown hair is slightly past my shoulders, and I have curtain bangs that compliment my diamond shaped face. Luckily, I'm good at doing my own hair. I know my hazel eyes and ivory skin tone complete my look. I'm average height for a girl. Wash is at least almost two heads taller than me.

We take our seats as our waitress comes over. Classic Wash orders his Coke while I order the same as him hoping the bubbles from the soda will ease the nausea coursing through me at what I have to ask. I can't believe I have to grovel to Wash. He's my last hope, the only option I have left, and I don't know what I'm going to tell him exactly. I'm not sure where to draw the line between what's too much and what's not enough. My life has been shit for the last six years, and I don't know how to finally tell another person the pain, hurt, and fear that has plagued me for far too long.

"I'm happy you reached out, Lexi. I always wonder how you are doing. After you moved, you only texted for a few months, and then you went dark. I was seriously worried about you." His voice is even, and there is slight disapproval in his tone. Guilt eats at me. I never wanted to stop talking to him.

"I'm sorry, it wasn't my doing. Mom flipped when she found out I was still talking to you," I watch his face twist in confusion because he knows my mom likes him. Sadly, he's not the problem. "Not because of you, but because of me. She was afraid I'd ruin your life like I ruined Jesse's. She erased your number and broke my phone to ensure I'd lose all contact with you. I only recently got on social media, and that was mainly to find you because I didn't know any other way to contact you. I didn't know if you even still lived in Union City." I answer honestly. I know honesty is something Wash appreciates. He's never been one to accept bullshit answers.

Through the Flames of Desire

His face twists from confusion to serious. "Lexi, be honest. Did she hurt you? How many times did she relapse?" Wash's voice oozes concern as he sits up straighter in his seat.

I sigh. "A lot, Wash. I almost got placed into foster care a few times, but being older, they didn't really want to stick an older kid in foster care who would age out of the system in a couple of years, so I just fell through the cracks of the system. Her last relapse ended with her being drunk and behind the wheel of a car. She killed someone and severely injured someone else. She's been in prison for about a year now. I'm on my own, and I'm struggling. I have no education to back me up other than high school, which I barely fucking graduated from. College never happened due to money being tight all the time. My shitty full-time job at a retail store isn't cutting it. I was fine at first, but with money going to court fees, lawyers, and other shit dealing with my mom. I'm broke. I can't afford my rent, and my landlord kicked me out because it was either pay him what I owed or sleep with him as compensation. I couldn't do that to myself. It was hard enough watching my mom do it. I'm twenty-one now, and there is no program to help me out. Trust me, I looked. If I was a minor or freshly eighteen, maybe, but not a twenty-one. I spent everything I had just to get back to Union City to meet with you. I hate to ask for your help, Wash, but I don't know what else to do." I hold back the tears threatening to spill from my eyes. I didn't think it would be this hard, and I haven't even told him the really bad shit. Fiddling my fingers on my lap as anxiety weaves through my system, wondering if Wash will help along with hating how pathetic I sound.

Wash's face is etched in concern. "Damn it. I was hoping Judy got her shit together and did right by you. I should have never let you go with her. I should have fought harder to be your guardian. I'm sorry, Lexi. You can stay with me. I have a nice three-bedroom townhouse in a nice part of the city. I will help you find a decent job and get into college if you want. I'm not going to let you drown in this." He pauses and takes a deep breath. "I need to know, Lexi, do you need to talk to someone about what you've gone through? I won't judge you if you do. I've had to see a therapist myself to cope with what I've seen as a firefighter. I know some great therapists." His voice is soft as his eyes shine with earnestness.

I sigh once more knowing damn well the answer is yes. I don't feel ashamed or embarrassed about it. I simply have dozens of thoughts swarming in my head. "I need to talk to someone. I know I have trust issues, and some bad things were done to me. It would be smart of me to talk to someone to cope with what happened, as I've been forced to push it all aside so I could survive." I answer honestly.

Wash nods his head. "Okay, I can help you get set up with a therapist. I've met some great doctors working as a firefighter and a paramedic. I'll get you hooked up with the best. Don't worry about the cost of anything. Whatever you need."

"Thank you, Wash. I really appreciate it." Relief floods me. Maybe I have a shot at actually getting my shit together.

"Of course. Anything for Jesse's little sister." I try not to cringe at those words. I don't want him to see me as Jesse's little sister or some poor pathetic girl who needs saving. Sadly, I fear that's all I'll ever be.

The waitress comes over and takes our orders. Wash, being the knight in shining armor he is, tells me to order whatever I want. Of course, he's paying because I'm not even sure I have two cents to my name. Pathetic doesn't seem to be a good enough description of how I feel right now. This is a new low to experience, and it hurts. Right now, I can't seem to think of a positive description for myself. I feel like the walking definition of a loser. No job, no home, no car, no money, and no family. Yeah, I'm a real keeper. No guy is going to want to get involved with me or cross tracks with my crazy train that has gone so far off the rails I'm not sure I can get it back on track.

After we order our food, I want to turn the topic away from my sad ass because I don't like how Wash is looking at me like a fucking wounded puppy he found in a dumpster. "So, what's been new with you? I see you made Lieutenant. That must have made you happy." I comment, nodding to his shirt.

A proud grin comes across his face. "Yeah, I was pretty happy about that. It's gotten me places. In fact, I'm actually leaving the action soon to go into fire investigations. They recruited me, and I accepted. I'll still be a fill-in if they become short-staffed for whatever reason. You came at a good time. I'll be following a more stable schedule in fire investigations, or that's the idea at least. I'll have time to help you."

"I never thought I would see the day where you left the action. You and Jesse were all about the action." I comment as I take a sip of my drink.

"Well, things change, people change, and shit happens that makes you see things differently. Part of the reason I'm headed to fire investigations is because I've been struggling since I lost a few firefighters in a bad fire. I need a break from the action for a bit. That doesn't mean I won't ever get back out there, but for now, I need time away. Wash replies as he tries to hide his sadness at the loss of his brothers.

"I'm sorry you lost some of your brothers. I know Jesse was always sad when he lost a fellow cop. You guys have a special brotherhood."

"We do. There is no denying that." Wash agrees.

"By the way, I'm grateful you are helping me. You were my last hope. I hope I'm not intruding on any girlfriends you might have. I don't want to cause issues if you have a relationship." It's the smoothest way I can think to ask if he's seeing someone.

I need to know if I have to deal with a jealous girlfriend or not. Shit, maybe even a wife. I have no clue where Wash is at in his life. As much as I want Wash to be mine, I also don't want to ruin a relationship he might already be in. I'd feel horrible crashing his life and ruining his relationship. Then I really would be the thing to ruin his life like my mom feared I would. Suddenly I feel on edge. I try to steady my breathing. I can't freak out right now. I don't need Wash thinking I'm deranged.

"I'm single, Lexi. You don't have to worry about a crazy girlfriend. I was engaged a couple of years ago, but Kate and I broke it off. She's a paramedic, so I still run into her, and it's always a disaster when that happens. It sucks that we hang out at the same spots, but like you said, it's a brotherhood, so we all support the local firefighter-owned bar. I'll have to take you to Fireball."

"They named the bar Fireball?" I ask, trying not to laugh at the slightly ridiculous name.

"I didn't say they were smart firefighters," I giggle, and Wash laughs. "The name is definitely questionable, but the drinks and people are solid. I'll take you down to station ninety-one too. I usually go down to make them my famous Mississippi pot roast."

"I forgot you like to cook. I remember Jesse would always call you when he was trying to cook. I always tried to help him, but the stubborn fool wouldn't let me. Good thing you put the fire extinguisher in the kitchen." I joke as we both laugh at the memory.

"Your brother couldn't cook for shit. God love him, the man tried," Wash says with a laugh. Damn, his laugh is sexy. It's low and rumbly. Wait, seriously, rumbly? I'm losing my mind because I can't have feelings for Wash. I can't mess this up. He's going to help me, and as much as I hate to admit it, I need his help. I need to let go of my girlish crush especially because the innocent girl who fell in love with him is gone. She's been replaced with an anxiety ridden adult with her life in shambles.

My future isn't bright if Wash doesn't help me. I'll either become a striper, a prostitute, or a drug runner. None of which provides a safe life. I can't end up like that. I have to keep my feelings in check. Maybe the therapist will help me talk through it so I don't fuck this up. I can't think with my heart right now, no matter how much it swells with joy at the man in front of me. My brain is screaming at me not to fuck this up. At least he's single, and I don't have to worry about a girlfriend. Although, his ex-fiance sounds unpleasant, and I don't want to meet her. I'm sure I will have to at some point.

We eat our food and spend time catching up. I decided to tell Wash a little bit of what happened. I told him about the losers Mom would date, how she blamed me for Jesse's death and told me she wished I died instead, and I told him about her endless string of jobs. Sometimes Mom was good, and she would keep her job for months. She had one for almost an entire year, but once she started drinking, that was it.

Of course, my life sounds like shit compared to Wash's. He's done a lot in the UCFD. He teaches courses and classes at the fire academy when they need him to. His parents still live a lavish life, but he really doesn't talk to them much anymore. From what I can tell, he's pretty wealthy independent. I doubt he even uses his parents' money anymore. Wash was always so determined to make it on his own, to prove he didn't need his parents' money to make it in life. From what I can tell, he's succeeded. Wash is accomplished, respected, and a great guy. I'm just used up trash with a shitty past. I will never fit into his world.

It's better if I look at him more like my guardian and a lot less like the man who has my heart. I can't believe he affects me this way all these years later. I tried to tell myself I was chalking my feelings up to be more than they were. That Wash was just my brother's friend, and I was so desperate to feel important to someone that I focused on Wash. I tried to tell myself I was a stupid, naive fifteen-year-old who believed her life would be better someday.

After we eat, Wash takes me to a food store. I buy myself toiletries, snacks, food I want, and whatever else I need. I don't have many clothes. I have what's in my backpack, which isn't much, but I'll get more clothes once I get a job. I don't care if I have to shop at thrift stores. There are good finds there, and I don't care if I'm seen in one. I've never been one to care about what others thought, except for Wash. He's the only person I've ever cared about what he thinks about me. I didn't even care what Jesse thought of me, and I certainly never cared what my mom thought knowing I would never be seen as good enough to her.

We head back to Wash's place. Of course, Wash has a Mustang, a nice one too. Wash and Jesse always said they would buy a Mustang. I guess Wash got his. From what I can tell, it's a special edition one too, or is customized to the T. Either way, it's nice, and if his car is nice, I can imagine his home is just as nice. By the time we get to his townhouse, it's early evening. The garage is in the back of the townhouse. Wash has an end unit. It looks like a fairly new remodeled area. The garage door opens into the kitchen. It's an open-concept kitchen, dining area, and living room. Everything is grey and white and looks fucking brand new.

"Down that door is the basement with a mini workout room. The three bedrooms, laundry room, and two full baths are upstairs. There's also a little sitting area up there." Wash tells me as he sets the bags on the small island counter.

"Your home is really nice." I compliment, suddenly feeling like Tramp from Lady and the Tramp. Jesse would read that story and watch the movie with me all the time. It was my absolute favorite childhood movie. The concept of a fancy dog falling in love with a dog off the streets appealed to me. I wanted so badly to be Lady. Looks like I'm Tramp instead.

"Thank you. The living room has a working brick fireplace. I like to light that up when it gets cold, which it should soon. Fall is turning to winter pretty quickly. I'm glad you came to me before winter hits."

"I'm just glad you didn't turn me away. I know you said if I ever needed anything to contact you, but I wasn't sure it applied to adult me." I say honestly as I help him unpack the food bags.

"Of course, it applies to adult you. From what it sounds like, things weren't easy for you. I wish you had reached earlier, but I understand why you didn't."

"It wasn't that I didn't want to. I never really had a chance to. Without your number, it took a little more to track you down. I had to end up at the library just to make a social media account. I don't have a smartphone. I have those prepaid phones. It's about all I could afford at the time, and mom never allowed me to have a smart phone anyway. I'm so used to prepaid phones, I don't even think I would know how to work a smart phone."

Of course, I wanted a smart phone. I wanted a laptop too. My mom never would buy me electronics. I think she was afraid I would get in touch with Wash for whatever crazy reason, or she thought I would post shit about her. I don't know her real reasons besides electronics cost too much money, and they do. I looked into getting a phone plan that I could afford. I was about to get one before my mom killed someone drunk driving. She talks about how I ruined her life, but the truth is she ruined my life.

"You can go on my phone plan. I have open lines. You need a reliable phone for a job. Why don't I order some takeout, and you can settle into one of the guest rooms. I don't care which one you pick," Wash offers.

"Okay, thank you again, Wash. I'm not sure how I'm ever going to repay you for everything, but I'll try. I'll help you cook and clean, whatever you need." I spit out anxiously. I don't know what to do now that I'm actually getting the help I asked for.

I feel desperate and helpless. I hate that I'm failing as an adult and as a person too. I don't want Wash to think I'm taking advantage of him. He's being so kind, and all I can think about is how I'd love to suck his dick as a way to pay him back. What is wrong with me? It was one thing when I was a naive teenager, but I'm not naive, nor am I a teenager anymore. Yet I can't help the feelings this man invokes in me.

"You lived with me before, Lexi. You were a wonderful house guest. I was honestly surprised a fifteen-year-old cleaned up so well, and I remember you baking me tasty treats. I know this is going to be longer than before, but I don't care. I'm happy to have you here with me. I was days away from getting a dog." Wash jokes.

I laugh. "So what? I'm the stray you brought home?" I joke back, trying to laugh off the fact that I am actually Tramp. Wash chuckles at my joke.

"You are far too pretty to be a stray, Lexi. Who knows, I still might end up with a dog anyway." He shrugs his shoulders. Did he just call me pretty? Get it together, Lexi.

"I wouldn't say no to you getting a dog. Doggy snuggles are the best." Even though I totally wish I could snuggle with him. Oh seriously? I need to get my hormones together. I can't have desires and feelings for Wash. Not now. How does he still affect me like this after all these years? It doesn't seem fair. I'm totally in over my head. I thought I could handle this. I need to keep my shit together.

    Wash goes about putting the food away while I go upstairs. The upstairs is huge. There is a small sitting area with a loveseat and coffee table with some book shelves nearby. I see the double doors that lead to the laundry. A door in the middle of two other doors is a full bath. On either side of the bathroom are the two guest bedrooms. The one door to the left must be Wash's room. I chose the room closer to Wash's. Silly, I know, but I want to be near him. I feel safe with him.

    For the first time in months, I feel like I can breathe. I'm not worried about anyone breaking in, a creepy landlord sneaking into my apartment while I sleep, and it's quiet here even though it's in the city. No loud neighbors, no cops being called, and no gunshots. I'm safe here. Wash won't hurt me. I know he would never take advantage of me. Although, I wouldn't care if he did. I doubt he will see me like that. Besides, a relationship is the last thing I need right now. I need to focus on getting my life together.

    Taking in the room, it's simple with a double bed and a large dresser. There is a nightstand on either side of the bed and a decent sized closet. I settle into the room by unpacking my backpack, which isn't much. By the time I head back downstairs, Wash has everything put away and has ordered us pizza.

We crash in the living room watching some action movie. We eat our pizza when it arrives while we finish our movie. Afterward, I head to take a shower and rest. I haven't had a good night's sleep in a while nor have I had a quality shower. I make sure I have all my grooming products as I turn on the hot water.

Once the shower is warmed up, I let the delightful shower wash away the worries and fears. Right now, I'm safe. I'm going to get back on my feet. Wash is back in my life, and it's like we haven't been separated for six years. I always got along with Wash. I hung out with him and Jesse as often as I could. They would indulge me from time to time. Let me hang with them and let me feel like I was part of the dynamic duo. Wash was in my life from the day I was born, and I grew up thinking I had a second brother. That was till my raging teenage hormones kicked in and I started crushing hard on him. Even now, he makes my hormones go crazy. I couldn't stop thinking about kissing him and what it would be like to be with him.

My first experiences of sex aren't really great, but I bet Wash could erase all the bad shit and replace it with something so much better. Washington was always my hero, my knight in shining armor. I don't think I'll ever stop pining after him. I'm sure he sees me as a hot mess and his best friend's little sister. I can't be more to him than that. Wash is helping me for the sake of what he thinks he owes Jesse.

I have no doubt in my mind Jesse made Wash promise to look after me if something was to ever happen to him. Jesse and Wash knew that they would be putting their lives on the line with the careers they chose. Jesse had to fear that he might not make it home one day. Even if Jesse didn't make Wash promise to look after me, Wash would do it because he's a good guy who looked at my brother like his own. They were best friends. They grew up together, knew everything about one another, supported one another, and had a type of friendship I could only hope to find one day. I never found it, though. Maybe there is still a chance that one day I will.

After a nice shower, I change into a simple T-shirt and panties. I climb into bed, feeling the exhaustion from my anxiety take its toll on my body. I'm glad Wash is going to get me help. I need to talk to someone. No doubt the rape, sexual assault, and abuse from my mom and her loser boyfriends is enough to give me years worth of therapy sessions. Not to mention losing my brother and mourning him. Sometimes I feel like I've never been able to really mourn Jesse. I've been so caught up with survival since he died that I don't think I've really properly mourned how much it hurt to lose him.

Sometimes I wonder why, if he was going to die young, why couldn't he have waited until I was at least eighteen. Then I would have been able to leave my mother behind. I would have been able to stay with Wash. That's not how it happened, though, and at the end of the day, I'd still rather Jesse be here with us. I often think about the family he would have had, the woman he would have married, and the life he could have had. His future was bright. Right now, my future is undetermined. I know Wash will help me, but I just fear I won't be able to pay him back. He's going to drop so much money, time, and resources on me. Part of me feels like I don't deserve his help, and the other part of me feels like I do.

Pushing all the swarming and all consuming thoughts from my mind, I focus on the soft mattress, the fluffy pillows, a warm place that is safe, and I get to reconnect with someone important to me. Wash is all I have left in this world. Thankfully, he's the knight in shining armor I always knew he was. I wish it was a romantic thing for us, but right now, I'll settle with being Jesse's little sister.

Chapter 2
Wash

Hearing the water turn on, I take a deep breath and exhale. Grabbing a beer from the fridge, I slip on my hoodie on and step outside on my deck. Fuck, today didn't go as planned. I was surprised when Lexi popped up on my Facebook messages. Relief washed over me knowing she was still alive. I never trusted Judy, but I never had enough against her. DSFS was convinced she was sober. I knew she wasn't. There wasn't much I could do without proof, and she was Lexi's mom, which gave her more power than it should have.

It's no secret that Judy started losing her touch as a parent when Jesse and Lexi's father, Jerry, walked out. Jesse stepping up was huge. He supported his mother's choice to keep his baby sister. Jesse didn't understand until we were older what his father was really asking. I can't believe he asked Judy to get an abortion. Judy chose her child, but over the years, it became clear she regretted it. She struggled as a single mother. Their father was horrible at paying child support. Jesse started working as soon as he could. I gave money where I could, but I was limited because I was a kid myself. Even as an adult, I tried to help them, but by then, it became a point of pride for Jesse to not accept money.

Right before Jesse died, I told him he better be prepared to use his gun on the boys that were going to be swarming his sister soon. Even then, I could tell Lexi was going to be a looker, a classic heart throb that would have the guys asking for her number. I was right. I almost couldn't control my dick when I first saw her. Her profile picture was simple and a little blurry. Seeing her in person, well fuck. She is definitely not little anymore.

Now the pretty thing is under my roof, and I have to control myself. I know I'm good looking, and I'm used to girls tossing themselves at me. I haven't hurt for sex or dates. I took a break from dating after Kate and I broke off our engagement. That was a doomed relationship from the start. We worked together. She was a paramedic on the ambo in my station. She isn't anymore. She transferred after we got engaged and stayed away after we ended things. That was a few years ago. I'm not sure why I ever proposed to Kate. Probably because everyone was putting pressure on us. Both sets of parents were desperate for their child to marry. Since my epic failed engagement, I've just done one-night stands.

It's not that I don't want to settle down, but I haven't met the right woman yet. No one I meet strikes my fancy. Not even Kate really got my blood pumping. Kate is pretty, but I could not stand her need to be in control of everything as I like to be in control especially in the bedroom. Then I see Lexi after six years all grown up, and I can't seem to stop thinking about all the things I want to do to her. I realize how familiar she feels to me. She might have been a teenager, and I did watch her grow up, but still, I can't deny the attraction. However, I can only imagine the shit Judy put her through. I don't know everything she went through, and I'm not sure I want to. I'm glad she is willing to get help. That's a positive sign.

Part of me was afraid I'd have to fight her on certain things like doctors, therapists, and possibly medication. However, Lexi is level-headed. She wants to get back on her feet. She isn't mooching off me, and she isn't using me. Not that I think she would, but I don't know what Judy instilled in her. However, Lexi has always rebelled against her mom. I know Jesse did his best to raise Lexi, but at the end of the day, he was a child himself. Judy sucked at parenting even before her husband left. Judy was that mother who is great at putting on a show to everyone else, but I saw how she neglected Jesse and later on how she did the same thing with Lexi. Judy had no problem letting Jesse help and take over with Lexi. Jesse was more her father than her brother. We are only eleven years older than Lexi. It's not that much when you think about it. We were older kids when she was born, but still kids. Jesse grew up faster than he should have. It would seem Lexi has also been forced to grow up faster than she should have.

    Lexi is trying to get her life together. The last thing she needs is me trying to date her or have sex with her. She needs me to help her get things on track. Help her find a job, gain savings, and maybe get her into college. She needs support and a friend, not a boyfriend. Still, it's hard to deny the burning desire I have for her. This is dangerous. She's living with me now. I risk catching feelings for her, and I can already see that happening with how she makes me feel. No one has ever been able to get such a strong reaction out of me when it comes to sex. I want her under me, screaming my name as I bring her to pleasure over and over again. Fuck, I'm going to need a lot of cold showers to keep myself in check.

I pull out my phone and text Hunter and Kevin. They are my best friends since we started the fire academy together. I'll need their advice on this one. Hunter ended up working fire investigations after a bad accident in a fire caused him to not be physically fit to firefight anymore, so he moved on over to the white shirt's territory. Kevin and I stayed on truck, and each worked our way to squad. Kevin is staying at the station. No matter what Kevin sees, no matter who he loses, he is always ready to get back out there. I don't know how he processes it and moves on so quickly, but he does. This time around, I couldn't get past the loss. I know I'm not responsible for what happened to my fellow brothers, but the guilt that I survived and they didn't eats at me. Survivor's guilt, it's a real fucking thing, and so is PTSD. I need a break from the action. It pains me to admit that, but fire investigations has been trying to get me over to their department for years now ever since I impressed the Chief fire investigator by helping him with a case no one else could figure out. They were more than thrilled to take me on.

Seems like it's all the right timing for this career move. Lexi will benefit from me having a stable schedule. I'll be able to get her set up and stabilized easier. The doctors and therapists are easy. The job shouldn't be too hard either. All I need to know is what she wants to do. Does she want something more stable and full-time, or is she looking for part-time work and less commitment so she can pursue college. The truth is, I don't know Lexi anymore. It's been six years. While I might be mostly the same person, I don't know if that can be said for Lexi. Whatever she had to deal with was not easy. I will say it's nice how well we slipped back into being friends. I guess we've always been friends on some level. I just happen to be her guardian as well.

"There you are." I hear Lexi's sweet voice from behind.

I turn on my heels and face her as I lean on the railing of the deck. "All cleaned up?" I ask, taking a sip of my beer.

"Yeah. I feel like a person again. I tried to fall asleep, but my mind is refusing to take a break. I figured I'd come see what you were up to." She smiles as she shivers slightly. She's in sweatpants and a T-shirt.

"You need a jacket, Doll?" I have no idea why I just called her doll, but the slight red blush to her cheeks and her small smile suggests she liked it.

"Yeah, it is getting cold at night now. I guess I need to get serious about hoodies and maybe a light jacket. The first paycheck I get, I'll have to do some shopping." Lexi states, rubbing her arms.

"I'll get you what you need, Doll. Whatever you need, it's yours. You're going to need clothes for interviews, too," I take my hoodie off and toss it to her. "Put it on before you get sick. Your hair is wet, you definitely should be bundled up."

Lexi catches the hoodie and quickly slips it on. Fuck, I do like seeing her in my clothes. "Thank you, Mr. Paramedic." She says with a smirk.

"Be lucky I'm not a doctor." I joke.

My parents wish I was a doctor. Actually, what they really wanted was for me to follow my father's footsteps and carry on the family business of politics. My dad is a well respected and sought after political campaign manger. My dad's family is filled with politicians from mayors, governors, senators, and more. It's bad enough they stuck me with one of the most pretentious names they could come up with. They claim they named me Washington because they met in Washington DC while attending college, but I think they just wanted to name me something pretentious. They were not happy when I came up with my nickname. I made sure it stuck too, which added to their displeasure.

"Well, then you would just be insufferable." Lexi jokes back, coming closer to me.

I laugh at her remark. Alright, well, she's still a ball-buster. "You're probably right." I set my beer down on the ledge and wrap her in my arms. Her hazel eyes stare up at me. "Still cold, Doll?"

"I was, but you're really warm, so I'm all better now. I think you're just what the demanding paramedic firefighter ordered." Lexi takes another crack at me. Damn, I really have missed her. Even watching a movie was nice with her. Natural.

"Is that so?" I inquire as I raise an eyebrow at her. She nods her head up and down. "Well, if that's the case, I have some other orders for you too."

"Oh, really now?" She asks, snuggling more into me as she rubs her body against mine.

Fuck, I want to kiss her. Her soft sweet pink lips are begging me to kiss them. I can't. The girl hasn't even been back in my life for twenty-four hours. I'm not a predator, but shit, she makes me want to be one. Her hazel eyes sparkle with desire. If I didn't know better, this little vixen wants me like I want her. Now isn't the time. I need to show restraint. I can do this.

Deciding against telling her that I suggest she comes to bed with me so I can fuck her pretty body to oblivion and back, I decide to stick with a safer option. "Yes, like you should get some sleep. I'm sure you are tired from traveling. I have some melatonin that might help you sleep." I suggest instead.

"I am tired. It was a ten hour bus ride." She comments as she tries to hide a yawn by looking down.

"I didn't think you moved that far away, or did you have to move again?" I question. They were only moving to the state line. It should have only been about four hours.

"We moved a lot, Wash. Bouncing around from town to town. Going to different states. Leaving apartments in the middle of the night so Judy didn't have to pay rent. She changed her name and had fake IDs to cover her ass. Any money I made when I got a job went to whatever she thought it should be used for. I couldn't stop her. I tried. I tried to save and tried to pay our bills on time, but none of it mattered. Our last landlord was a sleazeball, so he let Judy get by without paying him rent because once a month, she let him fuck her. When Judy got arrested and tossed in prison, I was finally able to stay on top of shit. That didn't last long due to court fees and lawyers to try and get her sentence reduced. Before I knew it, creepy Marvin was offering me the same deal. I thought the streets would be better, but I knew it wouldn't be. Judy and I spent a few months on the streets at one point. It wasn't pretty. By the time I decided to find you, I had been on the streets for about a week. I spent all I had to buy the bus ticket. Just a week of sponge baths, and I'm already happy I have an actual shower, bed, and food. Thank you, Wash. Really, I don't know what I'd do without you." Lexi informs me. Shit, things sound like they were bad. I don't even know if that is the worst of what Lexi experienced.

"I'm sorry, it was hard for you. I'd ask how Judy got around DCFS, but I have a good idea of how. She was always charming and knew exactly what to say to get her out of shit. I'm happy to help you, Doll. I'm also glad you didn't sleep with that landlord. You're far too pretty to be sleeping with losers. You're with me now, so you don't have to worry about creepy landlords or other creepers. They come near you. Well, let's just say I know how to set fire to shit and make it look like an accident." I state seriously. Too much? Eh, maybe, but I think Lexi needs to feel protected. Judging by what she has told me, she hasn't felt safe since she was forced to leave me six years ago.

"I know that comment should probably freak me out, but it doesn't. It's comforting to know I have someone looking out for me. I haven't had that, well, since the last time I lived with you." Her voice is soft and quiet like she's afraid if she speaks too loudly, it will cause me to slip away from her.

"I'll always look out for you and protect you, Doll. Come on, it's getting cold out here, and we need to sleep. I'll grab you the melatonin and leave it in your bathroom if you want it." I state, letting go of her. I miss her body against mine. Fuck this is going to be hard. Cold showers are going to become my best friend.

"Thank you. By the way, I like it when you call me Doll. Goodnight, Wash." Lexi says as she kisses me on the cheek. It's adorable she's on her tippy toes. I'd much rather she be kissing other body parts other than my cheek, but that is not happening tonight.

"Goodnight, Doll. I'll get you up in the morning. I'm off tomorrow, so we can go shopping."

"You spoil me, Wash." She replies as we walk inside and head toward the stairs after I lock the sliding door.

"Well, a pretty girl like you deserves to be spoiled. Plus, I care a lot about you, Doll. Always have and always will. Now go get some sleep." I say, smacking her playfully on her ass.

"You really are demanding." She comments.

"Get that pretty ass of yours up the stairs and in bed before I punish you." I threaten.

"Tempting, but I'm not sure I'm ready for the punishments we both secretly have in mind. When I am, well, I'll be sure to not listen to your demands. Goodnight, Wash." She says as she blows me a kiss. Lexi saunters her sexy ass up the stairs tempting me to run after her and pull her into my bed.

I don't even respond. I'm honestly shocked she confirmed that she is interested in me. What did she mean she isn't ready? What the hell happened to her? I won't pretend I'm blind to how Lexi feels. It was obvious she had a crush on me six years ago. I'm surprised she still carries a torch for me. I assumed she'd have a boyfriend, but if she did, why the fuck would she run to me then? I don't think she is dating anyone. We are both single, and that can lead to a road I'm not sure either of us are ready to jump on.

After I'm sure Lexi is in her room, I head up the stairs and leave the melatonin on her bathroom counter. I notice she picked the room closest to me. I'm not sure if she did that to feel safe or because she really wants to be close to me. She was all too eager for my embrace, and her flirty little comments along with her body language, indicate she's interested in me like I am her. Still, I can't be that jerk. I can't prey on her while she is vulnerable. Her life is in shambles. Her mother is in prison, her father walked out at her birth, and her brother is dead. She's alone, and I'm all she has left. I can't fuck that up with sex or a relationship no matter how badly I want her. She needs support and a friend, not a horny boyfriend who wants to enjoy her body.

I take one hell of a cold shower to calm my ass down. Hunter and Kevin haven't gotten back to me yet. I'm trying to meet them for drinks. However, I have to make sure Lexi is okay here by herself. I know I don't need a reason to hang out with my friends. I don't owe her an explanation, and I sure as hell can't tell her I need to meet with them because I can't control my dick around her. I don't think I've ever had to take a cold shower before because I couldn't fuck the woman I wanted.

Lexi is a big girl. As long as she is comfortable here by herself, I can go out with the guys for a few drinks. I have to make a lot of phone calls tomorrow for her. I have to get her set up with Dr. Daniels ASAP. He's a great psychiatrist and therapist. It's rare to find someone who does both. Most just pick one or the other, but not Daniels. He's a huge help to the first responders in our city. He's great with PTSD and tough situations. He will be able to help Lexi. I have no doubt she has some form of PTSD. The way she lost Jesse and the treatment from her mother, well, it's enough to send any sane person off the rails. That doesn't include all the other shit she's been through, and I have a feeling I don't even know the worst of it.

I also need to get her a wellness check. No doubt she hasn't had a regular doctor's visit in years. Lexi needs to make sure she is healthy physically, mentally, and emotionally before she really claims her life back. I know how important it is for mental and physical health to be good. I know we all struggle, and sometimes we need help. Hell, I've had my fair share of therapy sessions and doctor appointments. It can't hurt to have her checked out on all fronts.

Then, once her health is sorted out, I'll focus on finding her a job. I'll have to feel her out for what she wants, but I know a lot of people in the city. A good portion owes me, and I have no problem calling in a favor for Lexi. I wasn't lying when I said she's important to me. She always has been. She was my best friend's little sister, and while some would think that's how I would view her, too, I never did. I've never seen her as my little sister. She was always just Jesse's baby sister.

When I was younger, she was just another kid we played with, but the older she got, the more I saw her in a friend way. Now, well now, I see her as a potential girlfriend. Someone I'd actually consider marrying. Crazy, but not really when you take into account how long we have known each other. Yes, dating would be different, but at the same time, our foundation is strong.

The problem is I can't look at Lexi like that, not now. Maybe when she is a bit more on her feet. I also don't want to make moves when she is vulnerable. I don't want her to regret being with me. At least she is able to admit out loud she isn't fully ready for whatever might develop between us, but that doesn't mean she doesn't want it. I can only assume she is willing to wait this out with me. I don't see either of us jumping to go on any dates any time soon.

Recently I have been enjoying single life, waiting for the right woman to walk into my life. Well, she didn't walk into my life that's for sure. More like crashed back into my life like a train off the rails trying desperately to get back on track. At least she came to me. I would have liked her to come to me sooner, but I know Judy made that hard for her. At first, when she told me Judy didn't want her talking to me, I was insulted. I took Lexi in when Judy couldn't take care of her. Who was she to act like she was better? Then Lexi told me it was because Judy didn't want her to ruin my life like she ruined Jesse's. That pissed me off, and I wanted to punch Judy in the face. I don't condone punching women, but sometimes it needs to be done to women who hurt their fucking kids.

The hurt in Lexi's eyes when she told me that, or really anytime she talks about Judy, crushes my heart. My mother may have not been the greatest mom, but at least she tried. My mom comes from old southern money, and she breeds races horses for a hobby along with running her own fucking stables.They weren't thrilled that I picked a dangerous career. Although, they don't shy away from using our son's a hero when it benefits them.

They couldn't fight me on it as it was a solid career. I planned on moving up, and I have over the years. I made Lieutenant, which was huge. I also became a paramedic, which isn't too unheard of. Many firehouses have ambos, especially in the city. Not only that, but you need basic life-saving skills anyway, so many get interested in being a paramedic that way. I did it because it gave me versatility within the firehouse. Strange to think I'll be moving out of the firehouse and to headquarters. I can't deny the part of me that is fascinated with fire investigations. Fire investigations get brought in anytime foul play is suspected. I'll have to work a bit more with the police, which is fine. I honestly know most of them one way or another. Even in a decent sized city, the first responders all seem to know each other somehow, which goes to show the world really is a small place.

After my regretful but needed cold shower, I hop out and dry off. I slip my black boxers on. I decided to check on Lexi to make sure she is okay. Lexi is passed out asleep. She's curled in a ball under the covers. I smile at how innocent and cute she looks. While she is cute, I doubt she has much of her innocence left. It seems we tend to lose our innocence faster than ever these days. Satisfied that Lexi is good, I head back to my room and climb into bed. Getting comfortable, I try to clear my thoughts and not think about Lexi. However, there is no denying the joy I feel that she is back in my life. There is no denying the attraction between us that I was hoping was just my imagination. It's not. The fire between us might just set everything on fire around us, and I'd light the match myself if it meant she was mine.

Chapter 3

Lexi

The sun coming through the curtains wakes me from my deep sleep. Rolling to my back, I stretch under the warmth of the blankets, refusing to open my eyes just yet. I collect my thoughts as they start swarming around in my head. I'm in Wash's townhouse. Damn, that man is fine, and last night on the deck, I don't know what that was, Then I remind myself that I'm the literal last person Wash would find sexy. I'm just a little sister to him, although I don't think Doll is a normal nickname for a sister. So, maybe I'm not a little sister.

What if Wash is interested in me? Would it be worth exploring? Oh, who am I kidding? It would totally be worth exploring. Wash is my literal dream guy, and I've been pining after him for six fucking years. I'd be insane not to take the chance to date him. I'd say it's not a good time with my life being in total shambles, but then again, there is never a right time to start a relationship. Why give up a shot at a relationship with my dream guy just because my life's in shambles? Dream guys like Wash do not fall in your lap more than once.

    Still, I'm not sure if I'm just reading into things that aren't there. Wash and I only reconnected yesterday, even though it feels like no time has passed. I know time has passed. I know I'm slightly different from the bright eyed girl he saw last. I'm jaded in many ways, but I'd like to feel alive again. I know I can feel alive again. I'm finally free of my mother and her toxicity that has plagued my life for far too long. She's rotting away in prison. There is nothing I can do for her, and honestly, I don't want to help her. My mother deserves what she got. She made a bad choice and killed someone. Even if it was an accident, she fucked up in a way she can't really come back from.

    I might not be able to help my mother, but I can sure as hell help myself. I can stay with Wash where I'm safe. I will get a job and start saving to be independent. I might even think about college if I can figure out what I want to do.

Sometimes I think I'm just not a school person. I'd blame my mom for my lack of love toward school, but this one is on me. Maybe I can find a trade to do instead. There are so many things I can do that don't have to result in college.

First, I'm going to talk to someone about all the shit that has happened to me. I know I have PTSD and serious trust issues. Trust issues are part of the reason I haven't tried to date. I used to use the rape and sexual assault as reasons, but I realized not every guy had bad intentions. When I stopped using the rape and sexual assault as reasons not to date, I found myself questioning the guys who took me on dates for other reasons. I didn't trust them for one reason or another. I struggled to feel comfortable doing things with them. I never let things lead to sex. As much as I wanted a good memory when it came to sex, I couldn't bring myself to have sex with someone I didn't trust. Trust is very important when it comes to sex for me. I can't do one night stands. I need commitment, trust, and desire. All three don't seem to happen all at once, except for one man. Fucking Washington Spencer. The one man I can't let myself think of in that way, but damn it, I can't help myself.

I roll out of bed because I'm tired of my endless thoughts already, and I need to get my ass moving anyway.

One minute I'm thinking positive, and the next minute I'm shitting on myself. Yeah, I need a vast amount of therapy to work through my issues. I have crazy train written in bold letters on my forehead. Grabbing my only pair of jeans, a short sleeve dark purple shirt with fresh panties, and my very worn out bra, I make my way to the guest bathroom. I brush my teeth, thankful to have a toothbrush. You never really miss the small things until you don't have them anymore. If anything, all of this has taught me to be grateful for everything, even little things like a toothbrush.

After I'm dressed, I grab my worn out sneakers and a pair of socks that have seen better days. Damn, I really need new shit. Wash is taking me shopping today. I would protest, but Wash is just going to buy my shit anyway. I know better than to try and tell that man no. I learned that years ago when I was a kid. Wash would always spoil me even then. Jesse would get so mad at Wash because he would buy my stuffed animals, toys, and as I got older gadgets. Jesse would scold Wash, telling him he spoiled me far too much. Wash would never listen.

The last time when I stayed with Wash he bought me clothes, shoes, stuff for school, books, and just about anything I needed or wanted. Somehow I have a feeling Wash will be doing something similar this time around. Wash is generous and also very smart with his money.

Even six years ago, I remember Wash was making smart moves with his money. I'm more than sure he has different types of investments. He is someone I'm glad will be helping me get financially stable because Wash is good with money. He knows how to save it, he knows how to spend it wisely, and he knows when to use it to spoil the shit out of me. Wash is going to end up giving me a pampered day out, and I'm not about to stop him or complain about it. If Wash wants to spoil me, I'm not going to do a damn thing to stop him because he will just do it anyway. Plus, I can't deny it sounds nice. What girl doesn't want to be spoiled rotten by a handsome man? I do, and I'm going to enjoy it while I have it because I know good things can easily disappear.

Heading downstairs, I find Wash dressed in jeans and a black hoodie with UCFD on it in dark red letters. There are flames in the background of the letters. Wash has on his black vans, meaning he is ready to walk out the door. Wash only wears shoes inside when he's about to leave. One might think it's odd that I remember that detail about Wash, but I'm secretly not so secretly in love with him and have been for a long time.

"Good Morning, Doll. Are you ready?" Wash asks with a million-dollar smile that is swoon worthy on every level.

"Yeah, I'm ready when you are," I reply.

"Good, let's head out. The first stop is coffee at your favorite coffee shop."

"Cool Beans is still in business?" I ask as we head out the door leading to the garage.

I loved this privately owned coffee shop called Cool Beans. They hand make everything from their coffee, to their syrups, pastries, and teas. The place is always packed. There is a cute seating area for people to enjoy their goodies, but many people get their stuff to go. At least, that's how it was when I was there last. Jesse and Wash would take me there after school for hot chocolate and a cookie on the days Mom was having a bad day. Wash would buy us our drinks and cookies. He was always treating Jesse and me whenever he could. Seems like today is going to be no different.

We hop in Wash's car and head downtown, where Cool Beans is located. Leave it to Wash to live only twenty minutes from my favorite coffee shop. As I got older, hot chocolate slowly got exchanged for mochas or cappuccinos. Of course, it's been awhile since I've had a fancy coffee like a cappuccino, and I am looking forward to going to one of my favorite places from childhood. Cool Beans and this one pizzeria that Jesse worked at for a bit were my favorite places growing up.

Entering the coffee shop after we park, I'm shocked to find the place is pretty much the same. Besides a few new tables or chairs in the seating area, there isn't much that's changed. The register is at the back of the shop. Dozens of different syrups line the back wall with various coffee machines, milk steamers, blenders, and espresso machines set up on a counter under the shelves of syrups. The two front counters on either side of the register are lined with baked goods. They have just about every breakfast pastry you can think of. They even have seasonal favorites. With Thanksgiving around the corner, they have pumpkin flavored stuff. I do enjoy a good pumpkin drink, but right now, I want something classic. It's been so long since I've had a good mocha cappuccino. Now do I want a blueberry muffin or a cinnamon chip scone?

The line is long, but it moves quickly. Before I know it, Wash and I are at the register getting ready to place our orders. "Good Morning, welcome to Cool Bean. What can I get you?" A very chipper blonde haired girl asks. Her hair is in pigtails, and the Southern charm comes off of her in waves. I keep forgetting that even though Union City is a large city, it's in the south, and not even the stink of the city can dampen the Southern hospitality.

"Hey, Meg, hope you are doing well?" Wash greets back.

Wash has always been very polite. I've been astounded by how Wash treats other people given it would be very easy for him to be a rich stuck up asshole like his family. Wash's family are the type of people who look down at the little folks. They have money, status, and power. They rule the well-oiled streets of Union City. Wash's family doesn't live in the city, but in the suburbs in a beautifully restored old southern manor complete with pillars, a fountain, and a balcony in the front of the house. It's beautiful, and I used to always find a reason to go swimming at their house in the summer. The beautiful flower garden that Wash's mom, Ilene, is anal about made me feel like I could be a princess. Their home has been featured in several magazines and TV shows. People pay them to film movies and shit in their house or property. Their property is all private and the literal perfect old southern manor, complete with a lake in the background and the horses that they breed as a hobby. It's picture-perfect.

"I'm good, Wash. You want your usual?" The perky blonde named Meg asks Wash.

Through the Flames of Desire

"Yes, please, and whatever my friend wants." Wash replies with a smile.

"Can I get a medium mocha cappuccino and a blueberry muffin, please." I order.

"Add two cinnamon scones too. Everything to go, please." Wash adds, and I stare at him, slightly dumbfounded. "What? You love them, and you need to eat, plus I'm totally stealing some." Wash says, shrugging his shoulders as he hands Meg his credit card.

"Thank you, Wash." I say, nudging his arm with mine as we walk off to the pickup area.

"Of course, Doll. After this, we are heading to the mall. You have a lot of shopping to do, and no money isn't a problem, so buy everything and anything you want and need. I'm serious, Lexi."

"I know you are. I know better than to tell you no, Mr. Lieutenant." I joke in a bratty tone.

That's the problem. I know he is serious, and while I want to enjoy being spoiled, I can't help but feel pathetic that I need a wealthy man to bail me out. One very hot, wealthy man. I have to stop myself from thinking dirty thoughts. I don't know if it's the fact that I've been denying myself any real sexual pleasure for a while now and I'm just in overdrive, or Wash really does have this crazy effect on me that shouldn't feel real. However, it's very real, and being confronted with it is overwhelming. I guess it was easier to ignore my feelings for Wash when I wasn't near him.

"At least you're learning that denying me is a waste of time." Wash jokes back in a slightly seductive way that has me questioning if I've lost my mind.

"Jesse always said you spoiled me." I quickly retort.

"Jesse forgets I spoiled him too, although I never really looked at it as spoiling you guys. You were two were people I cared about, and I wanted you guys to be happy like I was. We both can agree I was happy because my parents left me alone to do my own thing and let me spend whatever amount of money I wanted. I mean, seriously, who lets a sixteen year old have control over his own bank account? They are just lucky they at least raised me to be smart about money. That's about all they taught me. You and Jesse were different. You wanted your parents around, but they ended up disappointing you, and hurting you."

"You really never wanted your parents around?" I ask, hoping I'm not prying into a sensitive topic.

"Maybe when I was a kid, but I quickly realized I was better off without them being so involved in my life. I let them focus on my sister, who is literally the perfect child. Beauty pageants, business school, engaged by twenty-four and married by twenty-five. She literally is everything my parents made her to be, and she loves every part of it. I am the black sheep of my family. I know that seems insane because I'm the most normal out of my cliche family, but I am the black sheep because I didn't follow in my daddy's footsteps, or at least do something they deemed worthy. They spent so long ignoring me that when they tried to control my life, they found they had lost their control over me. I became my own person, and they don't like that." Wash's answers honestly. He's clearly had to explain this before.

Our drinks are called, and we grab them. I take note of what Wash ordered. "Since when do you drink cappuccinos?" Changing the topic to something lighter because I don't know if I can handle where this serious conversation is headed.

Wash chuckles. "You actually got me into them. I sometimes switch it up with a regular coffee or a cold brew, but you were right, Cappuccinos are the best." He answers as we walk out of the coffee shop. I smile at him. Jesse was all about Americanos and black coffee. He never understood my need for milk and flavor in my coffee. Not that I got to drink coffee a lot when Jesse was alive. I was still a teen, and coffee was only allowed when absolutely needed. Still, Jesse and I would argue over the better coffee. Wash would be oddly silent and never add his opinion. Now, I know why. Jesse would have been livid if Wash picked my side. I know Jesse saw Wash as only his friend. I was the annoying tag along.

We sit on a bench on the street and dig into our scones, and split the blueberry muffin. For a moment, we don't say anything, just enjoy our food and drink while the cool breeze of the morning rustles everything in its path. Luckily it's not a bitter breeze, but this is one of those warmer fall days. The temps have been dropping more and more at night. I wouldn't have lasted out on the streets very long. One never knows the type of winter the South will get. Sometimes it's like an extended fall and early spring. Other times it's cold for a few months where temps dip to the mid-thirties. With the way the winters have been in the past, we will probably end up with a mix of warmer weeks and colder weeks that alter on and off until spring officially makes its appearance with the pollen that will coat everything.

"This is better than I remember," I comment as I take a bite of my scone.

"I knew you would enjoy it. I come here almost every morning for my caffeine fix. I get a treat from time to time, but I usually eat on the healthier side. I have to keep fit to fight fires. Even with my move to fire investigations, keeping fit has just become my lifestyle."

"You were always pretty fit even before you became a firefighter. I remember Jesse was the baseball star, but you were the track and field hockey star. You two were such jocks." I jokingly recall.

Wash rolls his eyes. "It's not our fault you didn't like sports. You were always buried in a library book. Did you say you wanted to write children's books at one point?"

"I did. I thought I could write and illustrate the books. I'm good at cartoon-like drawing, but that's about it. I still like reading. The library was my favorite place. It was warm, and the smell of old books made me feel safe. The librarians would always give me snacks and give me older books that they were going to get rid of for whatever reason. Jesse would leave me there knowing I'd be safe while he went to his afternoon job mowing lawns and washing cars before he got his job at the pizza place."

"Well, I guess we are getting you some books to read while we are out today. We can get some journals and art stuff if you want to. I have a feeling you're going to need a creative outlet. While you are shopping, I will be making phone calls for appointments and maybe some jobs if you want to start work right away. You don't have to work right away, Lexi. If you need to take time to deal with your health, you can. You won't be able to really get back on your feet if you don't start to heal from your past."

"Thank you, Wash. I want to work, but let's keep it simple and part-time. There's no rush to find the perfect job right away, but there's no harm in looking. I need to see a therapist. I know that. I would also like to see a primary care doctor and gynecologist, you know, to cover my basics." Did I really just say gynecologist to Wash? Oh, who cares? The man is a paramedic and firefighter. I don't think things like gynecologists weird him out.

"Okay. I think that's a great start." Wash agrees.

We finish our food and drink, reminiscing about the old days and Jesse. It's hard for us not to bring up Jesse. He comes up consistently, even with little things. He was such a huge part of our life, especially mine. He was my older brother who gave up so much to raise me. Jesse was my hero. Wash and Jesse considered each other brothers. I always assumed Wash looked at me like a sister while I looked at him as my dream guy. Now, I'm starting to feel like Wash returns my feelings, but I'm a little crazy. So who knows. For now, I need to focus on keeping things chill while I figure my shit out.

Once we are done, we head to the mall. I haven't been to the mall in forever. I didn't really enjoy going to the mall even though it was a place to hang out for teens. Wash, Jesse, and I didn't really grow up in the city, but we visited it a lot. Our little hometown of Everton, which is in the suburbs. It's a large town with lots of hometown southern feels with a town square in the downtown area of the town. Union City is only thirty minutes away on the highway. I always loved the ability to be in the countryside or in the hustle and bustle of the city with a short ride.

Wash was determined to get out of our town and live in the city where he wasn't as well known even though his family still has influence in the city. Wash's parents are very well-known in our hometown. I remember going out with him and Jesse all over town, and everywhere we went, Wash was noticed. The Spencers are like southern royalty in our town, and Wash hates it. Wash has done everything to break away from his parents and the mold that they tried to form for him.

I admire Wash and his ability to tell his parents to fuck off. I never cared much for knowing my dad. He left and wanted my mom to abort me. I think I'm better off not knowing that asshole. However, with my mom, I wanted her to love me like she did Jesse. I wanted to be worthy in her eyes because I felt like I was the reason her life was ruined. I can't count the times I wished I was never born so that my family would have been spared the burden of me. I can't blame myself, it wasn't my fault my dad didn't want me, but I do blame myself. I blame myself all the time for ruining my family. At this point my mother's verbal abuse is deeply rooted in my soul. I'm going to need years of therapy to work past it.

Arriving at the mall, we park in the parking garage. In our hometown, we have a lot of shopping centers. Nice ones too, with fountains, pretty flowers, sculptures, and other things to make them unique. The main shopping center would often host things for different holidays. Trick or treating around the shopping center, going in the stores to get candy, followed by some type of fun activity of sorts. If it was Christmas time, Santa would show up at the main shopping center to take pictures. Everton is a huge on town community, and family values run high.

It was a good place to grow up, and there are times I miss it. Then there are times I don't miss it. It's nice avoiding people who know my family. It's awkward when people bring up my dad, it's depressing when people bring up Jesse, and it's annoying when they bring up Mom. Sometimes I like not being known, and I get the appeal Wash sees to living in the city. It's large, so much larger than our town. Union City is a large city, but not on a scale like Atlanta, Charleston, or Nashville, but it's still large. I'm not sure I'd want to live in a major city, but so far, I'm not minding Union City. It was always fun to visit growing up. An escape away from the boring suburbs that really weren't that boring. Living here is different from visiting, but so far, I'm not minding it.

Entering the mall, I decide it's best to start with basics, so I head to the lingerie store. I can't try on clothes without a proper bra on. I also hate clothing shopping and would much rather stall by going lingerie shopping. I enter the store, but I notice Wash hesitates.

"Please tell me the tough firefighter isn't intimidated by a lingerie store." I taunt softly, bridging the gap between us as we stand in the rather large entryway.

"It's not that. I wasn't sure you would want me to accompany you in such a store."

"Wow, could you be any more of a gentleman? I didn't think men still had such manners." I comment.

"Well, I guess my momma did teach me something after all. I might be a gentleman in public, but that doesn't mean I'm one in bed." Wash winks, and my mouth drops open slightly before I promptly shut it. "So, do you want me to come in with you, or would you like my card, and I'll wait out here for you," Wash asks, closing the ever so small gap that is left between us. His mouth is so close, too close.

"I do need someone to model for, you know, make sure I have the right size and all," I teasingly reply as I gather my composure. I know how to play with fire and two can play the flirt game. I'm not entirely sure where my confidence to be all flirty with a man, let alone with fucking Wash, is coming from, but I'll take it.

"I'm not so sure I'm the person you want for that job. I'm more skilled at taking lingerie off than knowing whether or not it's the right size." Wash counters.

Oh fuck. I might have let the fire get out of hand. I'm not sure I can play this game, but fuck it. If I'm going down, I might as well enjoy the burn on the way there. "Well, come on, Mr. Firefighter." I say, taping his chest lightly with my fingers before I turn on my heels and head back into the store.

Wash follows me in. Turns out all our little flirting was for nothing. After a few minutes of walking around, one of the employees found me. She measured me and made her suggestions. Now I'm in the dressing room surrounded by a pile of fucking bras. I start trying on the different styles and slowly eliminate the ones I don't like. I make a pile of the ones I do like. I get all basic colors like black and nude. I add in a sexy red one and a lace underline bra with matching sexy panties. Hey, I might not have been able to model for Wash right now, but I'm sure as hell hoping I do one day.

It's crazy to think that he has the power to heal my fractured heart. That somehow, he is a superhero capable of making me forget my screwed-up past. Everything that happened with my mom over the last six years, every single unpleasant part, is finally in the past. I've wanted to leave my mother behind for so long, but somehow I was chained to her. Her getting herself locked up is the best damn thing to happen to me. Dark? Yeah, a little, but I'm not innocent. I'm tainted and broken on levels I'm not sure I fully understand.

I can't help my insane heart and how it still yearns for Wash. I thought with time and space, my feelings would disappear, but they haven't. I almost hate how strong they are. I hate the pull I feel toward him. I hate how natural everything feels with him. I don't know why I hate it. Maybe I don't think I deserve it. Maybe there is a part of me terrified that the dream won't meet the reality. I'm used to not being hopeful and for things to end in disaster. Maybe just this once, things won't totally burn to ash. Guess it's a good thing Wash is a firefighter.

We hop around to different stores, and I lose track of time as Wash becomes my personal bag carrier. He ran to the car once already. I didn't realize all the things I needed. I knew it was a lot, but I didn't think it was this much. Of course, Wash keeps adding his own additions to the piles insisting that I get everything my heart desires. Wash is spoiling the shit out of me, and part of me loves it, while the other part of me is afraid I'm living in a coma and this is a blissful dream.

Chapter 4
Lexi

A little after two in the afternoon, Wash and I end up in the food court. I'm starving, but I manage to eat my food like a normal human being and not a crazed person. We have done a lot of shopping. I'm grateful to Wash for everything. I seriously have no idea how to repay him for his kindness. He's dropped thousands of dollars on me today. I know he picked up a few things for himself, but most of what he has spent is money on me.

"I know I can't stop thanking you, and you are probably sick of it, but I can't express how grateful I am, Wash," I say, taking a sip of my cookies and cream milkshake.

"I know you are grateful, Doll. You don't have to keep thanking me. I'm happy to spoil the shit out of you, like you deserve. You've had it rough, Lexi. Harder than I'm sure I fully know about, but life isn't going to be hard anymore. I'm back in your life, and I'm not going anywhere. Your mother can't stop you from living with me anymore. You are free of the burden that is your mother."

"Funny you call her the burden. To her, that's all I was, a burden. She placed so much blame on me, blamed me for everything she possibly could. I know how much she regretted not aborting me. It messes with your head, your self-worth, and seeps into other areas of your life. It's hard to see hope and positivity when that has been nothing more than a dream for so long. I have a lot of healing to do. I need this fresh start. It's my lifeline." I softly confess. I have to admit it feels good to express some of these thoughts out loud to someone who won't judge me.

"You live with the sins and regrets of your parents because they have wrongfully put them on you. You will heal with time, Lexi. I've already made an appointment for you with a therapist next week. Dr. Daniels is someone I have seen myself, along with many of my colleagues and friends. You will be in good hands with him. If there is anyone who can guide you in healing, it's him. Don't forget, you have me. I'm happy to help you with your fresh start. Fresh starts are liberating but hard."

"I look forward to talking with Dr. Daniels," I say with a smile. Relief floods me as I realize I'm finally going to get the help I need. The help to get me over my past and working toward a brighter future.

"Hey, would you like to come out with my friends and I tonight?" Wash offers.

"Sure, I'd like that. Good thing I'm old enough to go to a bar." I joke.

"How do you know we are going to a bar?" Wash asks with a raised eyebrow.

"I assumed we'd be going to the firefighter bar; Fireball, I think it was called."

Wash chuckles. "I guess you read me better than I realized. Yes, we are going to Fireball. You know, if you want to work a few nights a week there, I know they always could use some extra hands. I happen to be tight with the owners." Wash offers.

"Maybe. It's something to consider. I'll think about it." I reply, taking another sip of my creamy milkshake.

"No hard feelings if you don't want to, but being a silent partner, I get swayed on who gets hired on."

"You own the bar?" I ask in disbelief.

"Part of it. I was the start-up money for the bar. Stephen and Kyle didn't have enough to start up the bar on their own, so I offered to start it up for them as long as I could be a silent partner. They have full control over how the place is run, the menu, drinks, and just about everything really. I still have a say in it all. I just don't really add my opinion unless they need me to. The bar is their dream. I simply helped make it happen. Besides, the bar was a good investment option for me. It's also a backup plan in case I leave the UCFD one day. Options are never a bad thing to have. I'll text the guys and let them know we are coming out tonight."

"Sounds good. I guess we should finish shopping and get home soon. I have a lot to put away and wash. Plus, now I need to figure out an outfit for tonight." I say with a smile, happy to be having a real night out with friends. I know they are technically Wash's friends, but hey, I'll take what I can get when I get it. I've certainly learned that beggars can't be choosers.

Hopefully, with me starting over, I'll make some of my own friends. I do have friends. I always made friends everywhere we went, even if I knew the friendship probably wouldn't last long. Still, I did my best to be social, make friends, and go to social events. Things were easier when Jesse was alive. He was a great buffer between Mom and me. After he died, it was harder to be social or maintain friendships. I never made it to prom or just about any big social event in high school after Jesse died. I didn't live long enough with Wash then for it to make a difference. I was underage and not allowed to make my own choices. Now I'm an adult, finally free of my toxic mother. Free of bad friendships. It was hard to make friends with good people.

Unfortunately, the areas we lived in often weren't the greatest. So I ended up being friends with drug addicts, drug dealers, and some gang members, but I never went near gang shit. I was never going to have that be my life. Still, those were the kids that were around because my mother could never afford somewhere decent to live. Still, I took what I could. Not everyone was bad. Most of the friendships fizzled away after I'd moved since I was forced to be stuck in the stone age, thanks to my mother. We never had the internet, I never had a smartphone, I was lucky if I had a prepaid phone, and we didn't have cable or any TV. It's why reading became my main entertainment.

What else is there to do when you don't have access to regular teen things? I like reading, and I found an escape in my books. The library was always free no matter where I went. Sure, I could use the internet at the library, but it was hard to maintain a true social media profile. Books were easier. I didn't have to impress the books. Having social media meant having to keep up with my peers on all the latest fads. There was no point. I wouldn't be able to afford any of the fads that were considered cool. By the time I'd save enough to afford whatever the latest fad was, there would be a new fad that had replaced it. It was pointless, so I gave up and stuck to what was easy, books.

Wash and I finish shopping and then head home. I can't believe Wash spoiled the shit out of me. I mean, I'm not that surprised. I knew Wash would go out of his way to make sure I had more than what I needed. It's sweet. I can't deny it's nice being spoiled. I almost feel like I deserved it. I know that I do, but it's hard to undo years of being told you're worthless. Maybe I can finally change that line of thinking. I'm ready for the change that is going to happen now that I'm free of my past. Now, I need to figure out what I'm going to wear out tonight to meet some of Wash's friends. I don't know what to expect, but I'm glad that Wash is taking me out. I guess there was a part of me that assumed he wouldn't include me in his personal life.

I settle on something simple. Dark wash skinny jeans, a simple nice black top with lace trim. I put on black knee-high dress boots to embrace the impending autumn weather. I grab a black zip-up hoodie in case I get cold. Heading downstairs, I find Wash looking handsome in black jeans, a dark blue v-neck t-shirt, a black leather jacket, and black boots. It's not fair that he looks hot in anything he wears.

"You look cute, Doll." Wash compliments as we head to the car.

"Thanks. I wasn't entirely sure how to dress." I confess.

I was afraid I would either overdo it or underdo it. It's been a while since I've hung out with friends. I only turned twenty-one a few months ago. I've never really been to a bar to hang out. I was usually at a bar to drive my mom home, if we had a car, or I was there because the bartender called me to come get her before the cops were called. I'm actually curious about what it's like to hang out at a bar with friends. You know, for what a bar is actually intended for, not peeling your mother off the floor, hoping you make it out before the cops show up.

"You look perfect, Doll." Wash reassures me with his million-dollar smile as we get into the car. I smile back because I suck at taking a compliment. I guess I should get used to them because I have a feeling Wash is going to give them often.

The car ride is quiet, which is fine because I'm nervous. While I'm happy that Wash is including me in his personal life, I didn't expect to meet anyone so soon. I guess it's a good thing Wash wants me to meet his friends so quickly. I don't know why I thought he would be embarrassed by me. It might be good for me to see myself through Wash's eyes.

We arrive at Fireball, which in high traffic area for the business. It's an average-sized bar. Not too big, not too small. Firefighter memorabilia is everywhere. I notice there are cops hanging around too. It's not uncommon for fighter bars to welcome cops and vice versa. At least in Union City that is. I don't know if every area is like that. I know cops and firefighters are often painted as enemies, and sure they do compete on some level with each other, but it's always friendly and civil.

The moment we enter the bar, Wash is being flagged over by a group of people. There are four guys and four girls. They are all clearly couples, as they are paired up in intimate ways. I didn't realize all of Wash's friends were in relationships. I only thought it was some of them. Wash brought me here as a friend, right? There's no way that Wash brought me as his date. We have been flirting on and off, but there is no way I'm his date. Still, I can't deny that it would be nice if I was.

We join Wash's friends in the corner. He introduces me to his friends. There's Stephen and Kyle, who own the bar with Wash. Julia is Stephen's fiance, and April is Kyle's wife. They are both nurses and work together. Then there is Kevin and Hunter. Keven still works in the fire station while Hunter works fire investigation with Wash. Ashley is Kevin's girlfriend, and Maddie is Hunter's girlfriend. I lost track of what Ashley and Maddie did for a living. I'll have to clarify with Wash later. Honestly, the introductions felt like they went by in a weird blur as I fought off my unwanted social anxiety. I forgot that social situations often give me anxiety, but thankfully being near Wash is helping ease my anxiety.

I hate to say it, but Wash placing a beer in my hand is the thing that started to help me relax. I shouldn't need alcohol to socialize, but sadly right now, I do. I'm sure the more I'm out in public and exposed to proper social interactions, it will get easier. I'm not completely invalid. I've had friends of my own, and I even went to a party a couple of times in high school. It's just being with Wash and his friends. I feel like a loser. They all have good jobs, they are in stable relationships, and they are regular adults.

Thankfully, Wash doesn't leave my side. I'm comfortable with him as I try to avoid the uncomfortable questions his friends are asking. I know they are curious about me. I wonder if Wash has ever talked about me to them? They seem to have some idea of who I am. If anything, being the dead cop's little sister somehow never seems to get old. I know I can get through this. I'm ready to move forward with my life, and part of that is being social and acting like a regular twenty-one year old at a bar having a drink with peers.

Chapter 5

Arsonist

Wash always shows up at the bar at least once on the weekends. He's always enjoyed hanging out with his brothers. It's one of the many things that bonded us once upon a time. To say that Wash is someone important to me would be an understatement. I've been out of his life for a while now, but I can't help but keep tabs on him. Wash wouldn't recognize me now. My appearance has changed, and I stay hidden in the dimly lit corners to be sure no one notices me. I usually have on a hoodie or baseball cap to help obscure my appearance. When you are someone who lives the life I do, it's best if you never run into people from the past.

I like knowing Wash is doing something good with his life like we always said we would.

I was always secretly the bad apple of the two of us. I tried to keep up with Wash and his honorable ways, but it's easy to be honorable when you come from a wealthy family. That's one of the admirable yet annoying qualities of Washington Spencer. He's well aware of his family's wealth, and he's managed to not be a rich, douchey asshole. He's done good things with his life. He's even become wealthily, independent from his parents. Granted, he doesn't have their level of money, but he doesn't hurt for it, either. I'm sure he's still in his parent's will. He might not be the golden child like his sister, but Wash's parents wouldn't cut him out of the will.

Although, I'm not sure how his family would feel about him taking in Lexi Martin again. I didn't think I'd see that bitch around Wash again after she left six years ago. She's pathetic, pretending she fits into Wash's world. She's trash that I thought would be left on the street. Even now, she's acting like she's totally not using her drink to make her feel better about socializing with good people because she knows she doesn't deserve to be among them. I can't believe given her mother's history she's using alcohol as a crutch. Then again, I shouldn't be surprised since she is a low life.

I don't know why I'm surprised Lexi would find her way to Wash's doorstep. She's always admired him. No doubt she fed him some sob story to guilt him into taking her in. Wash was always a sucker for her, even back then. I think he enjoys being her hero. With Lexi, he can be a hero twenty four hours a day. Wash likes being a hero, and Lexi is a walking charity case.

Lexi is good at getting Wash to her side. She's always had a little crush on him, and somehow she uses it to her advantage to wrap Wash around her finger. The two of them have always had a special bond that I always despised. It never seemed fair that they bonded so easily. It often made me jealous to watch their friendship flourish while my friendship with Wash seemed to suffer.

I don't like that she's back in his life. I was hoping once she left with her mom she wouldn't show back up again, but I guess that was wishful thinking. Lexi is nothing but a distraction for Wash. I need to make sure she doesn't hold Wash's attention for long. I might just have to find a way to distract him at work. I know he's starting in fire investigations. I've become good at setting shit on fire, and what better way to catch a firefighter's attention than fire.

Chapter 6
Wash

It's hard to believe it's been a couple of weeks since Lexi moved in with me. We have easily fallen into our own swing of things. It amazes me how natural things are with Lexi. Even six years later and it's like no time has even passed. It's not like it's not clear that time has passed between us. It sneaks up on us in moments that we don't expect.

The first time it became clear that six years had past was when one of my friends, not in my main circle, made a comment that Lexi is sexy and cute, but she's too young to pursue. I've never looked at Lexi as too young. I know eleven years seems like a lot to some people, but it doesn't to me. I was still just a kid when Lexi was born. We have been in each other's lives forever. We know each other.

Even when Lexi lived with me previously, she was only fifteen, but we fell into a routine like it was nothing. Lexi is certainly not fifteen anymore. She's grown into a sexy woman. I always knew she would be a looker, but fuck me, I didn't think she would turn on me like she does. Cold showers have become my best friend. I'm glad that I work because I wouldn't be able to control myself around her. She's sexy without even trying to be, which just makes her adorable.

The weekends are the hardest because I want to go out without Lexi, but it's hard to hang out without my friends with her. My friends judge her, and she knows it. She's not stupid like they think she is. Lexi has always been observant to how people are around her. She knows they are just pretending to like her. It's not even her fault that they are acting like that. It's Kate's.

Kate and I are in so many of the same social circles. We dated for almost three years and was engaged for another six months before I ended things. I wasn't happy with her, and I couldn't marry her. I thought I loved Kate, but I realized I was in love with the idea of what she represented. I want a wife and eventually a family. The stupid house with a white picket fence dream. Kate filled the role, but that's all she did. We never really clicked even when we lived together for those six months of engagement it felt forced. I was happy when I got my townhouse. Yet, Lexi is here for a couple of weeks and nothing about her being here feels forced.

The downside to not marrying Kate is that our friends are still our friends, they just don't hang out with us together anymore unless it is a special occasion. I know half our friends, including my parents, hope that Kate and I fix things, but we won't. Kate has tried to get me to come back to her. It's been well over a year and half after our breakup and she still texts me if I miss her from time to time. I know she's gone on dates with other guys. Our friends tell me in hopes to make me jealous when I'm just hoping the guy catches her attention. I want her to find someone else, and move the hell on with her life. I should have never proposed to her. I don't know why I did. I think it was because so many people were asking us when we would get married. Instead of breaking up with her, I gave in and brought a damn ring.

A ring that I let her keep. I don't know why I let her keep it. I didn't want it. I wouldn't propose to someone else with it. I could have returned it, but that didn't feel right either. So, I just told Kate to keep and sell it. At least she could use the money to set herself up nicely. Unfortunately, she hasn't sold it. She's taking it that because I gave her the engagement ring, I'm not really over her. I acted out of guilt and somehow she read it as me still having feelings for her. Now, I do everything I can to make it clear to everyone including Kate that we are never getting back together.

This is the first time after Kate that I've brought a girl around my friends. Granted, only the guys know that I'm interested in Lexi. Still, it was a test, and they are failing. It's disappointing to watch. They think if they push Lexi away eventually I will go back to Kate. The only reason I told the guys about my feelings for Lexi is because I needed someone to talk to about these crazy feelings. I don't know why any of them are judging her. It's not like them to give the cold shoulder this way. They don't know full details, but they know enough that they know Lexi hasn't had an easy life.

It's not that I'm expecting them to feel bad for her or like her right away. I am expecting them to give her a chance. To actually get to know her as a person. They aren't even giving her the benefit of the doubt. It's been making going out with my friends hard, but Lexi will get suspicious if I stop hanging out with my friends. She's even offered to let me go by myself and stay home. I don't know why I feel odd doing that. I shouldn't, but I think I'm afraid of losing her. It was hard when she moved away with her mom. I kicked myself constantly that I didn't fight harder to keep her with me. I don't want her to leave because she falsely thinks she is ruining my life.

Lexi has taken to doing everything around the house. She's even doing my laundry. She doesn't have to, but she insists. She was the same way when she lived here before. She really tries to earn her stay even though she doesn't have to. Lexi can't help it, though. It's what years of neglect and abuse will do to someone. I do my best to make sure Lexi knows she doesn't have to do anything. Honestly, I enjoy having her live with me.

While things might be smooth at home, things are rough elsewhere. If things being awkward with my friends wasn't annoying enough, I'm having issues at work. Well, not real issues. More like I'm in this weird transition and finding my footing. Going into the office is totally different from the firehouse. I'm not even on a case right now. I'm still learning the computer systems and the proper way to do things here.

Part of me misses the action. I hardly felt like I was sitting around at the firehouse. I worked at a busy firehouse, and I loved it. Right now, I'm not seeing any action. I know I will eventually catch a case. I guess I didn't think I would take so long to settle into my new position. Hunter warned me there would be a transition, but I guess I didn't heed his warning properly. It's only been a couple of weeks. I'm sure I'll adjust soon enough. As much as I might miss the action, I know I needed the change. I knew it might not be an easy change, but sometimes what we need isn't always easy. I've learned that lesson a couple of times already.

I've gone through a lot of changes in the last couple of years. They were good changes in the long run. I have to trust that these recent changes are also good. I know that I love having Lexi back in my life. I never fully realized how much I missed her. I don't want to lose her again. I'm realizing that Lexi is someone I need in my life, and I would gladly set shit on fire for her.

Chapter 7
Lexi

Wash has just left for work. I made him breakfast and coffee before he left. I know I don't have to do it, but I like being helpful. Plus, Wash has been wonderful. He's stuck to his word and got me help. I've already seen a primary doctor who did a pap smear for me. Everything came back good. I need to gain a few pounds, which I already knew. I'm also now taking vitamins. I'm overall healthy, which I'm relieved my health didn't take too hard of a hit. My mental health is another story, but I'm working on it.

I even have a list of some part-time jobs to look at. I don't know if I'm ready to jump back into work. Part of me still needs a minute to catch up from the chaos. I'm still reeling from getting away from my mom and that I actually got myself somewhere safe. I also feel like my emotions are swirling around me, hitting me in tidal waves. I can finally step out of survivor mode, and while that's freeing, it's also terrifying.

Today I'm meeting with Dr. Daniels. I'm looking forward to therapy. I need someone to help me process and someone that will simply listen to all my problems. I trust Wash with everything, but I'm not fully ready to open up to him about what happened to me. One day, I plan to tell him everything, but right now, it feels like it's too much to unload. I just got him back in my life. Everything is smooth between us. It's casual and natural.

I can't deny that it hasn't been hard keeping my feelings in check. My crush on Wash has come back in full force. I'm not sure it ever left. I always compared other guys to him. He's my dream guy. It was easier to hide my crush at fifteen, but I'm an adult now. I actually have a chance with Wash. It might be a small chance, but it's there. Wash is struggling too. I've noticed the increase in cold showers he claims he takes to help with his workout. We both know it's complete bullshit, but we pretend his excuse is valid.

The one downside that I've run into is Wash's friends don't like me. At first, I thought it was because of my anxiety.

I chalked it all up to overthinking, but I wasn't. I was right. His friends bring up his ex, Kate, as often as possible. They quickly change the topic when I walk over to them. I was in the ladies' room last week. Ashley, Maddie, and April walked into the ladies' room, talking smack about me. I was in the stall, so they didn't know I was there, or maybe they did, and they wanted me to hear them. Either way, what they said was I was too young for Wash, and he's only interested in me because he's having a midlife crisis. Wash is thirty-two. I doubt he's having a mid-life crisis because he might be interested in me.

 I don't really care if they think I'm too young for Wash. It's just some lame excuse because it's clear they want him back with Kate. I was shocked to find out they thought Wash was even interested in me. It confirmed that the sexual tension between us isn't in my head. Washington Spencer, the man of my dreams, is actually interested in me. We might have a chance. I know I can't be thinking about a relationship right now. It's hard not to. I'm doing everything I can to get myself on the right path so that I can be in a place to start a relationship.

 I've always liked the idea of being in a relationship with someone. I never had anybody I was really interested in being with because they never compared to Wash. Never in a million years did I think Wash would be interested in me like that. It's weird having it unofficially confirmed. It leaves room for doubt and overthinking, which I hate. Still, the idea of being with Wash is something I definitely desire.

I get ready to leave. My appointment is an hour. I'm taking the bus to my appointment. Wash said he would get me a cheap car, but I just can't bring myself to accept something that huge. It's bad enough he bought me clothes, a laptop, a phone, and tons of other things. I'm fine taking the bus. Wash gives me money for the bus until I get a job and can afford it myself. He's being so generous. I wish I could thank him with sexual favors. Damn it, I need to stop thinking like that, but damn, is it hard not to.

Pushing thoughts aside, I get dressed for my appointment in skinny jeans and a black hoodie. It's getting chilly out. It's November. Thanksgiving is a week and a half away. I'm not sure what Wash plans to do for it. He hasn't talked about it. I assume he's going with his family. I don't mind staying by myself. I don't want to intrude on any of his plans. Besides, I've spent my fair share of holidays alone. At least this time, I have TV and food.

My appointment with Dr. Daniels goes well. He started me on some antidepressants and an anti-anxiety pill in case I need it. Most of the first talking session was mostly me giving him a background of everything that happened. We agreed I have PTSD, major depressive disorder, and some other anxiety conditions. I wasn't surprised to get my diagnosis. It did feel good to talk to someone. I think with Dr. Daniel's help, I can heal. For the first time in a long time, I feel like I can breathe.

I decide to make homemade fried chicken, mac and cheese, mini corn on the cobs, and rocky road brownies. Wash loves brownies. I love baking for him. I enjoy cooking for him too, but I actually have more fun when we cook together. We normally cook together on the weekends. The weekends are fun with Wash. We alternate from staying home to going out unless there is something special going on.

Before I know it, I get a text from Wash saying that he will be home soon. I finish cooking just as Wash walks through the door. "That smells delicious, Doll." Wash compliments, setting down his items down on one of the counters.

"Thank you," I reply with a smile. "How was your day?" I inquire, making our plates.

We usually eat out in the living room, and watch TV while we eat. It's probably not considered proper, but Wash and I don't give a shit. We both are about what makes us comfortable. Wash is a relaxed person to live with. I always felt like I was walking on eggshells with my mom. Even when Jesse was alive, I felt the need to be perfect. I couldn't be the reason they blamed me for something. I was eager to earn their approval. It wasn't until after Jesse died that I realized I compared myself to him. He was the golden sibling. He made a huge sacrifice by helping our mom raise me. I was this shared burden between them. Wash is the only person who doesn't make me feel like I'm a burden. I feel wanted by Wash, and that is a good feeling. It makes me all warm inside when I think about it. Cliche? Maybe?

"It was okay. I'm still getting the hang of a new department. It's an adjustment from working in a firehouse. I'm sure I'll catch a case soon." Wash answers as he takes his plate and glass of ice unsweetened black tea that I poured earlier.

"Be careful what you wish for, Lieutenant. You might get more than you bargained for." I warn as I take my plate and glass and walk out to the living room with Wash.

"You are probably right, Doll. I've seen this in the firehouse. Sometimes we hit these lows where it feels like we barely get any calls. We are downright bored on shift, hoping for a call. Then you feel shitty for hoping for a call because that means someone is in trouble. Then there are times when it feels like it never slows down. There is just one bad call after a rough call after a brutal call, and it goes like that until finally, something gives, and you catch a break. Once in a while everything is balanced between calls and time spent in the firehouse. That's why I'm positive something is going to drop on my lap, and I'm probably going to wish it hadn't." Wash explains as we get comfortable. We have our TV trays permanently set up since we use them so often.

"It will work out, I'm sure." I reassure him.

"I'm sure you are right, Doll," Wash pauses as he turns on the TV and puts on a TV show from our list to stream. "How was your appointment?" He asks before digging into his plate of food.

"It was good. I have to pick up my prescriptions tomorrow at the pharmacy. I think going to Dr. Daniels is going to be good for me."

"That's good to hear. By the way, this is really good. I might let you cook the turkey breast for Thanksgiving." Wash compliments.

"Thanks. I doubt your parents would want me cooking for them." I reply, taking a bite of mac and cheese.

"My parents? Lexi, I'm not going to my parents for Thanksgiving. I haven't gone in years. I only go for Christmas Eve, Christmas Day, Mother's Day, and sometimes we do a vacation with each other for the Fourth of July. I try not to do much with my family for obvious reasons. I thought we could do dinner here. Haven't you noticed I've been buying Thanksgiving meal stuff over the last couple of weeks?"

"I guess I didn't put it together. I thought maybe you did a friendsgiving or something." I shrug my shoulders. It's safer to assume Wash isn't including me in his plans. I've completely invaded his life. He's allowed to do things without me.

"No, silly, it's for us. I thought we could cook it together." Wash says, taking a sip of his drink.

"That sounds like the perfect Thanksgiving to me. I haven't been able to celebrate any holidays in a few years. Even better that we can do it from the comfort of your home." I say with a smile, totally loving a day with Wash. Spending any holiday with Wash is ideal. Here I thought I was going to sit at home alone while Wash has been planning for us to have the holiday together.

"You know this is your home too." Wash comments. Of course, he would tell me this is my home too. He's too sweet sometimes. Wait, did I seriously complain about that?

"You'll get tired of me eventually." I retort.

"What makes you think I want you to ever leave? Having you here is the happiest I've been in a long time. You don't have to move out unless you want to. You'll always have a home with me." Wash counters as he lightly nudges me.

"That's good to know because I don't want to leave. I like being here with you." I reply, hiding the pink tint to my cheeks by ungracefully shoving food in my face. Wash chuckles, and we eat the rest of dinner in comfortable silence, enjoying our show.

I'm glad Wash doesn't want me to leave. I truly want to stay with him. Not just because I feel there might be a chance for us as a couple but because I know I'm safe with him. Being safe isn't something I've had in a long time. It feels good to be with Wash. I feel like I'm finally getting my life back on track. I'm starting to heal. I'm ready to move forward from my past and actually leave my past behind me.

Chapter 8
Arsonist

Thanksgiving is tomorrow. I'll be spending it with my dad. The two of us have grown very close over the last several years since reuniting. I wish I had him in my life for a longer period of time. I always hated his absence in my life because it always felt like I was missing something. Something I was forced to be for the person who was responsible for making my father leave. I'm glad to have him back in my life. I made a huge sacrifice joining him. It was worth it.

While I'll be spending time with Dad, Wash will be spending it with Lexi. I, unfortunately, overheard him telling his friends at the bar that he would be doing Thanksgiving with Lexi. I couldn't believe he wouldn't be with his family. I knew he was never overly close with his family. I didn't think he would skip holidays with them because I know how much his family values holidays as family time. It's a big deal that he is skipping Thanksgiving dinner, and I blame Lexi. He's ashamed of Lexi, and I don't blame him.

It seemed his friends weren't thrilled about him spending it with Lexi either. I know they hate her living with him. Some of them think she is a little leech and trying to seduce Wash, so she can live off him for as long as possible before he picks up on her games. I wouldn't say they are wrong. That's exactly what that little bitch is doing. Of course, some of his friends think she is okay and don't mind her. Those are the ones that think she might be a bit young for Wash. One of them described it as Wash is in the fine wine stage of life whereas Lexi is still in the wine cooler phase of life. It was something along those lines. I sometimes tune out his friends when Wash isn't around. They are usually annoying, but listening to them talk about Lexi and compare her to Kate is always fun. I don't know why Wash ever broke up with Kate.

I wish Wash would get back with her, but he won't. He definitely won't while Lexi is around. Those two are getting harder to watch. They aren't screwing one another yet. I hope they don't because once they do, Lexi will certainly dig her claws into Wash. Them spending holidays together might be a problem. I honestly thought Wash would be with his family.

Wash was always big about family. He gave me the speech often enough. There were many times I didn't want the responsibility that my family was. It was hard after my dad left. I grew up so fast. At the time, I thought my sacrifice for my family was worth it. Then I reconnected with my dad, and I realized it was time to stop being the sacrificial lamb. So, I left my family in an unexpected way. My family will never know that I'm alive. That's the point of faking your own death. It's morbid, sure, but I gave up being the good guy a long time ago.

Wash is finally settling into his new position in Fire investigations. I can't believe he went to the white-shirt side of things. Wash was always about the action. He loves the thrill of having his life hang in the balance. He gets off on it just like I do. It's why we chose the careers we did. Wash might be in fire investigations now, wearing his white shirt, but that doesn't mean I can't make things interesting for him. Time to distract Wash from Lexi and set his new career ablaze.

Chapter 9
Lexi

It's hard to believe it's only been a month since I moved in with Wash. There are moments it feels like I never left at fifteen. I know I left and some bad things happened in that time. I'm learning to heal from that. I've been seeing Dr. Daniels once a week. He's helping me heal and move forward with my life in a positive way. I have a lot of work to do on my journey of healing, and I'm willing to put the work in. I want to feel like I have some control in my life and over my life.

There was a big part of me terrified to ask Wash for help. I feel like my whole life, I've needed help from someone for something. I needed help from Jesse to raise me, which isn't technically my fault. Still, I needed his help. I've needed Wash's help in the past. I've needed others' help for food, shelter, and other supplies. I've been to my fair share of food banks and shelters over the years. When we had to skip town because Mom couldn't pay rent anymore, we would leave in the middle of the night and sometimes go to a shelter for a couple of days.

When my mom went to prison, I felt free for the first time since she went to rehab. I wanted nothing more than to stand on my own two feet and prove I could do it without anyone helping me. What I didn't account for was her somehow saddling me with her court and lawyer fees because she just couldn't go with a public defender. I'm not even sure why she bothered with lawyers, and took the whole thing to court. Her ass was guilty, and the jury convicted her as such. I didn't account for my sleazy landlord raising the rent price because he wanted to be a dick. Then my job cut my hours with no luck in finding a second job. It was one punch after another, and before I knew it, I was drowning. I couldn't keep up on bills no matter how hard I worked. I thought I had failed and was a loser. However, Dr. Daniels pointed out that I wasn't given a fair deck of cards to play the game of life with in the first place.

He is right, I wasn't given a fair chance. I don't know how I thought I would get ahead when I was already so far behind to begin with. There was no way I was going to be able to keep up. I didn't have a good enough job making nearly enough money. I tried, but I wasn't totally where I needed to be.

I've accepted that I need help to get on my feet. As Dr. Daniels said, there's nothing wrong with accepting help when we need it. Dr. Daniels also pointed out that I have been given a chance to get myself on track. Not everyone gets that chance. So, instead of sulking about how I couldn't make it on my own, I'm celebrating Thanksgiving with Wash. I'm happy and grateful he is giving me a second chance to get my life on track.

Wash is a complex situation because my feelings for him romantically are only increasing. I think about kissing him more often than I should. I definitely should be thinking about sucking his dick or how badly I want him to have sex with him and replace every single bad memory with a good one. As much as I want to cross that line with Wash, I'm not sure I should. I'm fairly certain that Wash has romantic feelings for me too, but crossing the line from friendship to something more is not something I want to do lightly. Knowing Wash, he feels the same way I do about crossing that line.

I thought a four-day weekend home with Wash should be amazing, but on day one as we are preparing Thanksgiving Dinner for ourselves, I'm tempted to rub up against him. We are in the kitchen cooking up a storm. The two of us have fun cooking together. We always have. Cooking was always something we bonded over. Even when I was young, Wash would help me cook. Jesse couldn't cook for shit, but Wash was a natural. I learned a lot about cooking from Wash. I think I was determined to learn to cook because of Wash. I think it was my attempt to impress him while bonding with him.

It would seem it worked. Cooking together is now something we do often. Even after all this time it's something we still enjoy doing together. I think Jesse was a little jealous that Wash and I had something that only we bonded over. Jesse could never cook. He tried, but he was just bad at it. Wash started to teach me to cook because Jesse kept failing. I think Jesse took it the wrong way, but I saw it as a way to help Jesse out.

Thanksgiving is the biggest meal we have made together. We are making a turkey breast that we decided to fry. Wash even brought a damn fryer for us to do it in. Mr. Fireman made sure everything was set up safely. For our sides we are making mashed potatoes, sweet potato casserole, green bean casserole, corn, cranberry sauce, stuffing, and rolls. We have an apple pie that we got from a bakery because we knew we wouldn't want to bake on top of all the cooking.

I love Thanksgiving, but I've never had a proper one. Mom was usually too drunk to cook, Jesse couldn't cook, and even when I could cook we didn't have the money for a full feast. I made what I could, but it was often just Jesse and me. Then when he started working he would try to work the holidays because it would be extra pay. It's nice finally being able to cook a big meal and for someone that will enjoy it with me.

Wash and I plan on stuffing our faces and watching movies for the night. We are even in bum clothes. Wash has on dark grey sweatpants, a black t-shirt and his house slippers. I have on black leggings, a dark green tunic top, and my house slippers. We are keeping everything very casual, and I'm enjoying it.

After everything is done cooking we set up our trays and get comfortable in front of the TV with plates overflowing with food. Wash puts on an action movie. It's something we have bonded over for years. It was something we had in common with Jesse. However, even with Jesse gone, we still enjoy watching them together. I wasn't able to really keep up on shows or movies. So, I'm catching up now. Wash knows just the right ones to show me. He truly does know me.

We eat our dinner and then when we are done eating, we put the leftovers away. We will be eating leftovers for a few days. Once everything is put away, we decide to crash on the couch and watch TV while we digest our food.

I'm happy here with Wash. There is a part of me that fears I'll mess this up somehow. I worry Wash will get tired of me. I sometimes worry that I'm imagining his mutual attraction. I don't think I am. The problem is I don't know how much longer I can take being casual. I want to kiss him. Right now, I'm leaning my head on his shoulder while we watch our show. It's relaxing. I feel safe. Yet, I also want to make out without him. I want to be with Wash romantically. I also want it to happen naturally. I don't know how much longer I can take before I make a bold move I might regret.

The next day we sleep in. We are really taking our time to enjoy being home. Autumn has fully set in the city. The leaves are warm shades of orange, brown, yellow, and red. Hoodies, leggings, and warm beverages. It's my favorite time of year. So, today is about leftovers, playing video games, and relaxing. Wash threatened to bring out board games for old time sake. He has a collection of old board games up stairs in the mini sitting area.

Jesse, Wash, and I would play board games together often growing up. Jesse would get stuck babysitting me because Mom had to work. Wash would come over to help Jesse so he wouldn't have to be alone. Wash was an amazing friend to Jesse. I know Jesse and Wash had a special friendship. Best friends that shared a bond like brothers.

I enjoy spending time with just Wash. Jesse often made me feel like I was a burden. When I was little Jesse was my hero, but as I got older I started to feel like he resented me. I tried so hard to convince myself it was all in my head. However, Jesse had his way of making me feel like a third wheel in his and Wash's friendship. I like to think what the three of us had was a unique bond, but I'm not so sure Jesse saw it that way. Wash on the other hand saw everything with my family from an outsider's perspective. To him it was important I felt included. I think in some way Wash always knew I wasn't loved by my family, so he did his best to make me feel like I mattered.

The problem is my admiration for Wash has turned into a flaming desire of romantic feelings that are threatening to burn me from the inside out. I see opportunities all the time to make a move, yet I hesitate. I keep hoping Wash will make the first move, but I'm not sure that he will because he is a gentleman. Perhaps if I made the first move he would take the lead after that. Knowing Wash he just wants to know I'm on board with us taking things to the next level. The next time I get an opportunity I'm going to take it.

It might screw up everything, but the risk is worth taking. I believe Wash would understand why I took the risk. The best is if he truly does return my feelings then we have a chance to be together. Being with Wash is something I've wanted for far too long, and I'm going to be brave and put myself out there. I know I still have to tell Wash about the sexual assault and rape. I plan to do that soon. I'm tired of carrying it around like some heavy weight. Telling Wash about it will help things between us romantically. I'll tell him this weekend. Then I'll move forward with my plan to make a move to show Wash I'm ready.

Chapter 10
Wash

It's been nice staying in for the holiday with Lexi. I've been looking forward to it since we made the plans for Thanksgiving. I haven't enjoyed Thanksgiving in a while because I hated going to my parents, but I didn't want to be alone. This is the first year I felt like I had a good reason not to go. My parents weren't totally thrilled I was blowing them off for Lexi. It was either be honest, or lie and say I was on call. I was only going to lie so I could be sure to get out of my family obligations, but I hate lying. So, I went with the truth. It didn't matter what they said because I wanted nothing more than to spend this time with Lexi.

I love watching Lexi come alive. When she first got here, she was quiet. She didn't talk much about the years with her mom. Not that I expected her to open up right away about what happened. From what she has slowly started to share with me, I can tell it wasn't good at all. I know something bad happened. I know the look someone carries when they have survived something horrible. I see it in so many of my friends, sometimes even in myself. I certainly see it with Lexi. I want nothing more than to protect her.

    She's my Doll, my responsibility because I want her to be. I might even be slightly possessive over her. I'll do anything to keep her safe and make sure she is happy. Even if I'm not the person she wants to be with. I can't ignore our flirting and all the fucking moments that I want to kiss her. Lexi still has feelings for me that much is clear, and this time I return them. I couldn't back then. Lexi was so young and she needed a guardian. Now, it's different because she is older and ready for a boyfriend. She wants to be with someone she trusts and is comfortable with. I want to be that person for her.

    The problem is, I don't know if she is fully ready for us to cross the threshold from friends to lovers. It's a delicate thing that I don't want to get messy. I want to make the transition as smooth as possible and help Lexi with whatever she needs in the process.

I have to confess it's getting harder and harder to not give into those tempting, little moments of desire. Too many times I"ve wanted to fuck her, too many moments of lost kisses, and a case of the blue balls like I've never had before. I don't know why I thought I would hold out longer. I truly thought I could make it until after the new year before I would dare give in to temptation. Yet, Thanksgiving has barely passed and I'm about to be a damn daredevil.

Lexi is hard to resist. She has this way of intoxicating me in the best ways possible. I'm happy with her. I didn't realize how vital she was in my life. Lexi is my light. Those six years I kept feeling like something was missing. I tried to convince myself it was Jesse because I wasn't willing to admit that Jesse and I had a less than perfect friendship. In many ways our friendship was toxic. Jesse and I often disagreed with how to raise Lexi. I always thought he needed to step down and force his mom to be a fucking parent. Instead Jesse took the hard road. He enabled his mom. He helped her get whatever she wanted. He supported her smoking cigarettes and drinking whatever she wanted to numb the pain. He made his life miserable trying to enable his mom while doing her job by parenting Lexi. It was a fucked up situation.

There were many times I wanted to walk away from Jesse. He was so stubborn on making things harder than they had to be. He had victim syndrome hard. He didn't have to stay a victim. If he couldn't have changed his mom and got her to do her job as a parent then he should have left her. I told Jesse to get emancipated so many times. I was even willing to pay for the lawyer he would need to do it. I knew how toxic their mom was. She was a stink bomb always going off in the worst ways possible. I know she was abusive to her kids. Maybe not physically, but mentally and emotionally for sure. Jesse just sucked it up because he felt he had to be the man of the house. Their dad walking out like an asshole did so much damage. He destroyed their family and never looked back.

It was honestly sometimes hard to watch him suffer. Jesse held the weight of the world on his shoulders. He struggled mentally. Jesse was depressed to say the least. I think that was only half of his mental issues. Jesse never seemed totally stable. I worried about him more often than not. Sometimes I wanted to walk away from Jesse. At times his friendship felt toxic. Almost as if he enjoyed our spats because it added to his victimhood.

What I'm now realizing is I stuck around for Lexi. I couldn't leave her to her unstable family. Her mother was a mess, and her brother didn't know how to handle the shit storm that was tossed on his lap. In many ways, I didn't blame Jesse for his attitude because he did have a lot of shit dumped on his lap. I did my best to be his friend, and support him. I could never truly walk away from Jesse because that meant I'd have to turn my back on Lexi too. I stayed to protect her the best I could. Even then I was Lexi's guardian. Now, I want to be more than a guardian. I want her to be mine in every way that matters.

It's Saturday night. Lexi and I did some online shopping. I wanted to get a few more things for her to make her more comfortable here. I'm determined to make her love living here so much she never wants to leave. I can't lose her again that much I know. I know I promised to help her get on her feet. While I plan on doing that, I don't want her to move out. I know that in helping her get on her feet, I'm risking her leaving. In the end I want Lexi happy, and it's not too much to ask that she wants to be happy with me. Of course, I will let her go if she wants to, but I'm keeping her in my life no matter what. I simply prefer her with me.

Right now, we are curled up on the couch watching TV. We are relaxing before bed. It's been nice being home with Lexi, but I am ready to get back to work, mainly because at work I'm not tempted to give into my desires. I don't know how much longer I can hold out.

"Hey, Lieutenant," Lexi snaps her fingers in front of my face to gain my attention, scattering my desirable thoughts.

"Yes, Doll." I answer.

"It's time to play the next episode." Lexi gestures to the TV. Sure enough the autoplay has timed out.

"Maybe we should watch something else. I'm kind of in a movie mood." I confess, not wanting to admit I'm in a movie mood because I'm a little tired.

As much as I've enjoyed lounging around, tomorrow we have to do a food run, and do some meal prepping for the week. Our lazy days are over, we have to get ready to get back into our regular routine. Plus, if I'm sleeping it doesn't matter if I have a hard on or not. It's getting harder to hide my hard dick. I have to pretend to be cold so I can hide under a blanket. It's getting ridiculous, and I know Lexi isn't buying my silly excuses.

"No, I want to watch the next episode. I'm super into this show." Lexi protests as she crosses her arms under her chest, making her boobs pop a little in her scoop neck t-shirt. I love when she is playful. Suddenly, I'm not so tired.

"Then I guess you better get the remote from me before I pick a movie." I taunt as I quickly pick up the remote from my tray. I begin to act like I'm going to exit out of the show we have on, and Lexi falls for my playful trap as she reaches to snatch the remote from my hand. However, I'm faster and move the remote up higher, and on the opposite side of her so she can't reach.

Lexi counters me by straddling me. The moment she starts to straddle me I quickly move my arm up higher while my other arm wraps around her waist to stop her from reaching. I had to counter her move, but it backfired because Lexi is playing dirty by rubbing her pussy and ass on my lap as she attempts to wiggle free from my grasp. She keeps trying to reach for the remote but she can't wiggle free from my hold. She's making me hard and I can't fucking hide it because she's straddling me. I laugh at her attempt to get the remote to distract myself from how good she feels grinding against me.

"You think it's funny, Lieutenant," Lexi challenges as she stills before she playfully slaps me on the chest.

The moment she stills, realization that my dick is semi hard crosses her face. It's hard to ignore it as my dick twitches itching to get past the fabric that separates us. Lexi sucks in her breath as she appears to contemplate something. Is she thinking of making a move?

"I do think it's funny," I taunt as I wiggle the remote in my hand away from her. "So what are you going to do about it, Doll?" I challenge, holding her tighter so she can really feel what she does to me.

That's when a determined look crosses her features before she crashes her soft lips onto mine. Holy shit, she actually crossed the line. I didn't think she was ready, but clearly I was fucking wrong. Her lips are sweet from the cream cheese icing from our red velvet cupcakes. Lexi loves her red velvet cupcakes. I decided to treat her to some cupcakes from a very well known bakery. I love watching her face light up with happiness. When I got her the cupcake I didn't think I'd be tasting it off her lips.

Instinct takes over and my hand slides up her back before I grasp a fist full of hair in my hand. I drop the remote, not caring what the fuck we watch because Lexi has my full and undivided attention. Shit she tastes like heaven and it's not the damn cupcake. She feels like home, like she is all mine. I'm finally getting to taste the sweet desire between us.

Fuck, it's intoxicating. My free hand slides under her shirt, and I gently squeeze her breast.

To my surprise Lexi puts her hand on mine under her shirt. I release her hair and her lips before placing my hands on her hips to steady her. "What's wrong, Doll?" Shit, did I go too far?

"Wash, before we go any further, I have to tell you something before we proceed sexually." Lexi's voice is quiet. This is it. This is where she tells me the thing she has been holding on to. This is where she bares her pain to me. This is the part where I become her rock. This is where I wrap her in my love, comfort, and protection. "I don't mean to stop us from fooling around. Trust me, I want nothing more than to keep going, but we have to talk first. It's important. I was hoping to have this conversation before we gave into our desires." She cautions.

"It's okay, Doll. Whatever it is, it's your past. Right now is what I care about. Just tell me what it is, and we can fix it together." I rub her back with one hand to soothe her.

"You're going to be angry, but not at me." Lexi barely whispers.

"I never thought you did anything wrong, Doll. I know whatever happened, you were the victim." I continue to rub her back because she's slowly relaxing. I want her to feel safe because she is safe with me. I'm her fucking guardian first and foremost.

"When I was seventeen my mom's boyfriend raped me, twice. He never touched me after the second time because she broke up with him over something else. We ended up moving from the town he lived in a few weeks later. I thought the nightmare was in the rearview mirror, and in some ways it was. While the string of sleezy boyfriends after didn't rape me, they took advantage in their own ways. Some of them even did inappropriate things in front of my mom, and she didn't care as long as she had her fix. I tried to get past it all by dating. I thought if I had my own boyfriend I would be safe. The problem was I never felt safe with any of the guys I tried to date. They either pressured me, expected things from me, or accused me of things that weren't true. It was more drama and jabs to my already fragile ego, so I just stopped. I promised myself I wouldn't do anything with a guy unless I felt safe. You're the first and only guy I've ever felt safe with. I think I've been fairly obvious over the years how I feel about you. That never went away, Wash. I want to do things with you sexually, but I need to do things slowly. I need you to ease me into all this because I don't know how. My experience is not the experience I would have chosen, but it's what I got stuck with. You have to take the lead from here because I don't know how, but I trust that you do." Lexi confides in me.

She's right, I am pissed, but not at her. I'm pissed at her piece of shit mother. How could she let her boyfriends take advantage of her daughter? That woman really is the scum of the earth. I will never understand Lexi's parents. I'm not sure I'll ever fully understand Jesse even though he's dead. Lexi, on the other hand, her I fucking understand. The innocent victim that got placed in harsh surroundings. The tragic tale you read about in the newspaper. Yet, she never plays the victim card. If anything she downplays what's been done to her.

My one hand moves from her breast that Lexi was still holding, more like gripping by the end of her tale. My hand caresses her cheek. "We will go as slow or as fast as you want. Do you trust me? Do you trust I won't do anything to hurt you?" I question. If we are going to do this I need to know she trusts me not to hurt her.

"I trust you, Wash. I've always trusted you. I think you are the only person alive I do trust." She answers with such sincerity that I have no doubt she means it.

"Just so we are clear, you understand if we cross this line there is no going back. I don't want just sex, Doll. I want everything with you. You're mine, and only mine." She has to know what she is signing up for with me because once I own her, I'm never letting her go. I will let her be her own person. She can have whatever career she wants if she wants one, but at the end of the day she belongs to me. A spark is never just a spark, eventually it will start a fire.

"I've only ever wanted to be yours, so make me yours, Lieutenant."

"It's Sir when we are being intimate. Do you understand, my Doll?"

"I do, Sir." She replies and it makes my dick twitch.

"Good Girl. You'll have a little control at first until you are fully ready to give me total control. Only give me full control when you are ready to have sex," I pause and Lexi nods her head in acknowledgement before I continue. "Do you want to keep fooling around, and stop when you are ready, or stop right here?"

"Keep going until I'm ready to stop, but I have a request."

"What is it?" I ask, curiously.

It's a little bold of her to make requests immediately, but given her past she needs to feel like she has some control, so she gets a pass. Lexi is my exception to many things when it comes to women. I've never acted this dominate with other women, not even Kate. With Lexi, I don't have to hide anything. She brings out a side of me that only she sees.

"Can I sleep in bed with you? I think I'd sleep better with you by my side." Her voice is soft, and she looks down. She's afraid I'll reject her request. Her request is innocent. She wants to be close to me because I make her feel safe. She feels vulnerable after opening up to me.

I grin pulls on my face. "I like the sound of you in my bed even if it's just sleeping. Why don't we forget watching TV, and fool around before bed." I suggest.

Lexi nods her head yes. Normally, I would want her to verbally respond. However, I'm easing her into things. We've already set the spark a flame. Now it's time to let our fire burn. I waste no time wrapping my hand in Lexi's hair and grabbing a fist full of it before I slam her lips back onto mine. My other hand slides up her shirt and doesn't stop until it's softly touching her breast. Lexi doesn't stop me this time. Instead, her hands lay on my chest before sliding up around my neck. I stick her nipple between two fingers before I squeeze gently. Lexi moans into our kisses. I play with her nipple some more, earning more moans. Lexi begins to rock her hips gently grinding her pussy onto my cock that is back to standing with full attention.

    I move my hand to her other breast, playing with her nipple. I'm enjoying Lexi's sweet little moans of pleasure. She hasn't seen anything yet. I know she isn't ready for sex, but I can't deny there is something sexy in taking it slow while showing Lexi exactly what she deserves. I will erase every bad thing those bastards did to her. I know that I can't fully erase it or make her forget. Trauma is tricky, and I will do my best to make sure she doesn't think about it ever again.

    Deciding I want to increase Lexi's pleasure, I remove my hand from her shirt while my other hand releases her hair. I don't remove my lips from hers as I push my tongue into her mouth. Lexi lets me dominate her. I know she isn't ready to fully give me control, but right now she is lost in her desire for me.

    I use my hands to pull her pants down just enough so I can get to her pussy. It goes smoother than I anticipated because despite Lexi not having the best of experiences, her flow is perfect with me. My hand cups her pussy while my other hand holds her hips to hold her in place. My fingers slide between her folds finding her clit. I begin to rub her clit in small circles. Lexi moans as she begins to ride my fingers.

My mouth catches her moans as my tongue swirls around hers. Lexi is intoxicating. Being intimate with her is so intense and easy at the same time. We flow smoothly together. I'm more than ready to see where this goes because I can already see it ending with a ring on her finger. I know it's crazy to think that so soon, but it's not given how long Lexi and I have known one another. We have always been connected and drawn to each other.

Lexi gets wet quickly as I play with her clit. I'm sure this is the first time she has ever been able to enjoy her pleasure. She will always enjoy herself with me. Lexi rides my fingers and I can't wait for her to ride my dick. I'm willing to wait for that experience. My lips move down to her neck where I nip her skin causing her to moan and arch her neck to give my better access. I bite a little harder as I rub her clit faster driving her closer to the edge. She's close to her orgasm as she rides me hard chasing her release. Lexi's body tenses and shakes slightly as she crashes over the edge as her hands grip my shoulders for support.

"Good girl." I compliment as I kiss her forehead. "Are you ready for bed, Doll?" I question as I remove my hand from Lexi's pussy. I lick my fingers enjoying her taste. I can't wait to eat her pussy. That's for later. We have plenty of time to explore. Lexi needs things slow, and I will respect that. I will need to ease her into things, but I'm okay with that. I'm going to be the one to give her all her first good experiences.

"Yes." She says, slowly catching her breath.

"Come on then, Doll. Let's get you to bed." I say, rising from the couch as I scope her up in my arms and carry her to bed before I go back downstairs to turn everything off. Once I'm sure everything is good, I head back to my room.

I'm glad Lexi asked to sleep in my bed. I like the idea of her in my bed. I have since the first night she was here. I don't care that we aren't having sex right away. Some men might feel annoyed or teased, but I don't care. I understand Lexi needs to go slow as she overcomes the damage that was done to her. I hate that I couldn't protect her from it. I regret letting her go, but I didn't have a choice. I had no real evidence against Judy. She was too good at charming and putting on shows. She also used Jesse's death to her advantage as much as she could.

I felt I had no choice but to let Lexi go with Judy. I had to trust that she would do the right thing. Unfortunately, my worst assumptions about Judy came true. Judy getting locked up is a blessing. Lexi can finally get away from her toxic mother. As much as I wish I hadn't let Lexi go six years ago, the important thing is she is here with me now.

I climb into bed and pull Lexi to me. She snuggles into my arms as she lays her head on my chest. I'm glad we decided to get changed for bed early tonight and lounge around. It worked to our advantage. Lexi is fast asleep in no time as I feel her body fully relax in my arms. I hold her close to me. She is where she is meant to be, which is with me.

Chapter 11
Lexi

It's been a couple of weeks since Wash and I jumped the threshold from friends to lovers. I can't believe we are being intimate. We still haven't had sex because I'm not ready. However, I'm enjoying fooling around and exploring Wash's body as he explores mine. I'm comfortable with Wash. He's definitely the guy I was waiting for. I knew being with Wash would help me heal and give me the sexual experience I've desired for so long.

Wash and I have been sleeping in the same bed. Well, that's on the nights he's not working late. Wash caught a case, so he's been busy investigating. It's even starting to cut into our weekend time. While I'm glad that Wash might have a case, I miss having him around so often. I know the break isn't necessarily a bad thing. I am taking the time to do things I enjoy. So, I'm reading all the books I've wanted to catch up on. I'm working on my art. I'm enjoying my cartoony drawings. It feels good to create.

When I'm not doing self care, working on my DBT exercises, or with Wash, I'm up keeping the house. I do all the laundry, cook during the week, and clean. Wash helps where he can, but with him being busy I'm doing most of it myself. I don't mind it because I know Wash works hard and right now I'm not working. Wash does help around when he can. I don't have to worry about proving I'm a good house guest. Now, it's about proving I'm good house wife material.

Some might say that's too soon to think about, but news flash, I've been thinking of being with Wash for so long now. It's hard not to think about it now that fantasy is reality. I know I don't really have to prove myself to Wash. Wash already wants me for me. I simply want to make sure he is taken care of too because he's doing so much for me.

Tonight is a rare night that Wash is coming home at a decent time. I'm going to make a nice dinner and hope that we fool around tonight before bed. I want to put on a little show for Wash. I think touching myself in front of Wash will allow me to take a step toward being ready for sex. Wash got me a book to read to help me learn how to express my desires. It's been helpful. It's written from an abuse survivor who became a therapist. I'm not usually a self help book person, but this one has my attention. Plus, I can't deny it did help inspire tonight's idea.

So, I figured I would make a nice dinner. I have a pork roast in the oven, roasted red potatoes, mac and cheese, rolls, and apple sauce for the pork roast. I have a double chocolate cake with chocolate icing. I also have Wash and my favorite beer. I plan on wearing a sexy black silk baby doll nightgown to help entice my sexy firefighter.

I haven't done anything like this for Wash before. I'm a little nervous, but I know Wash will love it. I'm learning what he enjoys, and I know he will appreciate the gesture. I'm also enjoying branching out and trying something romantic with a sexy twist. I'm finally comfortable exploring my romantic and sexy side without having to worry I'll be taken advantage of. I know I'm safe with Wash.

Glancing at the clock I realize Wash is going to be home soon. So, I head upstairs to change into my sexy nightgown. I contemplate putting on makeup, but I know Wash prefers a natural look. I don't even know why I bought makeup since I don't use it daily. I do use it on nights we go out, especially at the bar because his friends' girls wear makeup. I don't wear a lot because I prefer a more natural look, but I want to try to have something to talk about with them. It's my pathetic attempt to have something in common with some of his friends. I've even thrown out my street hockey days just to attempt to bond with his friends that love hockey. I know Wash enjoys hockey, but he's not obsessed with it like his friends are. Wash even took me to a couple of hockey games. It was fun. I was hoping the one time we went with some of his friends it would be a good bonding experience with them. Instead, I got the cold shoulder, which irritated Wash because he knows I'm trying while they are not. Whatever, I enjoyed some beer, hot dogs, nachos, and popcorn during the game. I won't let his friends ruin my good time. For the first time in forever, I am able to go out and be a regular person. I'm enjoying it because it gives me a sense of freedom. I'm not sure I've ever felt so free before.

    Pushing thoughts of Wash's friends to the back of my mind, I head back downstairs to get to plating the food and setting up our trays in the living room. I set up our trays with plates of food and our beer. I set up the Tv with the current show we are watching. Then I perch myself in a sexy pose on the couch just as hear Wash is walking in the garage door.

"I'm in here, Lieutenant." I inform him, so he knows where to find me. I know he will ask since I'm not in the kitchen where he would enter.

"Dinner smells delicious, let me get out of these clothes, and we can eat. I was back at the crime scene today, and I feel a little dirty." Wash says as he walks into the living room. He stops dead in his tracks when he sees me on the couch. "Or, that can wait." Wash manages to say as he walks over to me.

"I wanted to surprise you with something romantic and a little sexy at the same time. I also want to try something that will help me be more comfortable with sex." I inform him, trying to avoid biting my lower lip.

Wash smiles. "I love it, and we can definitely try whatever you want." Wash plants a kiss on my lips, and I have to remember this is real and not my dreams.

"Do you want to clean up first? Our food still needs to cool down a little." I offer as we break our sweet, but short kiss. The love and admiration in Wash's eyes wraps me up in the best of feelings.

"I will go change and then I will be back down here to spend the rest of my night with you. You have no idea how much I need tonight." Wash says before he kisses me briefly once more on the lips. Then he turns and sprints up the stairs. I giggle at his eagerness.

Within five minutes, Wash is changed from his jeans and nice black shirt that had UCFD Fire Investigations embroidered on it. On the days he's out in the field investigating, he dresses more casually. Wash is now in black and red plaid PJ pants and a black t-shirt. Wash joins me on the couch before he kisses me passionately on the lips. Wash gives swoon worthy kisses that make me way too weak in the knees.

"I'm going to finish devouring you later, but I'm starving and your food smells good." Wash says breaking our kiss. I giggle.

"Eat up, Mr Lieutenant. There's chocolate cake for later."

"Shit, I really did need this." Wash says picking up his beer as I pick up mine. We clank them together before drinking. It's fun being able to drink with Wash. I was never able to do it six years ago, but so much has changed between us since then.

"Was work rough?" I ask as I hit play on the remote so our show will start.

"Eh, a little. The case is to investigate possible insurance fraud, except it's looking more like an arsonist is actually the culprit. We just don't know who the arsonist could be and why he's trying to set up a business to look like they are doing something dirty to get money." Wash informs me. He's barely talked about the case. I don't mind if he talks about work or not. I leave it up to him because I know he deals with hard stuff in his line of work. I was the same way with Jesse. I never expected him to tell me everything he saw as a cop.

"I don't envy you. I wish I knew how to help, but I know nothing about what you do." I confess.

"Talking and things like this help a lot, Doll. I'll figure it out. Enough about work. I want to enjoy my time with you." Wash replies, taking another swig of his beer. I don't argue. I'm used to first responders and how they don't like work and home life to collide. At least that's my experience.

Wash and I eat our food and then curl up on the couch together to finish a couple more episodes of our show. After a bit of TV, Wash declares it's time to go upstairs. I know we are headed to have sexy fun. I'm nervous for my request, mainly because I know I'm going to feel very exposed. Yet, I know I need to do this. I plan to have sex with Wash somewhere between Christmas and New Years. I'm confident I will be ready by then. I have a month give or take. It might not seem like much time, but I know with Wash I won't need a lot of time. I've never felt so comfortable sexually with a guy before. I've tried, and it was never like this.

We are in Wash's room, which is where we also stay when we stay in bed together. I don't care who's room we stay in. I will say, I like the master bathroom a lot. "So, what is it you want to try, Doll?" Wash asks, pulling me into his arms. With Wash being two heads taller than me I have to crane my neck to see him.

"I want to pleasure myself in front of you while you pleasure yourself in front of me." I say quietly. I don't know why I'm suddenly feeling shy. Probably initial nerves.

"I like the sound of that. After all this teasing, it's going to be amazing when we finally have sex." Wash cups my cheek with his one hand. "You know, I like going slow with you, exploring everything that brings you pleasure."

"It's good to know I'm not totally torturing you." I comment with relief. Part of me feared Wash would hate taking it slow even if he knows I need it. That doesn't mean it can't be annoying for him. Thankfully, Wash is understanding.

"You're not torturing me at all, Doll. Now, get undressed, and decide if you want me on the bed with you, or if you want me standing while we watch one another." Wash playfully smacks my ass with his free hand before he separates our bodies.

"I want you on the bed with me. Can you lay on your side, and I'll lay on my back?" I ask as we head over to bed, striping our clothes along the way.

"Works for me, Doll. The important thing is you are comfortable." Wash casually replies before he pulls back the comforter.

We get in bed and take our positions. I love how easy going Wash is with this. I was nervous that someone with his experience would hate taking things slow. However, Wash has the patience I need and he's giving it because ultimately he wants me to feel completely comfortable when I hand him complete control. That is why I'm comfortable with Wash because he's respectful and dominating at the same time. It's incredibly sexy.

Wash props himself on his side with his arm propping up his head. I'm on my back right next to him. We are close to each other. I could reach out and touch him, but as much as I want to I don't. Right now, not being able to touch him adds a bit of sexual tension that I'm enjoying, and judging by the look that Wash is giving me, he likes it too. I gaze at Wash as he wraps his hand around his wonderful cock. I can't help but admire his cock. He's a little above average length wise and has nice girth. I'm personally a girth girl. I might not have had many experiences with sex, but I have a pretty damn good idea of what I like. I've seen my share of dicks, and Wash's is definitely one of the best ones I've seen. Lucky me because Wash is finally all mine.

    I move my hand between my legs and slowly rub circles around my clit as Wash pumps his cock. Our movements are slow as we drink one another in. My eyes roam Wash's body admiring his defined muscles, his smooth skin, his sexy tattoo on his arm, and landing on his hard cock. I swear he's perfect like a Greek god. Wash could easily have been a model, but that's not Wash's personality. He actually hates attention. We have that in common along with Jesse. It was something that bonded the three of us. Wash might be a pretty boy, but he doesn't act like one, which honestly makes him even more attractive. He's kind, caring, and genuine. Plus, good looking, he's the complete package to me.

    Taking in the handsome man in front of me, I can't help but think of how badly I want him inside of me. I might not be ready for it, but damn, I like thinking about it. I especially like thinking about it as I touch myself while he watches me. This wouldn't be my first time touching myself to images of Wash or of him watching me. However, usually the images are in my head and pure fantasy. To my great delight, fantasy has merged with reality creating a bliss I didn't know could exist.

My free hand moves to lightly pinch one of my nipples as I rub my clit. I glance at Wash's face to see his eyes on my body as his gaze moves from my hand playing with my nipples to my hand between my legs spurring him to rub himself faster. I rub my clit a little faster, but I'm not trying to cum too quickly. I'm enjoying this and I want it to last a little bit longer, so I slow down a bit trying to edge myself because I can already feel my orgasm building and threatening to send me into sweet bliss.

Sometimes when I've masturbated in the past, I've struggled to cum. I don't know if I would just get to in my head or what, but there were times I just couldn't get there. I was a tad afraid I would freeze up during this experiment of mine or that I wouldn't be able to cum because I'd be too in my head, but thankfully none of that is a problem, not with Wash. I've never ignored the raw emotions he can invoke in me. His ability to make me feel comfortable, safe, and even loved has a type of power over me that I can't explain. However, I don't care if I get an explanation because I embrace the comfort his control brings me. I'm not even totally sure it's control, but it's certainly something that's for sure.

Wash and I are both enjoying the show we are each putting on for one another, but I can't take not touching him anymore. My hand that is switching between my nipples reaches out to Wash and lands on his chest. It's about all I can manage as I'm getting lost in my fantasies turning into reality. Wash takes my hint and moves so he is slightly leaning over me before his lips land on mine. Wash doesn't stop rubbing his cock while I continue to rub my clit faster than I was before losing to the heat of the moment. Wash's free hand goes to play with my nipples while my free hand grips behind his neck to deepen our kiss.

Part of me wants to give in and tell Wash I'm ready right now, but I know it's the passion of the moment. As much as I want to be ready, I'm not there just yet. I'm close to being ready and this is helping. Every time Wash and I are intimate in some way, it's a step closer to breaking down all the walls I built to protect myself with my fears of being intimate with someone and it being my choice. I didn't even realize I had built walls with sex, it doesn't matter because Wash is breaking them down and brings me to a place of bliss, pleasure, and safety. I chase my orgasm, rubbing my clit a bit more aggressively while Wash's fingers play with my nipples. Wash is also chasing his release as he rubs himself faster, our kisses grow more wild and erratic as we both chase our bliss. I feel warm, wet liquid on my belly knowing Wash has found his release, and knowing he's satisfied, I'm able to let myself crash over the edge. Wash and I break our kiss as we both relax, catching our breath.

"Damn, Doll. I needed this tonight. Thank you." Wash kisses me on the forehead. "Let's go get you cleaned up"

I can't help the smile that comes across my face. Wash is pleased with me and that makes me extremely happy. I'm also thrilled that I was able to give Wash a good night when things are a little rough for him at work. I love doing things that make him happy. I care so much for him, I always have. I know he is aware of how appreciative I am for him looking out for me. He's my guardian.

Wash and I clean up from our much needed fun before snuggling up together in bed. Maybe I have a shot at getting the dream I've always wanted. I have a chance to at least get my life together and be functional. It's even better that Wash finally feels the way I do about him. I don't care that it took him longer. I understand why it did, and somehow it makes it even better. I'm thrilled he even returns my feelings at all. Maybe I can have my happy ending, I hope at least that is where all this leads. For now, I'll enjoy the moment and let myself gain some much needed rest.

Chapter 12
Wash

I can't believe Christmas is just around the corner. I normally dread Christmas because my parents throw a huge Christmas Eve party that I have to attend every year. The only time I've gotten out of it is when I was working. Christmas for my family is a big show. It's about the big, elaborate party complete with Santa, a giant decorated Christmas tree, fancy party bags for guests, fancy food, being dressed your best, and alcohol. Then there's who can give the best gift in the family, who can donate the most amount of money to charity, and pretend we spend massive amounts of time together. It's a show my parents put on for their friends, coworkers, and so on.

This year, I plan to bring Lexi as my date. I've gone single since I broke up with Kate. Before Kate, I always made sure I had a date to bring even if I wasn't serious with them. It's actually how I started to date Kate in the first place. I needed a last minute date, Kate was free, and after that one thing led to another. By Valentine's Day, I found myself dating Kate. After I broke off our engagement, I promised myself I wouldn't bring a date unless I was serious about the girl. Well, I'm very serious about Lexi.

I'm sure my parents will add their opinions about me dating Lexi. I'm sure they will find fault with her for one reason or another. My friends have found reasons not to like Lexi. Everyone is so convinced Kate and I are perfect together that they will disapprove of Lexi. Honestly, I don't think it mattered who I dated after Kate, my friends and family would give them a hard time. I hate that they are giving Lexi a hard time. I'm used to my family being difficult with girls that I date, but I'm not used to my friends having an issue.

Personally, I don't care what people think about Lexi and me being a couple. It's not their relationship. I certainly don't need my friends and family to approve of her. It would be nice if they did. What matters is that I'm happy. I'm the happiest I've ever been with Lexi.

Some guys might get annoyed that they have to take things slow with Lexi. I know some of my friends would hate not being able to fuck a girl right away. If it was someone else, I might care. However, with Lexi, it's not like that. I'm enjoying taking our time exploring our bodies. I know when we have sex, it's going to be amazing. In a way, I like fooling around like teenagers. I was always in a rush with girls in my teens. I wanted sex and didn't care much about foreplay. As I matured, I found myself engaging more in foreplay. I realized it was my need for control. It was easy for me to control sex but I had to learn to control the foreplay part. I had to learn how to be a dom. Now, I've mastered my version of being a dom, and I finally get to enjoy it with someone who embraces it while reliving experiences I rushed through previously.

Not that I can think much about sex or anything with this case that I caught. I didn't think this case would be this crazy. It started off with the possibility of insurance fraud, but when we dug deep with security footage of the business with the fires we realized there was an arsonist involved. The problem is, the guy is smart. He never shows his face because he knows where the cameras are and how to avoid them. He oddly even knows how to avoid street cameras and always has a hoodie on with a baseball cap and the hood of the hoodie up.

The only reason we know it's a guy is because of build. The guy is going above and beyond to hide his identity, which I get because he doesn't want to get caught. However, it feels more like he doesn't want us to know who he is.

He poses as a worker or a handyman of sorts to get in. It was two fires that have now turned into three. We can't figure out the arsonist's motive or the connection the three businesses have. We know he targets the water heaters. The business are all random. A laundry mat, an arcade, and a flower shop. We are struggling to figure it out. Even the detectives we are working with are struggling to figure it out.

When I said I wanted a case, I didn't want something so complex. Insurance fraud seemed easy enough. A good, easy case to get my feet wet with a proper case that was mine. Instead, I got this overly complex case that is consuming my time. I don't mind working overtime, but it's a bit hard when I'm trying to build a new relationship. In some ways, it's good Lexi needed to take things slow with the way this case is turning out.

After a day of not getting anywhere with the case, I'm glad to be heading home. I was going to stay late, but I decided against it because I need the break. I thought I fully knew what I was getting into with fire investigations, and I know it was still the right move. Yet, it's different and I'm adjusting. Then having this case that is turning into a headache is making me glad the holidays are coming up, so I might get some type of a break. Although like Jesse always said 'Criminals never take a holiday'. I hope this one does.

Lexi wanted to get a Christmas tree, so I let her get one. We bought decorations for the tree and stockings to hang over the fireplace. Lexi didn't go too crazy. She wanted a little something to enjoy because she can. I've noticed Lexi is enjoying the little things in life. She was denied so much for so long, and now with everything she desires at her fingertips, she chooses to enjoy simple pleasures. It's one of the many things I love about her.

With Lexi, I find myself looking forward to everything with her. Even holidays I didn't enjoy before. I wonder what it will be like to have her on my arm at the party. I'm excited to show her off while showing her a good time. Well, the best time I can be surrounded by my judgemental family and their friends. Still, I'm oddly looking forward to the event, which I normally dread. Seems Lexi is changing my life in very positive ways, and I know I'm changing hers. Not just because I gave her a place to live, but because I'm showing her how much she is wanted. I don't think Lexi has ever felt wanted, not even by Jesse, but it doesn't matter because I'm going to change all of that. I'm not letting her go now that she is mine, and knowing Lexi, she doesn't want me to let her go. Not a second time. Over my dead body will I lose the only person who knows who I really am. I won't lose the only girl I can show my true dominating self to. I play for keeps, and keeping Lexi is starting to become non negotiable.

Chapter 13

Lexi

I can't believe I'm shopping for a cocktail dress to wear to Wash's parents party. I've heard tales of their famous Christmas Eve parties. They hold them at the ballroom of their town and country club. It's a big deal to be invited. All the high class of Union City and then some get invited to this party. The governor even attends the event. It's huge, and I'm going to very much be out of my league.

However, I'm excited to go. The downside is, I have to deal with Wash's family. Not that they are bad people. I've met them a few times before. They didn't pay much attention to me as I was just a kid then. I'm not sure how they will feel about me attending their fancy party, but I don't care because I'm not there for them. I'm going for Wash, and to experience the Spencer's ever popular Christmas Eve Party. I used to hear about it when Jesse would go as Wash's guest. Jesse painted it in such a fairytale way that I wanted to attend. Jesse always said I was too young even though Wash was willing to let me go. Jesse guilt tripped me into staying home to watch our mom and to make sure she didn't drink herself too hard into oblivion.

Sometimes I think Jesse hated me tagging along with him and Wash. Wash never seemed to mind. I always assumed it was normal for Jesse to get annoyed at me for tagging along with him because I was his little sister. I did tag along often. A lot of times Jesse didn't have a choice because our mom wasn't responsible enough to watch me.

When Jesse first died, I was so angry that he left me with our mom. Yet, at the same time I was devastated he was gone and never coming back. I was torn between being angry that he left me and the fact that he was dead. I know it wasn't his fault that he left me. Despite everything, Jesse was a good brother and he did the best he could. He was just a child himself. I always admired and loved him for all his sacrifices. Sometimes, I fear I wasn't good at showing it, but I did try. I wasn't sure how to show my love and admiration to him, but I tried in my own ways.

The holidays always make me think of Jesse. I haven't visited his grave since I left six years ago. I don't know why I haven't been to visit. I've thought about it, but going to his grave always felt so raw. It was hard to accept my brother was gone when it often felt like he was the only family I had. It was hard to consider our mom family, especially now with everything she put me through. I always knew Jesse was the buffer between us, but it became so harshly apparent when he died.

Maybe it's time I ask Wash to take me to Jesse's grave. I'm not sure how often Wash has visited, but knowing Wash, he goes on Jesse's birthday, which is coming up in February. It might be nice for us to go together. Perhaps I can find some closure. One thing about therapy is that I'm learning I have my fair share of wounds to heal. That's okay, I'm learning to embrace the scars that I have.

It's been so nice finding my own path. I even got a job at Cool Beans as a barista. I can't believe I'm going to be working at my favorite coffee place. I know that might seem lame to be excited for what many would consider a dead end job. However, when I was a young teen, and thinking about my first job. I always thought about working at Cool Beans.

So, it's kind of cool to get to do what young teenage me dreamed of even if it was just working at the local coffee shop.

I wish Wash was shopping with me because I have no idea what looks good on me, or what is appropriate. So, I decide to try on some dresses and send pictures to Wash for guidance. He's at work, and I know he's been busy, but if he can respond he will. If he doesn't respond in time, I'll have to pick something on my own and hope it's good.

With a few dresses in tow, I head to the dressing rooms to try on dresses. The dress code is that guys have to wear tuxes, and the ladies have to wear green or red. I like red, especially dark red for a dress color, but unfortunately the options in that color aren't my style. So, I picked dark green dresses to try on.

The first two I hate and don't even bother to take pictures to send to Wash. I slip into a satin long sleeve cocktail wrap dress with a cute little bow that ties slightly off the hip. The trim of the skirt and sleeves have ruffles. It's a little low cut, but it makes my boobs look awesome, and the cute key hole back makes me instantly fall for the dress. No need to take pictures. I know this is the one. As I'm slipping out of the dress, I hear a voice I know. It's Ashley, one of Wash's friends and Kevin's girlfriend. I can hear her talking with another woman. I peak my head out and realize it's Kate. I've seen a couple of pictures of her, and I know that's her. Jealousy stirs a bit in me because I know she is the one those closest to Wash have picked to be his wife.

"So, tell me about this girl living with Wash." Kate says as her and Ashley enter the dressing room. I quickly put my head back into my changing room and shut the door. I can't go out there now, but I can get changed. I'll hide out here as long as I have to.

"Oh, she's some young girl that was his dead best friend's sister." Ashely answers casually.

"That's right. I've heard him talk about her before. Lindsey, or Lisa. Something like that. He was always annoyingly fond of her." Kate comments.

"It's Lexi, and yeah he's more than fond of her. I'm pretty sure they are screwing one another. Wash is definitely into her and she's all over him like some desperate teenager hitting on her crush. It's hard to watch because of how cringe it is." Ashley notes as I hear them enter their own dressing rooms. I should make a run for it, but I can't. My anxiety is winning because I'm paralyzed with the fear that they will see me. Trust me I don't want to be stuck here listening to all the nasty things they are saying about me.

"Let him have his fun with some young chick. He will get tired of her. I mean the man gave up a great career at the fire station to go work fire investigations. He's clearly not thinking straight because Wash is going to hate working with the white shirts. I don't know why he thought that was a good idea. Now, he's shacking up with some chick who's probably barely eighteen." Kate says. Well, they're not being quiet about their conversation. Of course, they don't know I'm here, and there aren't many other people in the fitting rooms. Hell, for all I know it's just the three of us. I can't believe this is actually happening. What are the chances I would run into them here? Shouldn't they be at work? Or at the very least somewhere I am not.

"She's twenty one. At least she is not freshly eighteen. Still, I can't believe he took her in. She was apparently homeless before she arrived on Wash's doorstep. Her mom's in prison and her dad ran out before she was born. Talk about not ideal material for someone like Wash. She's clearly using him to get a free meal ticket." Ashley states in a disgusted tone. Wow. I knew they didn't like me, but damn, it's brutal hearing their thoughts out loud. Is this what the Christmas Eve party is going to be like? I'm not so thrilled to attend now, but I won't back out. I'm going even if it might not be the magical night I want. I'm going for Wash because I know how much he struggles around his family. I'm his emotional support for the event and I want to be that for him.

"I bet Wash is totally blind to her little schemes. He's always had a soft spot for her. I wanted to gag when he would talk about her because it was clear how much he cared about her. I told myself it was just because she was someone from his childhood. She's his dead best friend's sister. It's the only piece he has left of Jesse. I didn't want to believe he could look at her in a sexual way. I guess she grew up." Kate replies bitterly.

"Didn't you two argue all the time over Lexi?" Ashley probes. I can't tell if she digging for juicy gossip or genuinely curious. Ashley is snobby, so I'm leaning toward the juicy gossip. However, what now has my attention is what Kate just said. They argued over me?

"Yeah, he was almost obsessed with finding her. He kept trying to find a way to contact her. He didn't believe she would just stop talking to him out of nowhere. Wash was scared she wasn't in good hands with her mom. Something about him not trusting the mother because she was a lush. So, he would spend time trying to find her. It would get in the way of our time together. It was ridiculous. I guess he might have been right about the mom if she ended up in prison. I'm sure this Lexi girl is nothing but white trash from the wrong side of the tracks. I'm sure she came crawling back to Wash to mooch off him. It's disgusting how low people will go." Kate's tone is far too judgemental for my liking.

Although, it's nice to know Wash looked for me. He never mentioned that he looked for me, only that he was worried about me. It's not surprising he had a hard time finding me since we moved around a lot. We either didn't have cell phones or if we did, it was a burner phone. We only had the internet if there was free wifi somewhere. I wasn't on social media. Then you add my moms fake identities. Shit, I think she had made me fake identities too because many times she would tell me I had to go by a different name or last name. In many ways, I always felt like a ghost because of how invisible I felt with my mom.

Deciding it's best to get the hell out of dodge while they are still in their changing rooms, I grab the dress I want, and leave the others hung up on the hanging on the hook. I practically run out of the dressing room because I don't want to risk them coming out and I'm also trying to ignore my anxiety that is threatening to leave me motionless. I head to check out as quickly as I can. I don't want to run into them at all. I quickly buy the dress and head to another store for accessories.

Relief floods my system as I feel my body relax knowing I'm no longer near Ashley and Kate. I can't believe I ran into them. At least they didn't see me, or I don't think they did. I push them out of mind and focus on my task of finding accessories. I need shoes, some type of jewelry, and a clutch. Thankfully, the stores aren't terribly busy since most people are at work. I like going shopping when people are at work and school.

I get my accessories. I decide on light gold shimmer pumps, gold pearl teardrop earrings, with a matching necklace that will go well with the neckline of the dress, and a gold clutch. I'm happy with my outfit for the party even if I'm a little more nervous now. At least, I found out Wash was looking for me. It's comforting to know he didn't forget about me as I feared he would. It's a shame what his friends think. Maybe one day I can change their minds about me. I don't want to come between Wash and his friends. I care about Wash, and I know I'm falling deeply in love with him. Maybe I'm already in love and not wanting to admit it because it's no longer a daydream. I also don't want to ruin Wash's life like my mother said I would. I don't want to hate myself like that.

So, I hope his friends come around and give me a chance. It's Christmas after all, maybe there will be a Christmas miracle.

Chapter 14
Wash

Lexi looks gorgeous in her dress. She did well picking it out. I'm glad she was able to confidently pick something out. However, since she's gone shopping she's been a little off. Initially, she was excited for the party, which honestly surprised me because I didn't think being surrounded by judgy people was something that would interest her. Then she told me how badly she always wanted to go, but Jesse always told her no. She understood why he said no when she was a kid, but when she reached teenage years, she thought for sure she was old enough to go. However, Jesse never budged. Instead, he made her stay home to watch their mom. Jesse made the Christmas event seem like a fairytale to Lexi, and she wants to experience it for herself.

I always wondered why Jesse never brought Lexi to the party. I knew she would enjoy it and the age limit was thirteen as long as they could behave. My parents didn't want to be unreasonable knowing many of their friends had children. However, they also didn't want little punks ruining their fancy party either. I know Lexi would have behaved beautifully. She was never one to act out. Even as a kid she was fairly well behaved. She had her moments like all of us do, but overall she was mature for her age. I had asked Jesse to bring her, but he made excuses. I chalked it up to him needing a break, and the party was a great chance for him to have a break. Jesse deserved to enjoy himself too. It's unfortunate Lexi had to pay the price. In my opinion, he could have let her go at least once.

As much as I wanted to include Lexi in everything Jesse and I did, I also knew Jesse needed a break. He was often stressed. I know he often felt overwhelmed with raising a younger sibling on his own. On top of that he had to care for their drunken mom, which was like having another child to care for. So, I never tried to push him too hard. I figured it was best to let him have some events that were just him and I. Even if I wanted nothing more than to include Lexi. Jesse was my best friend. I felt this sense of loyalty to him, and it often made me choose Jesse over Lexi. I hated choosing between the two of them.

 I break from my memories to go check on Lexi's progress on getting ready. I find Lexi in my bathroom putting finishing touches to her makeup while lightly curling her hair. I'll never understand how women can do their hair and makeup at the same time. For some silly reason when I would watch Kate get ready I found it overwhelming. However, watching Lexi doesn't overwhelm me, it provokes something in me because Lexi looks stunning. I simply can't wait to show her off tonight. I still wish we could bail out of the event and stay home instead, but I promised my parents I would come. Plus, I still think Lexi wants to go even if something has her a little slightly off kilter. I've tried probing to see what threw her off, but Lexi keeps saying it was nothing. Maybe it is nothing or maybe she isn't ready to share. I won't push her. She doesn't have to share every emotion or thought with me. I know she is processing a lot as she goes through therapy. She is healing, grieving, and forging ahead with her future. I trust that if it's something important she will tell me when she is ready.

 I'm glad Lexi is healing. I still want to hunt down the assholes who touched her against her will. I especially want to get my hands on the asshole who raped her. She wasn't even eighteen making it statutory rape. Rape is bad no matter how you look at it. However, when it's done to a minor, it only adds insult to injury. Knowing Judy, she didn't even care what her boyfriends were doing to her daughter. In her twisted mind, I'm sure she thought Lexi deserved it. At least, Judy is in prison, and she's not getting out for a long time, if ever. If Judy ever gets out of prison, she is never coming near Lexi again. I will make sure of that. I'll also have to restrain from punching her in the face for being such a shitty parent to both her kids.

 Now that we are ready to go to the party, we start our drive to our destination. The country club is about twenty minutes outside of the city limits. It's the weird area in between the county and city where it's almost the perfect mix of both. With having to fight city traffic it will take a good forty minutes or so. That's providing the holiday traffic through city isn't outrageous. The drive doesn't bother me. I always enjoy a good drive, especially in the country or near the coast. What I don't love is fighting the city traffic on a holiday. Luckily, when we come back home, most of the traffic should be gone.

Through the Flames of Desire

We make it before the guests arrive. My parents insisted I come at least thirty minutes early before their guests were to arrive. They like to show a unified family front, which I don't know why they care when my sister is in Paris with her family. She's the one they love to show off, not me. I guess because I'm the one actually home for the holidays, I get stuck being showcased by my parents. Although, I'm fairly certain they aren't expecting me to bring Lexi as a date. I did tell them I had a plus one. I simply neglected to tell them who so I didn't have to deal with them trying to convince me to not bring Lexi. This night is going to be rough enough as it is. Them not knowing actually plays to everyone's advantage.

Getting out of my car, I toss the keys to the valet before heading to the passenger's side to open the door for Lexi. I offer Lexi my hand. Without hesitation, Lexi slips her hand into mind and I help her out. She smiles as I link my arm with her's before we enter the country club. The place is fully decorated for Christmas. There is a huge Christmas tree in the lobby, white lights are wrapped around everything they can be, ornaments strategically hung from the ceiling, and all the fireplaces have stockings hung over them while the mantels are decorated with mini poinsettias. In the ballroom where the party is being held hosts another overly large Christmas tree. Gold, red, and green are splashed everywhere they can be from napkins, silver wears, glasses, flowers, and gifts that are the party favors.

"Wow, this is beautiful. Please tell me, you will dance with me." Lexi pleads as her eyes light up with hope. Lexi loves to dance. She's a decent dancer too. Between dance and her art, she was always begging for classes and supplies. Unfortunately, they couldn't afford it. I helped her out where I could. I didn't want to piss Jesse off too much. He was never fond when I would help Lexi too often.

"I will dance all night with you if that's what you want, Doll." I reply with a smile. I know how to ballroom dance. My mother thought it was very important that I knew how to ballroom dance. I think she thought it would be a way for me to lure a suitable wife. Everything my mom has done for my sister and I was to lead us to suitable marriages that would benefit the family. Love is never a part to the equation, which begs me to question if my parents are as in love as they claim to be.

"I might just hold you to that." Lexi beams with a little mischief hidden in her tone.

"Be careful, Doll. You know I can give you exactly what you want," I lean into her ear. "You just have to tell me what and when."

"What about the where?" Lexi mischievously questions quietly so only I can hear her.

"I'll handle the where." I wink at her which causes her cheeks to turn a light shade of pink.

"You play a dangerous game, Lieutenant. What if I told you I want you to dance with me as much as possible tonight. Then we go back home so you can open your Christmas gift." Lexi turns so she's in front me. She puts her hands on my chest as my arms wrap around her waist.

"I told you not to get me a Christmas gift." I lightly scold. I got her a gift, but that's not the point.

"I didn't say I bought it, now did I?" Lexi counters as a mischievous grin crosses her beautiful heart shaped face.

"Are you sure, Doll?" I didn't think she would be ready for sex so soon. I'm not complaining. It's been fun fooling around and exploring each other's bodies. I love getting to know her intimately but for fuck sake I need to fuck her brains out soon. I would never rush her, but it's a relief to know she is ready sooner rather than later.

"I'm very sure. We might have to take it slow, but I want to. I trust you and I'm finally comfortable with giving you all the control." She confidently confesses.

"Well, now I really can't wait for this party to be over with." I reply before I kiss her deeply on the lips.

For a moment, everything fades away. I'm focused on Lexi. We don't kiss long, but it's long enough for me to enjoy the feel of her. She fits perfectly in my arms, and her body morphs to mine beautifully. I'm more than excited to get home. I was starting to pick up that she might be ready, but I didn't want to rush her. Of course, Lexi adorably picks Christmas to be ready for sex. Unfortunately, the cloud I'm floating on disappears the minute I hear footsteps behind us followed by someone clearing their throat. Lexi and I break our kiss before facing my family. Although, Kate walking in with my parents is something I did not expect. I didn't even think she would be invited, but I guess she is still on good terms with my parents.

"Washington, you made it, and you bought a date." My mother addresses us as she not subtly looks between me and Lexi. The look on her face isn't pleased. I can see the judgemental look on my father's face. Although, honestly, my father has what I like to call resting judgement face.

Meanwhile, Kate has the satisfied look of a cat who just caught a bird. The bird in the situation is Lexi. My guardian instincts kick in as I pull Lexi to the side, my arm wrapping around her waist.

"I told you I was bringing a date." I casually reply, trying to keep the fact that I'm already annoyed at them. I knew they would be judgmental pricks. However, I didn't see Kate being tossed into the mix. I know they invited her with intentions of her and I having some romantic reconnection. It's either that or they genuinely like Kate. Either way, it doesn't affect me like they think it does.

"I didn't think you were serious. You haven't bought a date since you and Kate broke up." My mother replies as if she's not trying to intimidate Lexi with my ex who happens to be standing right next to her.

The thing is, no one even knows we are truly in a relationship. The rumors are certainly there, but neither of us have felt the need to confirm it to the public, knowing people would be dicks. My friends are already proof that they aren't happy about my so-called midlife crisis. I know that's what they fucking think. It's what most people will think. It's what comes to mind when you hear about a person is dating someone more than five years younger than him. You go past ten and people instantly think it's a midlife crisis or the person is trying to relive their younger days. It's complete bullshit.

Clearly, my parents are on team Kate. Great. I was dreading this night, but now I want to walk Lexi out of here, get back in our car, and go home. I'm not against opening my Christmas present early. I'd much rather spend the entire night fucking Lexi into oblivion than spend even an hour of my night at this party.

"Well, I've moved on and now I have a date. Oh look, your guests are arriving," I nod my head toward several guests entering the ballroom. "You should go greet them while I take my date to get some champagne." With that, I move my arm from Lexi's waist, and link it with her arm before turning us away from my parents. "We are staying for an hour and leaving. We came, we saw, we left." I tell Lexi.

"I agree, but I get at least one dance." Lexi negotiates.

"That we will certainly do." I reply, a smug grin crossing my face. My parents and Kate will hate seeing me dance with Lexi.

For the next hour, my goal is to dance with Lexi, and get out of this party without losing my cool on someone. I'm not happy with my parents, which is nothing new. We tend to butt heads when it comes to how I live my life. You would think I ran off and become some drug addicted fuck up. I knew they wouldn't approve of Lexi. They only seem to approve of Kate. I don't know what everyone sees in Kate, or why Kate can't move on. However, I'm not staying stuck in the past like most people around me seem to be doing. I'm moving on and I'm doing it with Lexi whether anyone likes it or not. They can all fuck off for all I give a shit.

Lexi and I grab some champagne and mingle among the arriving guests. About twenty minutes after the party starts a string quartet comes up. They start playing music and couples flock to the dance floor. I lead Lexi out to the dance floor and we begin to dance. Despite the judgements from my parents, it is nice to be dancing with Lexi. Lexi is slowly weaving her way into every aspect of my life, and I wouldn't have it any other way. She's the missing piece that completes my puzzle of life.

Chapter 15
Lexi

The party is every bit as enchanting as I thought it would be. Well, except for Kate showing up. I guess that's why I ran into her in the dress store. I didn't even think about why she was there or the fact that she said something about attending the party. However, I was too busy trying to escape without being seen. Not to mention my anxiety was through the roof trying to get out of there unseen. I knew my chances of meeting Kate were higher than I would have liked. She was friends with Wash's friends and apparently she is chummy with Wash's parents. As much as I would have liked to avoid her forever, the reality is I was bound to meet her. At least, when I finally ran into her face to face Wash was with me.

Thankfully, Wash manages to keep us from running into Kate or his parents. We spend most of our time dancing while enjoying food and champagne in between dances. Wash mingles with a few guests, and keeps the conversations short and sweet. Wash is charming as he chats with guests. Wash may never want to admit it, but he's got the Spencer charm. I've only interacted with his family a handful of times including tonight, and they all have this charm and swag that entices people to want to be near them. I'm also enjoying Wash showing me off to the people he does meet. I'm certainly not Jesse's little sister anymore. After an hour and half of being swayed on the dance floor, eating and drinking amazing stuff, and being shown off, Wash leads us out of the party to the valet who gets Wash's car. Wash tips the valet, generously I might add, before opening my door for me to slide into the car. Damn, he's such a gentlemen, and I love being treated like a lady. Wash gets in the car and once he's ready we take off back toward home.

Wash is eager to get home. I am too. As nice as the party was, it wasn't worth dealing with dodging Kate. Still, I had a good time, but not I'm ready to get home to be with my sexy firefighter alone. Christmas was my goal to be intimate with Wash. I know I didn't need to set a goal and some might say it put unnecessary pressure on myself. However, it did the opposite for me. It gave me a goal to work toward. Plus, fooling around with Wash in the meantime to get myself comfortable helped in my horny motivations. There is a small part of me that's nervous because I'm afraid my PTSD will take over at the last minute and I won't be able to go through with it. However, I don't believe it will happen because I'm very comfortable with Wash. Every time we fool around I get closer to wanting to give into my need to have him inside of me. I don't think I can hold off any longer, and I don't want to.

The car ride home passes by in a blur as anticipation builds in my core. I've thought about being intimate with Wash so many times. I've played us having sex everywhere in his townhouse in my head more times than I count. I planned something special for Christmas. I did a little online shopping and purchased a sexy lace red bra and thong with a golden sheen to it. My original thought was to get a sexy Santa outfit, but I decided to go simple knowing Wash would prefer it that way.

Before I know it, Wash is parking the car in the driveway. I take a deep breath as anticipation makes my nerves jump. I'm excited for tonight. I've been thinking about it for weeks now. I'm giddy, which is good because I keep waiting for my anxiety to make an appearance. So far, my excitement is winning, and it feels good to know my anxiety is finally on the losing end of my emotions.

"So, how do you want to do this, Doll?" Wash questions, turning off the car.

"I have something I want to change into for you," I reply without hesitation.

Wash chuckles at my enthusiasm. "Okay, then. Why don't you go get changed? I'll give you ten minutes. Oh, and don't forget the position I told you to take, Doll." Wash reminds me as he turns of the car and wiggles the keys in front of my face.

"I won't," I say, kissing Wash on the lips before I snatch the keys from his hand and exit the car.

I can't get in the door fast enough as excitement pulses through me. I can't remember the last time I was this giddy with anticipation. I bolt up the stairs, and into Wash's room. I quickly head to the master bath to strip off my clothes and take off my makeup. I purposely didn't go overboard with my makeup or hair knowing that I would want an easy transition. I planned this night in my head for weeks. I went over every detail to make sure things went as smoothly as possible. I might have over thought it, but for once my over thinking paid off.

Once I slip into my bra and thong, I debate putting on my silk robe, but decide against it. I mainly want it for a security blanket, but I'm going to go against the need to wrap my body up so no one can see it. Wash has seen me naked plenty of times at this point, he clearly likes what he sees. Besides, tonight, I'm giving Wash full control. There's no sense in covering up when I know I'm going to end up naked. I'm only wearing lingerie because it makes me feel sexy, and the boost to my confidence is helpful.

Exiting the bathroom, I head over to the bed, and assume the potion next to it that Wash wants me to take. After our first encounter of setting fire to our desires, Wash gave me a couple of things he wanted me to do when I was ready. Wash wants full control in the bedroom. I can't deny his dominating side brings out my submissive side. A side I didn't even fully realize I had until Wash ignited it to life. The position I'm to take is kneeling with my head bowed and my hand resting on my lap.

My heart gallops in my chest as I hear the door open followed by footsteps and the door closing. I resist fidgeting with my hands. It's a habit I do when I'm nervous. While I wouldn't say I'm nervous, I am excited. I'm not used to being this excited when it comes to sex. Usually, anything sexual makes me uncomfortable, but not with Wash. Everything with him feels natural even with giving him control. I trust him. I trust that he won't hurt me. I'm not against things being rough and hard with Wash because I know that with whatever pain he gives, there will be pleasure. I also know he won't do anything I don't want or like. Trust is what I was missing with other guys. I never realized how key it was to making me comfortable with sex after my trauma.

I hate acknowledging my trauma. I hate even labeling what happened to me as traumatic, but it was. Part of healing from it is accepting what happened and knowing that it won't be my experience forever. I plan on doing my best to erase what happened to me even if I know I won't be able to fully erase it. It's scars to add to my ever growing badge of honor, but right now I'm not going to focus on that. Right now, I'm going to focus on my sexy firefighter and the pleasure he is about to give me.

"Good girl, Doll." Wash compliments as he dress shoes appear in front of me before his fingers slip under my chin forcing me to look at him. "One last chance to back out now,

Doll. Once I start I can't promise I'll be able to stop." Wash cautions.

This is exactly why I'm comfortable with him because I know he will always put me first. He will always make sure I'm comfortable. I do wish Wash could have been my first. It would have been nice to lose my virginity with someone I liked, knew, and trusted. Unfortunately, that's not how it happened. At least, Wash will make sure that I have a good experience now.

"I'm all yours, Wash. I was always all yours." I know I'm supposed to use Sir when we are in sexual situations, but right now I'm being raw with him. I want to give him every part of me I have left including my heart because I know I'm in love with him. I always have been. I'm not sure I'm ready to tell Wash I love him, but I am ready to be intimate with him.

"You have no idea how perfect you are to me, Lexi, and you are mine. Tonight is all about your pleasure, Doll. So, be a good girl, and get on the bed." Wash commands as his hand falls from my chin.

"Yes, Sir." I reply as the anticipation builds between my legs causing me to slightly rub my thighs together before I get up, and go over to the bed.

Through the Flames of Desire

Climbing on the bed, I lay on my back with my head propped up on the pillows. Wash strips off his clothes until he's completely naked. Wash climbs on the bed, and hovers over me. His muscular arms on either side of my head. "You have to trust me every step of the way, Doll. I have full control, but you can tell me if you don't like something. Do you understand?"

"Yes, Sir." I reply, nodding my head.

Wash doesn't hold back after that. His lips crash onto mine as he works on taking off my bra, which he gets off in no time. His tongue invades my mouth as it begins to swirl with mine. I want to touch Wash, but he hasn't said I can touch him. I'm still learning what is allowed without permission. Wash breaks our kiss before he trails kisses down my jawline until he's kissing my neck, but he's not just kissing. He's nipping at the skin lightly causing a smidge of pain to mix with the pleasure building between legs.

Wash moves his mouth lower, kissing my breasts before he sucks a nipple in his mouth, causing a moan to escape me. Wash switches between sucking and lightly nipping at my nipples before he trails kisses down my stomach. He's being romantic and taking his time to make sure I'm enjoying myself, and I am more than enjoying myself. Wash takes my thong off before parting my legs. Wash lowers his head between my legs with a mischievous grin. He hasn't eaten me out yet. I've sucked him off, but he told me he would only taste me when I was ready to be intimate with him.

With one lick of Wash's tongue between my folds, I know I'm in for a world of pleasure. Wash's tongue finds my clit and circles it before he sucks between his teeth sending pain and pleasure of dangerous levels of pleasure rippling through my body. Moans escape me as Wash assaults my clit with his tongue. It sends me into euphoria. I'm lost in my pleasure as my hips naturally rock against Wash's mouth. Shit, this is so good. I know the orgasm I'm going to have is going to shatter me because the intensity of pleasure building between my legs is unlike anything I've experienced. The pleasure intensifies as Wash sends me closer to the edge. Wash inserts two fingers into my entrance and moves them inside of me to the rhythm of his tongue on my clit. I don't even recognize the moans leaving me. I've never had this before. My body tenses before my orgasm washes over me, causing my body to shake from the intensity.

Wash removes his face from between my legs before he positions his amazing cock at my entrance. Wash doesn't hesitate before he starts pushing against my entrance as he slowly slips in, my juices coating his cock as he enters me. Wash gives me a moment to adjust. I'm tight. I've only been with one guy twice, and that was years ago. Once I'm adjusted to Wash's cock, he begins to move in and out of me at a steady pace. He looks me deep in the eyes as he moves in and out of me. I trust him with every fiber of my being. This man is my guardian, and the man I've been in love with for years. Yet I can tell he's holding back. I know why he is because he is being cautious. I've never actually gave Wash any details on the rape, so I'm sure he doesn't want to do anything that might accidentally trigger me. He's considerate, but the thing about damaged goods is we don't like sweet sex. No, we like it rough, hard, and primal because we are survivors who need to feel alive. Pain is a reminder that you're alive. When the pain of reality mixes with the pleasure of desire, it's the most intoxicating drug in the world. At least, that is from my experience.

"Fuck me like you own me, Wash. Fuck me, so tomorrow I have no doubt who owns me." I say slightly breathless because I'm drowning in pleasure that I've never had before. Pleasure I'm not sure I thought was possible. I thought I had pleasure when Wash and I were fooling around. However, this is totally different.

Wash takes my wrists and pins them above my head. "Be careful what you wish for, Doll." Wash warns before he picks up his pace, slamming into me hard and fast.

I had a feeling Wash would enjoy showing his passion through aggression. Wash might be level headed, but that doesn't mean he won't defend what he loves. Wash pounds into me hard as I wrap my legs around his waist giving him deeper access to slam into me. I want to feel every inch of his dick inside of me. Wash slams his lips on mine, devouring me. Our kisses cover up my moans and his grunts. Our bodies entangled in the perfect way as my ultimate fantasy of being claimed by Wash comes to life. The fire between us is ignited, and there is no putting it out now. We are in this fire together, and it will bind us in the best ways possible.

Wash grunts his release. He breaks our furious kisses before he softly kisses my forehead. Wash lets go of my wrists, and rolls off me. I quickly roll into his arms as I pull the covers around us. Best Christmas Ever! I'm going to be sore tomorrow, but I don't care. I don't ever want to forget that I belong to Wash.

"Are you okay, Doll?" Wash asks as I lay my head on his chest. Wash's arm wraps around me pulling me closer to him as we snuggle under the blankets.

"I'm beyond okay. I'm golden. Thank you for making tonight about me even if it was supposed to be your Christmas present." I joke as I playfully slap him on the chest.

Wash chuckles. "I'm glad you are happy. I wish I could have been your first just so it didn't have to be as horrible as it was.

"It doesn't matter because the first time I chose to have sex was with you. The man who raped me didn't give me a choice because if he did I would have never have let him near me. This was much better because the choice was mine to make, and that makes it my real first time." I reply, truthfully.

"That's a very good way of looking at it. Your resilience never ceases to amaze me." Wash kisses the top of my head.

My eyes grow heavy, and as much as I don't want to go to sleep right after sex, today was a long day. The party took a lot of energy mentally and even emotionally because it wasn't easy having Kate lurking around. People underestimate mental exhaustion and how it can make you tired. However, we are home now, and I can relax in Wash's arms knowing I'm safe. Wash is my guardian. He's always looked out for me.

He's the only person in the world that makes me feel wanted, loved, and safe. Wash is the one person I don't think I can live without.

Chapter 16

Lexi

It's hard to believe that a week ago Wash and I finally had sex, and we haven't been able to stop since then. Wash is busy at work with his case, but when he's home he's all mine in the best ways possible. I've pretty much moved into Wash's room. I was only sleeping in his room when he was home, but now his room is also my room. We are living like an actual couple, and it's a little surreal.

Christmas Day was amazing. We spent the day eating, playing video games, and watching Christmas movies. Sex certainly happened a couple of times. Wash even got me a gift even when he said he wouldn't. I can't deny I love the necklace he gave me. It's a white gold necklace with a diamond encrusted star charm. It's simple, and pretty. I wear it all the time now.

I stroke the star charm of my necklace as I look over my outfit for tonight. Wash and I are going to a New Years Eve Party at Fireball. All his friends are going to be there, and Wash wants to announce our relationship to them. I'm all for it, even if I'm nervous about how his friends will react to the news. It's surreal to think our relationship is official and real. It's what I've dreamed about. There is no denying Wash is my dream guy. I'm pretty sure I built my dream guy around him hence why he is my dream guy.

The problem with said dream guy? Nothing other than the fact that his friends and family think I'm using him. I'm a joke to them. Some gold digger from the other side of the tracks. I can only imagine how they believe Jesse ties into everything. As much as I miss Jesse, I'm glad he's not here because he would never approve of Wash and my relationship. He would just be one more person against us being together.

I truly don't get why they are so against me. I know I'm young, and much younger than Wash. I don't see the age difference, and neither does Wash. It's not even that big of an age difference when you think about it. Unfortunately, everyone else can't stop pointing out our age difference. It's the only thing they can sort of hold against us. Me showing up on Wash's doorstep broke and homeless certainly didn't give me votes. It's not my fault. I tried. I did. Asking Wash for help was my last resort, and if they can't see that, that's on them.

I always planned on reconnecting with Wash at some point. Especially when my mom had her accident and got arrested. I knew with her out of my way, I'd be able to safely reconnect with Wash. I wanted to contact him when I turned eighteen. It was my plan the moment I got in the moving van with Mom at fifteen. However, when eighteen came around I was still reeling from my rape on top of fending off the current creep my mom was dating. I didn't have the confidence to reach out. I wanted to be at least mentally stable when I reached out to Wash. I never planned on him seeing hot mess express me.

Unfortunately, I couldn't hack it on my own without turning to some unsavory things in order to survive. I tried living on the street and shelters, but that was dangerous. I had no choice but to turn to Wash, and I'm glad I did because it worked out. I never imagined when I reconnected with him that we would actually become a couple. I didn't think Wash would ever look at me in that way, and I honestly assumed he would be married by now, but I was wrong. I was very wrong, and for once I'm happy to be wrong.

I do hope that Wash's friends come around. I don't think Wash will ever care if his parents approve of us or not. Wash doesn't need their money. Not that it's all about money, but with Wash's family it sort of is. Wash confided he's been waiting for his parents to cut him off for years. It's why he made investments so that he would be good on his own if they ever wrote him out of the will. Wash tends to question his status in his family. However, with his friends, it's different. His friends are a much bigger part of his life than his family ever has been. I would hate to be the reason Wash stops talking to his friends. Hell, he owns a business with two of them. He's supposed to be the best man in Stephen and Julia's wedding, which is right around the corner. They are getting married at the end of August this coming year. Wash has already expressed he wants me to be his date to the wedding.

The truth is, I'm terrified I will ruin Wash's life just like my mom always said I would. I don't want to prove her right. The night she found out I was texting Wash was one the worst nights for me. My mom was cruel with her words, and I almost started to believe I somehow really caused Jesse's death. I can't even let myself think too hard about that night or her words because I will start to spiral. It's something I've been talking to Dr. Daniels about for weeks now.

    I push the thoughts from my head, and focus on simply getting through the night. It's exciting to announce our relationship. Plus, I look good. I have on a black long sleeve peasant style dress that comes to my knees. I've paired the dress with dark red red ankle heeled boots. My makeup is light, and my hair is done up in a cute messy bun with a few loose strands to frame my face.

    Wash is working late tonight and will be picking me up. It won't take Wash long to get ready. He's a guy. It takes them no effort to look good. The party starts at ten. It's almost nine, which means Wash is going to walk through the door soon to change so we can head out. I know he wants to get there a little early so we can help set up. It's a big party the bar is hosting, and it is an all hands on deck situation. That party is for any first responder and their plus one. The party is so huge they rent out the empty space next to the bar for overflow because the amount of people who show up would fill the bar past capacity. They even open up the rooftop bar that they open for summers.

Sure enough, Wash comes home and flawlessly changes into a black long sleeve cashmere sweater, dark wash jeans, and black dress boots. Flawless, sexy, and all mine. With Wash dressed and ready to go we head to Fireball. Wash and I walk in holding hands. It's not like we've exactly hidden that we are interested in one another. We've tried to keep our PDA on the downlow not wanting everyone to invade us with their thoughts on our relationship. However, the time has come where we need to put our relationship out in the open. Besides, hiding is only fun for so long before it starts to take a toll.

No one says anything about us holding hands, I didn't think they would. I'm not sure they are foolish enough to make comments about us holding hands in front of me because that would piss Wash off. Wash is very protective of me, he wants to shield me away from any hurt and pain that he feels he can control. He can control his friends rude, nasty, and snide comments knowing their words would hurt me. I'd love to say their words would have no effect on me, but that isn't the truth. Due to my years of mental, emotional, and verbal abuse from my mom I take what people say about me to heart like a sponge absorbing the unwarranted hate of others. Wash knows how I internalize things, so I'm sure he's already told his friends to keep their mouths shut around me about their thoughts of me to their damn selves. I'm actually thankful for that because I don't know if I could take hearing the mean things out loud. It's as if saying them outloud brings the terrible lies to life.

Pulling myself from my ruminating thoughts, I get to help setting up the buffet table while Wash starts helping set up kegs. I'm helping set the buffet tables with Julia, Maddie, and Ashley. April is doing stuff behind the bar. Things are awkwardly silent when Wash isn't around. At the very minimum the girls could be nice and strike up a superficial conversation. I know they like Kate and are friends with her, but they are all outsiders to the guys club of friendship. They all had to go through the awkward phase of trying to fit into the group of friends. They could be a little nicer and at least try to befriend me. I guess that's too much to ask.

It's like I'm back in fucking high school dealing with the mean popular girls. I thought people were supposed to grow the hell up after high school. I guess not everyone got the memo. The annoying part is it's not like they are better than me. They all work average jobs, and are middle class. They don't even compete with Wash's tax bracket, which is where I thought all the snobby people would be. I guess I was mistaken. I hate dealing with these mean girls that are all closer to thirty than high schoolers. For being supposedly older than me, they are the ones acting like teenagers while I'm the one acting like the adult.

Thankfully, finishing setting up for the party doesn't take long with so many people helping. Guests start pouring into the bar shortly after ten. The bar is closed for the party as a private event. The guys have been doing this party since the bar first opened. It's their tradition. It's grown over the years hence the need for extra space. It's a huge event that Wash looks forward to every year. I'm glad I can be a part of it this year and for the years to come.

After an hour or so of mingling and being introduced as Wash's girlfriend to people I will probably not see again for another year, I'm glad we are taking a seat at one of the booths. Wash's friends join us with the guys piling their respective girls on their laps so we all can fit. Wash wraps his arms around my waist as I lean back against his muscular chest. I let the safety of Wash's arms ease my social anxiety.

The group is chatting as we all take a moment to enjoy our drinks. The bar is hopping with guests. Some are dancing in the middle of the bar where they set up a little dance area. I wanted to dance with Wash, but we got caught socializing.

Maybe later on even though midnight is quickly approaching. The party will go until one and then we are going to stay and help clean up. So, we won't be getting home until very late. I'm glad we will be able to sleep in.

"So, any good new years plans, Wash?" Stephen inquires, taking a sip of his beer.

"Nothing spectacular. I do plan on going on a nice vacation with Lexi. It will be nice to have our first vacation as a couple together. I'm thinking of somewhere with a beach." Wash answers casually like he totally didn't just drop the bomb we are a couple. To be honest, I really didn't know how Wash planned on telling his friends. I didn't ask because they are his friends. He knows the best way to approach them with this. I guess the best way was to randomly drop it into conversation. Honestly, it's a relief to have it so casual. I was afraid Wash would make a speech or something that would put us painfully in the spotlight. I should have known Wash would do something casual, but anxiety is a tricky animal.

"Oh, you two are officially together?" Ashley asks, pointing her finger between the two of us like she can't believe we actually made things official. She's not the only one who's attempting, but failing, to act like we didn't just become the topic of gossip. I'm sure they will all talk about us behind our backs because their judgy looks are giving them all away. They could have at least pretended to be happy. Their reactions are certainly sending my anxiety to spike as I take a sip of my own beer trying to seek comfort in Wash's arms.

"Well, it's not a secret that Lexi and I have feelings for one another. We decided to make things official between us." Wash responds as he grips his beer bottle that's resting on my lap so tightly it's making his knuckles white.

"I guess that means Lexi is sticking around." Hunter adds, trying to joke, but it's clear it's not really a joke, which makes things a little awkward. Great. This is what I was afraid of.

"Sorry to disappoint, but I'll be around for a while. Let's face it, once Wash and I reconnected there was no separating us again." I add with my own little smug smirk before taking a sip of my beer again trying to drown their disgusted looks from my memory. I'm a beer girl, which clearly makes me stand out amongst the other girls of the group because they are all drinking wine or wine coolers. Just another thing to make me stick out like a sore thumb. Whatever, I won't change what I like to fit in with a bunch of stuck up bitches. Appealing to their likes and interests has only failed me in the past.

"That's right. I lost Lexi once, and I won't lose her again." Wash adds as he holds me closer to him. You would think his friends would be happy he reconnected with someone who is important to him. Unfortunately, to Wash's friends, I'm simply a ghost from his past back to haunt him.

"Well, that's great. I'm happy for you two." Stephen says as he tries to muster a smile. He's lying through his teeth.

"So, Lexi, anything good planned for the upcoming year?" Julia asks, directly targeting me as if I wasn't already the topic of conversation.

"I'm starting a job at Cool Beans next week. I'm thinking of looking into college courses. I'm not really sure what I would want to major in. I like drawing, so graphic design has always been an interest. There's also the idea of becoming a social worker or counselor, so that I could help teens and young adults with addiction, trauma, and mental illness." I reply, honestly.

It's true that I've been thinking about what I'd like to do with my life. Options were something I didn't have before. I never bothered to think about college knowing I wouldn't be able to afford it. I did try to apply for scholarships, but with moving so frequently my best bet was online courses. Unfortunately, having access to a computer was an issue.

Even if I did manage to get a computer and have internet, the chances of my mom pawning my computer were high. So, I stopped thinking about college, and focused on what I could do, which was work.

I don't know what I'd like to do just yet. The possibilities are endless, especially with Wash backing me. He's already offered to pay for college. Wash didn't go to college like his parents had hoped. Instead, he focused on becoming a firefighter while Jesse focused on becoming a cop. I'm not sure what I'd like to do. I want something I can make my own, which is why I like the idea of graphic design. It would be cool to illustrate kids books, covers, logos, and other stuff. Ever since Wash bought me art supplies, I've been honing my craft, and I'm proud that I haven't lost my artistic touch.

"That's great." Stephen replies, not really caring about my answer.

"Yeah, it sounds like you have some good options." Ashley adds with very little effort.

The rest of the group adds their half ass encouragements before the topic shifts to Stephen and Julia's wedding. Everyone at the table is involved in the wedding somehow. I think I'm the only one who isn't a bridesmaid. Not that I would really want to be a bridesmaid. Julia seems like she would be a real bridezilla. Then there's the fact that Kate is one of her bridesmaids, and that means I'd have to spend unwanted time around Kate. So, I'm good with not being involved. I will be Wash's plus one, and that's more than enough.

    Midnight rolls around as we all count down to the new year as we watch the ball drop in Times Square on the TV. Wash and I kiss at midnight, which I love because I've always wanted to kiss someone at midnight on New Years Eve. All the cute and romantic things I've always dreamed about doing with my boyfriend are slowly coming true. The best part is they are with my dream guy. The guy who has been my guardian for more years than I can count at this point. It's a new year filled with all kinds of possibilities, but it's also filled with new challenges. At least I don't have to face whatever the new year brings alone.

Chapter 17
Arsonist

I've always managed to sneak into Wash and his friends' little party. Every year since they started throwing it, I've either come as someone's guest, or I slip in with the crowd. It's not like they have security guarding the door and only letting people in that are on a list. Anyone from the street could slip in and join the party. It's easy enough to lie and say I'm someone's guest if anyone questions me, but since I stick to the shadows; no one even knows I'm here. I'm a ghost both literally and metaphorically. It's easy to be a ghost when everyone thinks you are dead.

Unfortunately, to my dismay I'm not holding Wash's attention enough. I thought I was doing a decent job at distracting Wash with a hard case to solve. It's his first official case, and I thought Wash was smart enough to not let anything or anyone distract him. I was wrong, and I underestimated Lexi. Something I won't do again.

That bitch has got Wash wrapped around her little finger. Just watching them fawn all over each other is gross. I can't believe Wash is falling for her act. I figured they would hook up and have sex eventually since they live together. I didn't think them fucking would turn into an actual relationship. Lexi is not wife material. She's not even girlfriend material. She would make a good whore though. Any pimp would be happy to have someone like Lexi working for them. She's got the looks, the body, and just enough innocence that men would pay to corrupt her. Shit, I'd be her pimp if that's that business I was in, but I'm not. However, I do know plenty of people in the criminal world that would be happy to take her on and against her will too.

Abducting Lexi is a last resort. It's risky taking her. I can't risk her or Wash figuring out who I am. I can, however, up my game with distracting Wash. I need to get more specific with what businesses I target. I was avoiding targeting anything that would have meaning to them or us, but Lexi has left me no choice. I need to unpry her claws from Wash.

I never took Wash as a guy who couldn't say no to a pretty face. Wash was always so resistant to girls. I used to be so jealous of the girls that would throw themselves at Wash. I'm not a bad looking guy. Granted, I don't have Wash's movie star looks, but I'm a catch. Well, so I thought. I guess it was hard to be considered a catch when you aren't rich, have a broken family, and are saddled with baggage.

The problem wasn't attracting girls. Wash and I were a good team, and we nailed it at being one another's wingmen. Wash was all about fooling around. He always said he would settle down when he met the right girl. The annoying thing was he could have been a playboy with a different girl every night. However, Wash is a gentleman. It's not that he didn't do one night stands, he simply didn't do them as often as he could have. Somehow that always annoyed me that he could have something so easily at his fingertips and trade it for the more noble thing to do.

My problem with girls was them finding out about my home life. Some would pity me, and sometimes it could be a great way to get sex. Some girls didn't want my baggage, and had no interest in carrying things forward. I couldn't seem to make relationships last because of everything I had going on at home. My mom and sister never made it easy for me.

Ungrateful bitches. They put a sour taste in my mouth for settling down. So, women are to be used for sex and nothing more. Forget getting married, having kids, and all that bullshit. It's overrated. I'll stick to primal fucking.

I guess I'll just have to take things up a notch. Time to start making Lexi pay for all the ways she ruined my life. I hate her. She's an ungrateful little leach who is soon going to learn her place in the world. All while keeping Wash distracted so he can't get too involved with Lexi. It's bad their dating. I don't want their relationship to flourish, so I must do everything I can to put an end to their relationship. I guess it's a good thing I'm good at causing chaos.

Chapter 18
Lexi

The new year is not fully turning out the way I would like. A few days before I was set to start Cool Beans, it burned down. Wash is actually investigating the fire because the fire matches those in his case. Wash is hunting down an arsonist, and he's been busy because of it. I can't be mad at him because I want him to catch the asshole who burned down my favorite place. Not to mention the person is clearly a menace to society and doesn't care if he is hurting people. I know not every criminal can be caught, that's simply reality. However, this asshole I not only hope he gets caught. but that he rots in jail. Bitter? Maybe a bit, but I'm tired of people fucking with my life even if it's indirectly.

Unfortunately, with Cool Beans burnt to a crisp, I'm out of a job that I never even got a chance to start. I know they will rebuild, but they have no idea how long it will take. They can't guarantee anyone's job, even the employees who have been there for years. I have no idea what to do now. Wash suggested working at Fireball, but I can't bring myself to say yes. It would be totally awkward working there because his friends hate me, and at least one of them is there every night. Not to mention Kate apparently shows up there when Wash isn't there. No doubt she would just love to make my job hell for me. It's an absolute last resort, and I'd almost rather remain unemployed at that point.

Even with Wash and I announcing our relationship, his friends still aren't accepting me. They pretend they are, but we all know it's fake. It irritates Wash with how they treat me. At least he's not blind to how they act around me. I hate that I feel like a divide between Wash and his friends. I thought maybe after the party and us officially announcing our relationship that they might start being nicer, but they are still fake. I know they aren't truly fake people. I've seen them interact with Wash and each other. I'm the problem because I'm not Kate.

Frustrated with Wash's friends, losing my job before I even started, and beating myself up over things out of my control, I decide it's best I head to my therapy appointment a little early. I need to get out of the house for a bit. Maybe I'll do some job searching after therapy. The new year is bringing its challenges, that's for sure. The bubble Wash and I were in with our relationship has been broken. I thought it was a good thing for us to be open about our relationship, but now I wish we never told anyone.

It's almost February. Valentine's Day is around the corner and I'm looking forward to it. Wash wanted to take me away, but with his case becoming more difficult with the added fire, Wash can't get away. So, he's planned a nice dinner out for us. We don't eat often together since the two of us love to cook, and we enjoy cooking together. So, we rather cook our meals at home because it allows us to bond. However, it's a romantic holiday, and Wash wants us both to take the night off cooking.

I catch the bus I need to take to get to therapy. Wash insists on getting me a bike or a car so I don't have to take the bus, but I don't mind the bus. The city keeps the buses clean. Much nicer than some of the buses I've been on in other places. The bus gives me a sense of freedom while being practical. I hate driving in the city. Maybe if we lived in the suburbs or country I'd take Wash up on his car offer. Thankfully, obtaining my drivers license was something I was able obtain thanks to the school I was attending right after we moved from Union City. They had a program for teens to take driving courses and obtain a driver's license. It was actually a nice program and I'm grateful for it because without it I'm not sure my mom would have let me get my license.

    My appointment with Dr. Daniels goes well, and I definitely needed it. I know I have a lot to process with my past and trauma associated with it. It's a process and I'm doing my best to remain patient with my change because I am changing through my healing in a good way. I'm gaining confidence slowly but surely, I'm making plans for my future, and I'm in a relationship with the guy I've been in love with for years. I'm determined to heal my wounds the best I can so that I can write the chapters of my future instead of rereading the chapters of my past. Wounds will turn to scars, and scars serve as reminders that I'm a survivor.

    After my appointment I head to the local library to seek some comfort in a place I know I can seek shelter in. To my great surprise and joy they were looking for volunteers. It's not a paying gig, but it does get me out of the house. I need to get out more and I need to do things that don't always involve Wash. I need activities that I personally enjoy that I can take pride in. It's a way to move forward from the past that keeps threatening to haunt me.

It's nice having independence for once. I always felt like I had chains holding me to my mom. I was her burden. I was Jesse's burden too, although he would never say it to my face. I've been thinking a lot about Jesse lately. I wonder how he would feel about Wash and I in a relationship. He would surely be against it. In fact, I doubt Wash would have made a move if Jesse was alive. I would have had to have been the one to draw him into the fire of our desires. I'm not sure I would have had it in me.

I don't know why Jesse is on my mind. Maybe it's because I feel like his ghost still haunts me. I'm the dead cop's sister to most people. To some I'm Wash's dead best friend's sister. To my mom I'm the reason my brother is dead. It's hard to escape his death. In strange ways it surrounds me serving as some reminder for something that I have yet to figure out. Strangely, Wash and I have not talked a lot about Jesse since I've come back. We mention him in passing occasionally, especially if something reminds us of him or something we did with him. Other than that he's a topic we almost avoid. I'm not sure why we avoid the topic of Jesse. Maybe it's because we are probably the only two people who don't remember him has the brave cop that died. We remember him for his neurotic behavior, short temper, and someone who was hard to please. Jesse had issues, issues that were untreated. Not that Jesse would ever dare see a doctor let alone a doctor for mental health.

    I've often wondered why Wash stayed friends with Jesse. Jesse certainly didn't make it easy for Wash to want to be his friend. It was as if Jesse was always testing Wash's friendship, and I know it drove Wash crazy. I'm starting to believe Wash stuck around for me. I was the one he couldn't leave behind. It makes me all warm inside to think Wash put up with Jesse's bullshit for me. Wash truly is my guardian so much so he wouldn't dare abandon me even if it meant putting up with Jesse and his bad attitude.

    After I spend some time at the library getting to know the librarians, other workers, and other volunteers, I head home to start dinner. While dinner cooks, I spend some time drawing cartoons to help with my anxiety over things. I have anti anxiety pills I can take as well as my daily antidepressants, but I try to take my anxiety pills as a last resort. I try to depend on my DBT skills that I've been learning from Dr. Daniels. Addiction is strong in my family. My mom is an alcoholic, Jesse certainly did his fair share of drinking and I assumed at one point he was on drugs, and from what I've heard about my dad he was also good at chugging bottles of alcohol. So, I'm a little afraid of developing any addiction, which is why I only drink socially or with Wash. I wouldn't dare drink alone, afraid of the temptation to get drunk to drown out my crazy thoughts. I don't want to end up like my mother because that is one of my greatest fears.

My next greatest fear is ruining Wash's life like my mom said I would. It's why I hope that Wash's friends eventually come around. They can't hate me forever for no reason just because I'm not Kate. They can't possibly want Wash to be unhappy with Kate. From what Wash has told me about their relationship it was like a chore. Maybe he's just saying that for my benefit. However, their relationship can't have been that great if Wash felt the need to call it off before he married Kate. Wash has told me that marrying Kate would have been a mistake and no matter how many times he tells people that, they still push her on him. He's even confessed that he only proposed to her because he felt the pressure from everyone to seal the deal with Kate, and regretted afterwards.

Wash wasn't happy with Kate, his friends have to accept that. At least, they should accept it.

To my disappointment, Wash can't make dinner, so I eat alone before heading to shower. I end up curling in bed with a book while I wait for Wash to come home. I did tell him in text about the library. I will say this, no matter how crazy Wash gets at work he always finds time to text or call me. I appreciate that more than he knows. Wash also keeps me updated on his schedule and what he has going on. I never have to worry about him skipping out on me like my mom did with many of her boyfriends. Watching the losers my mom would date made me realize very quickly what I wanted in a man. I guess my mom taught me something after all. My mom was never nurturing toward me. She was with Jesse, but never with me. Sometimes I'm jealous of how much my mom loves Jesse over me. I'm glad I don't have to deal with her toxic ass anymore. I took control of my life, and I'm liking the direction it is taking even if there's some challenges along the way. At least, I'm not facing the challenges alone.

Chapter 19
Wash

The new year certainly has taken a strange turn, and my work load is heavier than ever as I stare at the files laid on my desk trying to put the pieces together. Cool Beans burned down a couple of days after the New Years Eve party. Lexi was devastated she couldn't start. I'm upset for her because I know how much she was looking forward to the job. I certainly didn't expect the Cool Beans fire to fall into my lap as possibly related to my arsonist case. For some reason, it feels personal now.

I'm not sure if I'm simply taking the fire to heart because I actually loved that place, and I know how much Lexi adored that place. It's also filled with memories going all the way back to my early teen years when I first discovered that place while in the city for some event with my parents. I'm not sure why the arsonist would target a place that is close to me. Maybe it's a total coincidence. Somehow, I doubt it. If it's not coincidence that means the arsonist is now targeting locations that I value, or maybe it's about someone else. One of the customers, workers, or even the owners. Maybe the places weren't random to begin with. I'll have to see if there is someone I can tie to all the fires. There's no way the arsonist is targeting places because of me. That would mean they know me, and there is no one I know that would set fire to shit for fun. No one alive that is.

 Of course, with Cool Beans being a beloved community business there is certainly pressure to nail the bastard. Even the detectives we are working with are getting antsy to catch this guy. This case is certainly taking on a life of its own and it's consuming my life in a lot of ways. I knew fire investigations could be intense and that sometimes cases could be all consuming. I simply wasn't prepared for it right off the bat.

 I also didn't plan for starting a relationship with Lexi. I certainly wouldn't have planned for it to coincide with a crazy case. I am happy being with Lexi. She's a wonderful girlfriend, and I'm insane to be thinking about putting a ring on her finger so soon. I don't know why I have the urge to go buy a ring. It's way too fast, but I don't think Lexi and I do anything the way we should. I'm pretty sure there is some rule about not dating your best friend's younger sister, let alone your dead best friend's sister. There is an eleven year age gap, and while we don't think it's a big deal, there are plenty of people that care.

In fact, it's all I've heard about from my friends since Lexi and I announced our relationship. They all think I'm having some type of early mid-life crisis. That I'm over compensating for something. My dad texted me after Christmas asking me if I was having money problems. How having money problems and dating Lexi could even be related is beyond me, but my father somehow thought it could be connected. He's not the only one who made the crazy assumption. Stephen and Kyle also asked if I was having money trouble, and if I needed to pull out of the bar, they would buy my share. I had to hide the fact that I was completely insulted by their suggestion and offer. I get my dad, but my friends, I truly thought I knew them better than this.

I can't believe my friends are being so petty when it comes to Lexi. I didn't think it would be such a problem to date someone after Kate. I thought they were all mature enough to accept my choice. Not all of them are pushing Kate on me, and it's more the ladies of the group because they are the ones who are truly friends with her. The guys might have said something in passing, but ultimately they will learn to accept Lexi. In the guys' minds, they are testing to see how serious I am about Lexi. I'm not sure why they feel the need to test me with Lexi when they never tested me with Kate. Kate fit in so quickly, quicker than the other guys' girls. Kate almost reminds me of Judy because she has a way of convincing people of anything. Maybe that's why I never could take the plunge with Kate because she reminded me of someone I couldn't stand.

    I can see why my friends, and even my parents, might look at Lexi like some mid-life crisis. She's gorgeous, and younger than me. I don't know why when a man dates a younger woman it has to be considered a midlife crisis. However, age isn't the biggest problem they have with Lexi. I believe their biggest concern is her living with me because she was down on her luck. They look down on her for not going to college or at least doing a trade. They judge her for not having a penny to name. What they don't understand is that Lexi is getting her life back or really gaining her life for the first time ever. She's finding her footing in life, which is why I don't want to pressure her to move quickly with our relationship. I want Lexi to be a bit more established before I even feel her out for marriage.

Switching my thoughts, I focus on our first Valentine's Day together. I'm looking forward to it. It's truly a silly holiday, but I am a bit of a romantic. Lexi brings out my romantic side like she does my dominant side. I was never overly mushy or lovey dovey with Kate. It was harder than it should have been. Even with other girls I've dated over the years, I would try to be romantic and it always felt like it was an obligation or something. It never felt natural, but forced. However, with Lexi being romantic is easy, and I enjoy showering her with love and affection.

For Valentine's Day, I'm taking Lexi to a nice dinner at a hibachi restaurant because we both enjoy Japanese cuisine thanks to all the anime we watch. Lexi and I both enjoy anime and manga. I turned Lexi on to them when she was about twelve. She was so taken by the artistic style. It's actually what inspired her to start drawing in the first place. We bonded over something we both enjoyed as we still do now. I know Lexi has always loved Japanese cuisine, and I'm excited to have this experience with her even if I have gone to this restaurant several times. I never took Kate because she is simple with food and hates more foreign cuisine.

    Jesse never liked Lexi and I bonding over things. To him, it somehow took away from our friendship. Jesse tried to get into anime for my sake so that Lexi wouldn't be able to solely bond with me over it. Jesse hated it though. No matter how many different ones I would show him, he could never get into it. It was clear he was only attempting to like it for my sake, and to stop Lexi from having another thing that only her and I enjoyed. It was the same with cooking. He would beg me to give him lessons or pointers, but when I would, he would never pay attention. It was a facade and I hated it because we didn't have to have everything in common. It was as if Jesse feared I would end up having more in common with Lexi than with him, and for whatever reason that was a problem.

    When I finally get home, I warm up a plate that Lexi saved for me. She's incredibly thoughtful, especially when I'm working these long days. She's handling me being away better than I thought. I don't know why I thought she would struggle with me working crazy hours lately. Maybe I'm just used to how Kate would react when I would work doubles. I also think I had concerns about how safe Lexi would feel on her own, but she seems to be doing okay with it.

After I eat I head up stairs to find Lexi reading in bed. I thought she would be asleep, but I have a feeling she secretly struggles to sleep without me here. Lexi would never say anything because, knowing her, she doesn't want to hinder my job. She would also never complain about not having enough time with me even if we both miss each other a lot. That's why our Valentine's Day plans are that much more important.

Lexi beams as she tells me about her volunteering at the library. I'm glad she found something to do with Cool Beans burned down. I have no idea how long it will take the owners to rebuild. I hate having to find a new coffee joint because I've gotten used to having Cool Beans be a part of my morning routine for years now. That's why I think this particular fire feels personal even if it might not be. It's the inconvenience that irritates me.

I have no idea how to tell Lexi I think the fire might be personal. I don't want to worry her. I don't even know if it is, which is why I haven't even said anything to anyone on the investigations team. I'm probably over thinking and feeling the stress of the situation. There's no way the arsonist is targeting me. A good night's sleep is what I need to help clear my mind from the cloudy thoughts. So, I shower, and then curl into bed with Lexi, who is just as tired as I am. A good night's sleep is exactly what we both need.

Chapter 20
Wash

Well, to say things are truly starting to feel personal with the arsonist is an understatement. Not even two weeks into Lexi volunteering at the library, it burnt down. The old hot water heater gave, or that's how it was set up to appear. Except, I'm starting to think Lexi is the target and not me. I have no idea who would want to target her. Lexi mentioned her mom dated some unsavory types. It's possible that one of them is stalking her for some reason. There's a higher chance that one of the assholes that sexually assaulted her might decide to come after her. There's also the possibility that Judy made enemies who are now targeting her daughter now that Judy is locked up.

The problem is I don't know how to bring up Judy's boyfriends without raising suspicion. Lexi and I have only talked about what happened to her the one time. Even that one time of deep conversation over her sexual assault was hard for her. She ended up in tears and shaking. Now, that could have been a raw reaction to finally telling another person who wasn't paid to listen to her. Lexi has mentioned things related to the assaults a few times while we were easing her into being comfortable with sex, but it was brief and only enough for me to gauge how to better help her through the blockage she was experiencing. I'm never the one to bring it up either. It's not something I can pry about. I have to let Lexi come to me with it when she wants to talk about it. I'm happy she feels comfortable enough to talk to me about it at all. So, I don't want to push her, especially when she feels a little vulnerable with how rocky the new year has been so far.

Unfortunately, I need to know if any of her mom's exes could be our arsonist. A library burning down has the community even more devastated than before. Major pillars in our community are being targeted. It has people all up in arms, and they are getting restless for real answers because right now we have only been able to feed the public superficial information. We don't have enough to even make it appear we are doing something about it. That's how ridiculously good this arsonist is. I hate even giving the asshole credit.

    The worst part of this is that I haven't even told Lexi about any of it because then I have to tell her something that will completely devastate her and we are already having a hard enough time with my friends accepting our relationship. To my great dismay Hunter is wanting to look at Lexi as a person of interest. Hunter and I worked well together on truck, so I thought we would have no issues in fire investigations together. We were working well together until the other day when Hunter brought up Lexi being a person of interest at our meeting with the cops. Hunter painted Lexi as some wild twenty-something girl who can't control her liquor, and starts trouble wherever she goes. He made it seem like she was this homeless, leeching girl who craved attention. Hunter didn't flat out accuse her of possibly taking money for sexual acts, but he eluded to it. I was stunned silent as anger burned with fury in my veins. I'm not one to act on my occasional violent impulses, but I wanted to punch Hunter so hard that he woke up thinking it was last week. I had to restrain myself because we were at work. It was as if he finally was letting me know how he truly felt about Lexi and doing it in an environment where he knew I wouldn't be able to fly off the handle at him. He cornered me and I am not happy about it.

The craziest part is I'm not even sure what he was basing his inaccurate painting of Lexi on. It's not like she has a criminal record for him to go off of, although, the way he was talking about her sure made it sound like she had one. Lexi is not a lush. She tries very hard to control her need for alcohol in social events due to her mother's addiction issues, but likes the liquid courage it can give her when she is edgy out in public. Lexi does limit herself and she has even given me permission to cut her off at home or in public if I feel she is losing any type of control over her drinking. Also, Lexi is certainly not a whore selling tricks for favors or cash. It's exactly why Lexi came to me in the first place because of what her landlord was asking her to do for rent. Lexi hasn't caused one ounce of trouble since she arrived. If anything she's been a model citizen with getting a job, putting her mental health first, finding ways to channel her trauma and anxiety, and volunteering. Not to mention how much she is helping me around the house. If it wasn't for her I wouldn't have clean clothes to wear, a clean living space, and meals that I don't have to eat out because right now this case is just about consuming my life.

I can't figure out why Hunter even thinks Lexi could be a real suspect. Her only connection to the fires is Cool Beans and the Library. She didn't end up working at Cool Beans due to the fire. I highly doubt she would sabotage her chance to work at a place she was excited to start. Lexi barely even got a chance to volunteer at the library before it burned down. She was enjoying her time there too. Not to mention Lexi is a gentle soul. She wouldn't start a fire because it would risk hurting someone not to mention she wouldn't want to damage someone's property. Lexi is far too respectful for that. Lexi is also extremely caring. It's not in her personality to set shit on fire. That was more Jesse.

Jesse. I can't get him off my mind lately. This case reminds me of him for some reason. I don't know why other than Jesse was a firebug as a kid and teenager. Maybe it's because I wish Jesse was still alive and became a detective so we could be working this case together. I do miss him from time to time. He was a huge part of my life for so long. He was a very important person to me. I hate that he died, even if sometimes I admit it's easier without him here. I would never have been able to pursue Lexi so easily. Hell, I'm not sure Jesse would let me date her period. I could see him cutting me out of his life because of it. Still, I miss the asshole.

Of course, I'm getting home late again. We were interviewing more witnesses trying to get a shred of something that would give us a lead. We got fucking no where. I've never been so frustrated with work before. I also can't believe this is my first case. I feel like this is a case that someone gets well over a year into their career. Instead, I've gotten one hell of a case that could either make or break my career.

A career I'm starting to question if I even want. This is why I made investments in the bar, stocks, and a construction business. Perhaps, I'd be happier sticking to the construction part of things. I do enjoy getting my hands roughed up by working with tools, wood, and other materials thanks to my grandpa who was in construction himself and taught me everything I know. It's entirely possible my career as a firefighter is over. I'm in my early thirties, this is about the time guys start thinking about leaving. Some push it to forty, which is honestly when I predicted I would want to leave. Some never retire because they are true smoke eaters who live for nothing else. However, having someone I want to settle down with is making me want to move on to something that allows me a more stable schedule. Yes, I know it won't always be like this, but it will be more often than not. It's not necessarily the ideal job to have while thinking of building a family.

Walking into the kitchen I find that once again Lexi has sweetly prepared a plate for me and set aside for me to warm up. I pop my food in the microwave as I hear the patter of feet down the stairs. A grin spreads on my face. I don't even bother turning around to face Lexi because I know what she is going to do. Sure enough her dainty arms wrap around waist.

"I'm glad your home, Luitenentant." Lexi's sweet voice reaches my ears, but she sounds sad.

"Coming home to you, Doll, is my favorite time of the day," I say, turning in her arms. A small smile spreads on her face before it disappears. She hasn't fully been herself since the Library burned down. It was just another thing she was enjoying that was taken from her. "What's wrong, Doll?" I ask, stroking her cheek gently.

"I feel like I'm cursed. First Cool Beans burns down and then the Library. What's next Fireball, Dr. Daniels office, or another place that I've touched with my curse." Lexi answers, her voice slightly hysterical as tears brim her eyes.

Shit, I should have come home sooner. I knew she was struggling. However, this moment allows for two things. One, a sexy punishment to stop Lexi from thinking negatively about herself. Two, it allows me to bring up her mom's ex-boyfriends as possible suspects. I will not let her know what Hunter thinks.

"You're not cursed. I think the arsonist is trying to get your attention. Is it possible one of your mom's ex-boyfriends would be capable of the crime?" I ask casually as I continue to stroke her cheek. I want this part out of the way because the sexy punishment part is going to be fun.

"I don't know why any of them would want my attention. Not even the ones that sexually assaulted me would care. Most of the men my mom dated were the type of people who left things in the past and never looked back."

"That might be true, but you never know. Sometimes people look back if they think there is something in it for them. It's possible one of them came looking for your mom for whatever reason and figured out she was locked up. Then they could have decided to look for you. You're living in a nice part of the city. They might assume you have money now." I suggest, trying not to push too hard, knowing Lexi is vulnerable.

"Even if one of them did somehow track me down, they wouldn't set fires to get my attention. They would attack me like a mugger or something. Trust me, these guys aren't smart. They wouldn't know how to set a fire and get away with it. They would probably somehow end up killing themselves in the process." Lexi informs me. I can't say I'm not disappointed that my theory is wrong. It was a good angle that I could have used to counter Hunter's bullshit.

"Well, it was just a theory. You're still not cursed. I don't like you talking negatively about yourself, Doll. That's why I'm going to punish you, but in a sexy way."

"You think you can cure my insecure thoughts that have plagued me for most of my life?" she questions as her frown morphs into an amused grin.

"I think I can." The microwave beeps.

"Your food is done." She comments smugly, pointing behind me to the microwave as it beeps impatiently.

"It can wait. In the living room." I command.

Lexi scampers off to the living room with me hot on her heels. I strip to my boxers because after I smack her ass red, I'm going to put that pretty mouth of hers to use. Then I plan to bend her over the couch and fuck her so I'm the only thing she is thinking about. I sit on the couch as Lexi takes her position in front of me.

"That's my good girl." I compliment leaning forward as I slip my hand under her chin making her look at me. "I'm going to spank all the negative thoughts out of your pretty head, my Doll. Strip, and lay across my lap with your ass in the air." A shiver of excitement runs through her as her eyes light up with curiosity. I will never get tired of being with Lexi. She really is my perfect doll.

Lexi slips out of her silk shorts and cami. She wasn't wearing any panites. That little minx was hoping we'd have sex tonight. I've noticed that when Lexi is horny and in the mood she will go commando. Once she is naked, she climbs on my lap. I help position her with her legs slight parted so I can play with her pussy if I desire.

I stroke Lexi's ass gently. She has the perfect cute ass. Not too small, but not too big. Her ass is pale, which means her ass is going to turn a pretty shade of red. "Let's say ten spankings for your negative comments about being cursed."

Raising my hand I come down hard on her ass, which causes her to yelp and move slightly forward. I reposition her before laying my free hand on her back to help keep her stable. I smack her ass a few times in rapid succession as I keep counting out loud. Normally, I'd make Lexi keep count, but this is the first time I'm doing this with her. So, I don't want to overwhelm her. It's best to ease Lexi into sexual things as she recovers from her trauma, which clearly still haunts her.

With a few smacks to her ass, which is now turning varying shades of pink and red, Lexi's yelps turn to moans. Of course, my doll would be turned on by this. I finish off her spankings before dipping my fingers into her wet pussy. Shit, I wanted her to suck me off, but she's so wet and my dick is straining my boxers so badly I know it's poking Lexi in the stomach.

My mind is made up, I'm fucking her first then she can suck me. I help Lexi off me, rip my boxers off before positioning Lexi over the side of the couch, and then plunge myself all the way into her wet, tight pussy. Fuck, does she feel amazing. No other woman compares to her with sex, or anything really. I enjoy pounding into Lexi as she moans her pleasure. My one hand rests on her hips holding steady while my other hand snakes around and finds its way between her legs. I slide my fingers to her clit and begin to rub as I fuck Lexi roughly. Lexi's moans of pleasure are the sweetest damn thing to my ears. Lexi is close to coming, it doesn't take her much and I certainly plan on teaching her edging, but slow and steady is the best way with Lexi. I know with time I will completely immerse her into my world of sex and pleasure, and she will enjoy every damn minute. Lexi's walls clench around my dick as I keep pounding into her from behind. I keep rubbing her clit.

"Just because you had one orgasm doesn't mean I'm going to stop, Doll." I answer the thought I know she has running through her mind. I've never given her multiple orgasms in a row like this. Normally, I'd either stop and let her ride the wave of pleasure from her orgasm or I'd temporarily stop and go back later on. Not this time. This time Lexi is going to learn two things. One, just because she has an orgasm doesn't mean she can't have more back to back. Two, she's going to want to learn edging after this. I keep up my pace as I pound into Lexi taking out my frustration of the day while rubbing her clit sending us both closer to release. Lexi's walls tighten around my dick as her second orgasm washes over her. I almost cum myself, but I'm damn good at edging myself to a point to where I don't even need to slow down. I can keep going and hold back my orgasm. Something, I taught myself during my many lonely nights being a single man over the years. I keep rubbing Lexi's clit not letting up on bringing her multiple orgasms. I don't want to do more than three right now, so when Lexi quickly cums again, her walls tightening again around my dick send me to the sweetest oblivion as I find my own release.

Before we can catch our breaths, I pull out of Lexi before I spin Lexi around. "On your knees, Doll, and put that pretty mouth of yours to use." I command.

Like a good girl Lexi quickly drops to her knees, and starts sucking my semi hard cock. It takes no time for my dick to be rock hard again. Lexi's sweet, warm mouth is wrapped around my cock as she sucks while swirling her tongues around my tip when she can. I fist my hand in her hair to control her pace. Lexi keeps sucking until I'm satisfied and have a second release. Then I carry her up the stairs to shower before tucking her in bed. She's out in minutes. I chuckle to myself because my doll sure loves being used for my pleasure. I go back downstairs to eat before I take my own quick shower, and curl up with Lexi in bed. Hopefully, tomorrow I'll get answers instead of hitting dead ends on this damn case.

Chapter 21

Wash

A little over a week has passed and nothing new has happened with my case. Hunter is still insistent that Lexi could be a suspect, and of course the detectives don't want to rule anyone out too quickly. I haven't told Lexi they think she is suspect. I don't think she could handle the negativity right now. Even after my little punishment, Lexi is struggling to think positively. She came to me for a fresh start, and that's what I'm trying to give her. However, this damn arsonist, who I swear is someone we know, and my friends are making it hard to do that.

What no one seems to realize is that I'm trying to have a fresh start too. I needed to start over after the tragic accident of losing one of my men. It's why I went over to fire investigations in the first place, which I thought was the right move, but I'm not sure anymore. It's not just because this case is rough, and there's a high chance the case might go cold. It's a high priority now, but eventually another case will come along that will take higher priority. It's stressful, and while I can handle stress, fire investigations is a different type of stress than working in the firehouse. I'm doing my best to not let my stress show to Lexi even though she knows how to read me like I do her. I know she is aware of how stressed I am, but I also know she won't bring it up unless I do. I appreciate that Lexi doesn't force me to talk about work like Kate would. There's also the fact that I need a fresh start in a relationship. I have life goals of getting married and having kids. I thought those plans were with Kate once upon a time, but it never felt right.

Starting a relationship with Lexi is both our chances at a fresh start with a relationship that makes us both happy. She needs a positive relationship after her sexual assaults and rape, and I need a positive relationship after having one that was more negative than positive. Not to mention the pressure everyone put on Kate and me to get married. Of course, now I've got a different problem with my friends. They aren't pressuring me to get married, but instead they want me to end things with Lexi. Hunter even suggested kicking her out onto the street or setting her up in a woman's shelter. They truly believe that she is using me.

    The truth is, I love spoiling the shit out of Lexi. Kate never let me buy her shit. She was so miss independent. I'm all for women being independent, but I also like to be able to spoil the girl I'm with. I know even if Lexi had her own money she would still let me spoil her. Lexi secretly enjoys being spoiled by me. I know sometimes it's hard for her to accept things because she feels she doesn't deserve them. Years of being told you are a mistake and deserve nothing can take its toll. Not only that, but Lexi is grateful. She always says thank you even when she doesn't have to. In her own ways, she does things for me like keeping the house clean, doing laundry, and cooking when I can't. We take care of each other in our own ways, and we can recognize it. Too bad others can't.

    I hate to question my friends, but lately I can't help it. This whole thing with Lexi has really thrown a monkey wrench into my friendships. I don't blame Lexi. She has tried and tried to get them to give her a chance. She's gone out of her way to find things she can bond with them over, but they shoot down her attempts. They have, unfortunately, made up their minds about her. If it comes to it, I will give up my friendship, even my share of the bar, if it means keeping Lexi in my life. I choose her over my friends. I know some would say that's insane, but what people fail to realize is I've known Lexi longer than any of them. I literally was at the hospital the day she was born to keep Jesse company while Judy gave birth. I've known Lexi her whole life, and that adds up to be longer than any of my current friends. I'm also starting to believe that I've known for a long time Lexi is the person I'm meant to spend my life with. I think, for a while, I pushed it away out of respect for Jesse, and because Lexi was younger at the time. I tried to look at her as my little sister, but I looked at her more as my ward. Someone to look after and protect. I became her guardian without releasing it.

    It's Valentine's Day, and I'm looking forward to our date. Lexi has no idea what I have planned. I told her to dress nicely since the hibachi place is a higher end restaurant. I also got us a private table. I didn't want to have to share with other people. Some hibachi places don't like it if they have to have an entire table just for one couple, but this place has specific tables built for couples or smaller parties. I wanted Lexi's first experience to be just us because this is special to us. I plan for us to have Sake, something I know Lexi has wanted to try since she was fourteen. I also want to take Lexi to a raman noodle bar. We just haven't gotten to do it yet. My goal is to take Lexi to Japan. Maybe for our honeymoon, even if that's thinking way too far in the future.

I took a half a day at work just so I could make sure I wouldn't miss our date. Besides, I'm over this damn case. It's driving me insane. I'm going crazy trying to figure out how I could know the arsonist, and why they would target me or Lexi. It makes no sense. There's only one person I know who it could be and he's dead. Pushing the crazy thoughts from my head, I focus on Lexi. I may have taken a half day, but I'm not going home right away. Our dinner is at six, so I'll get home around five. First, I need to have an emergency session with Dr. Daniels. I'm starting to feel that I'm at some sort of a crossroads in my life. Between that, this case, and how my friends are acting toward Lexi, I need the session.

After I'm done, I head to the flower shop to pick up the dozen yellow roses I ordered for Lexi because I know she loves them. She's loved them ever since I gave her a yellow rose on her seventh birthday. I had forgotten it was her birthday due to just starting the fire academy, and it had all my focus. All I could get on my way to her birthday dinner was a silly yellow rose and her favorite candy, which hasn't changed. Lexi still loves her KitKats.

I don't want to overwhelm Lexi with too much romantic shit. It's our first Valentine's Day, and I have a feeling we have plenty more in our future. I also don't want to bring out all the stops in one night. Lexi is a simple girl, and she doesn't want the day to be a big deal because that's not her. Lexi would be happy if we stayed home and watched TV, but we do that most nights. I want tonight to be a little special.

When I get home, Lexi is finishing getting ready in our room. Our room, our house, our life, yeah I like the sound of that. Lexi is in a simple black dress that hugs her curves nicely. Lexi was fairly thin when she first came back, but now she has gained healthy pounds since then. Lexi smiles as I walk over to her with the roses.

"Thank you, Lieutenant. These are beautiful."

"You're welcome, Doll." I reply before kissing her on her lips.

"I should go put these in water while you get ready." Lexi says breaking our kiss.

"That's a good idea. We don't want to be late for our reservation."

"I guess I won't know where we are going until we get there?" Lexi inquires as she grabs her black pumps in her free hand as she heads to the door.

"That's right, Doll." I reply before smacking her on her ass as she walks past me. Lexi helps before she giggles.

Lexi heads downstairs with her roses and pumps in tow while I focus on getting ready. I don't have time for a shower, which is fine. I'll shower tonight with Lexi. I think a little shower sex is fun every now and again. Surprisingly, we haven't fucked in the shower. I guess it's time we do. Something extra to look forward to tonight.

I change into black slacks, a black button up shirt, and black dress boots. I head down stairs to find Lexi with her pumps on and her light black jacket on. It does get a little chilly this time of year. Thankfully, we don't have to deal with snow. I put on my light jacket, and we head out. No need for winter coats where we live. Half the time a hoodie is good, but we don't want to wear hoodies to this restaurant.

Lexi lights up the minute we enter the restaurant. Excitement is written all over her face with a wide smile as the hostess takes us to our table. We are seated. Our waiter comes over immediately taking our drink orders. I order us a bottle of Sake, which has Lexi grinning from ear to ear. We also order iced green teas to offset the Sake. We then order some sushi for our appetizers. I like that this place also serves sushi, not all hibachi places do. When the waiter comes back with our drinks we then order what we want for our main course.

"Wash, this place is amazing! Thank you so much for taking me here." Lexi beams, and I know I planned the right date for tonight.

"You're welcome, Doll. Maybe one day we can actually go to Japan. Maybe for our honeymoon." Shit, did I really let the word honeymoon slip. I cringe inside hoping I don't spook Lexi. However, she rolls with it.

"That would be fun. We totally would end up in Japan for our honeymoon. I would love to take a class to learn to draw anime style." Lexi replies, not missing a beat. Maybe she is ready for the marriage talk. Still, I'm not going to push too hard.

"You are pretty good at drawing anime characters, but I understand if you want to perfect it. Are there classes you can take online or something?" I inquire, happy that Lexi is talking about something she enjoys and furthering a skill she has.

"I'm sure there are. The internet is full of resources. I bet there are videos to watch, too. It's something to look into to help distract me from everything that's going, but I don't want to talk about that right now. Tonight is about us and just us." Lexi says with a smile.

"I agree. Tonight is about us. Well, if you need to pay for classes or anything you might need just let me know. You know I have no problem getting you what you want and need." I offer, taking a sip of my green tea.

"I know, and I'm grateful for that. I've been debating taking college classes online for art, but to be honest I'm not sure I'm a college material. Not because I don't think I can do it. I simply don't think I'll enjoy it. I never liked sitting in a classroom. I always felt there was so much more to learn than just studying. Plus, I read for fun anyway, so I'm sure I can find plenty of books to help me with my art. There are also videos, and other resources. Besides, if I'm going to go to college, I'm going to do something practical with it then like counseling or something. I do want to pursue my art at the moment. It's helping me so much with my trauma, and it's a healthy way to cope with things." Lexi explains.

I'm astounded by how much she has grown up and truly thought this through. I never doubted her maturity. She's always been more mature for age to begin with, but hearing her talk so confidently about her future, and what she wants is great to hear. I think I was worried she was being held back by her trauma, but it's clear she is healing. She is moving forward with her life, and I get to be a part of her future. It's a good feeling to realize we are on the same page after all. I was worried for no reason.

"I understand not wanting to go to college. I didn't go to college. I choose a trade job in firefighting and even construction and carpentry on the side. Granted, it's been awhile since I've done anything with construction and carpentry because I've been focusing on my career as a firefighter." Which I'm regretting because I'm not sure I want to stay and further my career like I originally planned. Part of me is almost craving quitting everything to do with firefighting, and going back to building things with my hands. I miss building furniture, and flipping houses. I need to start deciding what I want to do because if I'm going to make a big change, now is the time to do it. However, I'm not saying anything to Lexi about quitting until I'm certain it's what I want. "My parents were furious that I didn't go to college, but I've done well for myself despite their negative assumptions. There is no pressure for you to go to college."

"I know. I'm glad you aren't pressuring me to go to college. College isn't for everyone and I haven't decided if it's for me or not. Now, if I can just find a job, and keep it." Lexi says before taking a swig of her Sake.

"Something will work out. In the meantime, you can work on your art. Maybe try getting some commissions. You can set up a social media page for your art work, gain some followers. There's tons of local markets and events for people to sell their goodies at. I know plenty of people who do it." I suggest.

"That's not the worst idea. I'm not great with social media, but I bet I can figure it out. Thanks for the idea, Lieutenant." Lexi smiles. Good. For a minute there I was afraid she was going to head down negative lane. Not that I can blame her because things are a little rough right now for both of us.

The rest of dinner is great, we enjoy our food and Sake. For dessert, we get some tempura cheesecake and ice cream. It's honestly the best date I've ever had. Lexi and I haven't really done a fancy date like this. It's something I think we need to do more than just once a year on Valentine's Day.

After our delicious meal, we head back home. I'm ready to enjoy the rest of the night at home, naked, and fucking our brains out until we fall asleep. I park the car in the driveway. "Alright, Doll, you know the drill. Upstairs, undressed, and in your position." I command. Except this time Lexi hesitates as she looks away from me as if something is wrong. I have no idea what could be the problem. "What's wrong, Doll?"

"This is embarrassing, but I got my period this morning." Lexi shily replies.

Her period. Is she serious? It's moments like this that I realize Lexi still has some of her innocence left. It's not like I haven't known when she is on her period, but for some reason she hides it. She did the same thing when she was fifteen. Back then I got it because she was a teen living with a grown man she had a crush on. However, now she is an adult, and she is still shy about her period. It's cute, but I'm going to shred the last of her innocence. I should want to preserve her innocence as her guardian, but innocence is something we can't hold onto forever. We aren't meant to. Shedding our innocence allows us to become stronger and more resilient to how rough life can be.

"Doll, I ran into fires for a living. When I wasn't doing that I'm in an ambo. Now I investigate fires. Do you really think a little blood is going to stop me from having my way with you tonight?"

"Well, when you put it like that, I guess not." Her cheeks heat from embarrassment.

"Definitely not. Now, go get your pretty ass upstairs, and do what I told you to do because I don't want to punish you on Valentine's Day." I warn.

"Yes, Sir." Lexi replies before scurrying out of the car, and heads inside.

I can't help but chuckle and shake my head at her. Her period is not going to stop me. Besides, I planned on fucking her in the shower tonight anyway, so it doesn't really matter that's she is bleeding. That's exactly what I'm going to do. I wait about fifteen minutes to let Lexi fully get undressed, take her makeup off, and get herself ready for me. My dick is already straining my pants, needing to escape right into Lexi's tight pussy.

When enough time has passed, I get out of the car then lock it as I head inside. I make sure the house is locked up before I head upstairs. I enter our room, and find Lexi in her position. She's naked, but has a towel under her. I have to resist shaking my head at her. Yeah, I'm totally shedding the last of her innocence. At least, Lexi is considerate.

"Come on, Doll. It's time to introduce you to shower, period sex." I say, walking toward her and then offering her my hand. Lexi slips her hand in mine as she looks up at me. Her soft green eyes sparkle with desire.

I lead Lexi into the bathroom. I first turn on the shower to let it warm up. I quickly strip off my clothes, and then pull Lexi into my arms. I waste no time before my lips devour hers. My tongue invades her mouth as it begins to dance with her tongue. I push her back toward the shower stall before managing to open the door, and get us both under the warm shower stream. I push Lexi up against the wall before breaking our kiss. I take the detachable shower head and stick right between her thighs. I focus it on her clit, which has Lexi squirming as little moans escape. Lexi places her hands on my shoulders to help support herself. Lexi cums quickly, not surprising since she's on her period and I know it can make everything extra sensitive. Plus, we haven't started working on edging her yet.

Dropping the shower head, I lift Lexi up and she naturally wraps her legs around my hips. I position my raging hard dick at her entrance before I slam into her. Lexi moves her hands from shoulders. One goes to my hair, sliding her hands through my wet locks while her other hand rests on my neck. My hands squeeze her ass, supporting her as I slam into her over and over again. I trail kisses along her jaw and neck, nipping along the way before smoothing the bites over with licks and kisses. Lexi moans, leaning her neck back to give me more access to her neck. My sweet doll loves when I nip and kiss her body.

Lexi doesn't even care that my grip on her ass is going to leave light bruises or that she'll have little marks up and down her neck, on her chest, and breasts as my lips move over the parts of the body I have access to. Fuck me, sex with Lexi is something else. She's the perfect person for me. One day I'm going to marry her, that much I know.

I slam into Lexi harder. I know I should probably be sweet and romantic with sex given that it's Valentine's Day, but I can't control the beast that Lexi brings out in me when I'm fucking her. I don't mind sweet sex on occasion, but Lexi feeds the beast in me. It makes it harder to be sweet when fucking her, but my doll doesn't always like it sweet either. We really are a pair.

I find my release deep within Lexi. I lean my forehead against hers as we catch our breath. When our breathing is even, I slowly let Lexi down. We take turns washing one another, and getting cleaned up. After we are done, I dry off and head into the bedroom to let Lexi take care of her woman business. I slip on my boxers and get in bed. It doesn't take long for Lexi to come out in one of her cotton nightgowns. She hops in bed, giving me a kiss before she curls up next to me.

That's when I decided that this is what I want for the rest of my life. I want to build my life with my doll, and that's what I'm going to do no matter what anyone says. Now, to make up my mind about my career and to solve this damn case.

Chapter 22

Lexi

Valentine's Day was amazing. Of course, my dream guy would plan the perfect day. When Wash mentioned going to Japan on our honeymoon I got excited. It means he's thinking about a future with me. I'm thrilled Wash is thinking about marrying me because I have been thinking about marrying him for years now. Teenage me is doing one serious happy dance along with adult me.

While I'm thrilled Wash is thinking about marriage, I can't help but feel like he's hiding something from me. I know it has to do with his case. Wash told me they don't believe it's any of my mom's ex-boyfriends like he originally thought. I have to admit I was panicky when Wash thought it was one of the guys that sexually assaulted me. I didn't think any of them would come after me, but the thought that they might haunt me along with much of my past.

The only other thing I think it could be is something to do with his friends. They are clearly not my biggest fan. We don't go to Fireball as often as we used to. We would go at least once over the weekend, but now it's like every other weekend. Wash is using the case as an excuse not to go to the bar. I know he's slammed with this case. Still, I know Wash. He would find time to see his friends. It's clear he enjoys hanging out at the bar with them. I'm clearly the problematic factor with his friends.

It only feeds my fear that I might ruin Wash's life, or at the minimum ruin his friendships. Friendships he's had long before I came back into his life. He was friends with Hunter and Kevin when Jesse was alive. Jesse and Wash stayed friends, but they each developed their own groups of friendship within their respective careers. Wash certainly has more friends than Jesse ever did, period. Jesse was never as ambitious with making friends like Wash is.

The worst part about this is I can tell my trust issues are coming out with thinking Wash is hiding something. I'm sure if he is, it's for a good reason. Wash isn't someone who would hide something to be spiteful. Knowing him, he's hiding it to protect me because it will most likely hurt my feelings. I hate feeling like I can't trust when I know that I can. Every fiber of my being trusts Wash because I love him.

I'm falling fast and hard for Wash, but that's no surprise. The man makes me weak in my knees. He has for as long as I can remember. I want to marry Wash, have his kids, and build a life with him. I'm ready for our future, and judging by the way Wash was talking last night he's thinking about it too. We have some obstacles to work through, but that's how life goes. As long as we are doing it together that's all that matters.

I've also decided to take Wash's advice and start up some social media pages for my art. Wash has even let me set up a little art area in the small sitting area upstairs. I have a little desk filled with my art supplies. It's a nice little set up. I'd like to have my own room dedicated to my art and books. I can picture it. Shelves lined with books and nick knick knacks. A huge desk filled with art supplies. A little reading nook. A room that's just mine where I can let my creativity grow.

I looked up some videos and looked up local art classes. I found an artist group that meets up once a month at various locations to talk and support one another. I joined their social media pages, and have even posted some of my work, which is getting a positive response. I'm looking forward to the meeting that they have next month since I already missed this month's meeting. It's nice connecting with other artists and networking is important if I plan on making something out of my art.

I've also decided I'm going to work on a project for Wash. His birthday is in July, so I have plenty of time to work on it. I'm going to draw us as anime characters. I need to practice and figure out exactly what I want the piece to be. I know something romantic, but maybe a little badass at the same time since we love action movies. I want to combine all the awesome things we enjoy and love with a romantic twist. It's going to be awesome, and I'm already excited to give it to Wash. I should probably start the damn project before I plan all the cute ways I can give it to Wash. One thing I do know, it's going to be his birthday gift.

Wash is the person that likes gifts to have meaning. I think it's because his parents always tossed fancy gifts his way. The gifts didn't have meaning. They were more a means to buy Wash's love. I was the opposite. I was lucky if I got a gift. Most birthdays were spent with a box cake that Jesse would attempt to make. I say attempt because rest his soul, but he was horrible with cooking and baking. He would somehow mess up box dinners and baked goods. Still, I ate the damn cake, and I loved it too because I knew Jesse was trying. Forget Christmas gifts. They almost never happened. Granted, as I got older Wash would make sure to have gifts for Jesse and I.

    Deciding to be creative, I get to work on said project. It's a distraction from my wild thoughts that are leaning toward the negative side. I could always let them come out when Wash is around because I know it will lead to a sexy spanking. Sometimes, it's fun to provoke Wash's dominant side. He knows when I'm doing it on purpose too. It can lead to extra spankings or edging where Wash will edge me several times before letting me cum. Wash has been slowly teaching me edging. Wash brings out this sexual side of me that's been buried under the sexual trauma. I like bringing out that side of me and unburying it from under the layers of trauma. It's a side of me I feared I might not ever get to explore. Thankfully, that's not the case. I'm healing, and it brings a level of freedom I didn't know I was missing.

    Therapy has been so helpful in helping me heal. It's not just the sexual trauma I'm healing from, but the physiological and emotional abuse my mom did to me. I'm healing from her toxic parenting, and from Jesse's death. In many ways, I haven't properly mourned Jesse. Everything happened so quickly after he died. It only took a couple months before my mother was forced to check into a rehab. I think that's when my survivor mode kicked in, and I stayed in it for six years. Jesse wasn't even dead for a year before my mom moved us. I have only been to his grave at the funeral. I haven't been back since, and I'm not sure I'm ready for it. Seeing his headstone makes it real. A reality I know exists, but one I'm not sure I can face. Despite Jesse's flaws as a brother, I loved him. He was often the only family I had because I never thought of our dad as family, and over the years our mom stopped being my family too. With Jesse gone, I don't feel like I have a family anymore. It's not the worst thing because I know one day I will start a family of my own, and I will do things very differently than how my family did things. I have a feeling Wash is on the same page as me when it comes to this.

It's certainly a conversation to have, along with a few others. Wash and I haven't officially had the talk about marriage, kids, or anything along those lines, but they are coming. I'm not worried about it because Wash and I tend to be on the same page with things. Even if we aren't, I believe we can work through it. Some might think Wash and I are moving fast, but we aren't people who care what other people think. We are about living our lives the way we want because they are ours to live. Everyone else's opinions are nothing but background noise.

Chapter 23
Wash

I don't know how this case just took another wrong turn, but it did. Within days of Lexi and I having our date at the hibachi place, it burned down. It matches the other crime scenes. The arsonist is clearly targeting Lexi and me, but I don't know why. I don't understand why we are the targets. It made sense when I thought it was one of Judy's exes after Lexi. However, with what Lexi told me, and checking the dangerous ones off the list, my theory is wrong. Still, I swear we know the arsonist. I have to prove it, though.

With no real suspects, Hunter is still insisting it's Lexi. He's even spread his wild theories to our friends. Some of which agree with him, while others aren't so sure. The ones that aren't sure are trying to play devil's advocate for my sake.

Deep down I know they believe Lexi is the arsonist too. They think it's her twisted way of gaining my attention, which makes zero sense because she has my attention. They claim it's because she doesn't like me working, or because she is trying to sabotage me. Neither makes any sense.

Of course, Kate and my parents have jumped on the Lexi is the arsonist bandwagon. I got a call from my dad the other day expressing his concerns about me living with a potential arsonist. Kate used the whole thing as an excuse to text me her concerns, and to attempt to get me back. Seriously, at this point we broke up almost two years ago, and she still won't let it go. I don't know what I have to do to get her to move the fuck on. I've heard rumors she's been on dates, but either they are false or the guys can't catch her attention. There's also the possibility that the guys she is dating are ditching her because she's too high maintenance. Thankfully, Kate is not my problem. What is my problem is solving this damn case.

I still haven't said a word to Lexi about her being a suspect. It would upset her. I've even avoided going to Fireball and hanging out with my friends because I know they would somehow bring it up. They love pointing fingers at Lexi when she is around. It's like they believe if they make her uncomfortable she will stop coming with me. What they fail to realize is that Lexi and I are a package deal. If they can't accept the person I want to be then they aren't my real friends. This whole situation is turning into a test of friendship, and so far almost all of them are failing.

I know I need to tell Lexi the truth. I can't shield her forever. I was hoping to have a real suspect to pull the heat off Lexi, but now they are talking about questioning Lexi. I'm not sure I can hold them off for much longer. It looks bad that I'm not letting them interview her. I tried to explain why it wasn't a good idea and about her trauma, but they don't care. We all just want to nail the asshole. Unfortunately, Hunter and others want to nail Lexi for the fires. They are convinced she's the one even though she has no criminal background.

My next step is to talk to Dr. Daniels on how to approach Lexi about all this. I'm pissed that I have to talk to her about it in the first place. I'm angry that Hunter and my other friends are convinced Lexi is the arsonist. Hunter has the other investigators along with the detectives looking at Lexi. I can't help that my protective side is coming out. I'm incredibly protective of Lexi. That's no secret. I am her guardian, and I don't like people wrongfully accusing her. I guess it's time to call Dr. Daniels and figure out how the hell

I'm supposed to approach Lexi with this knowing how it's going to hurt her.

This might be the thing that shreds the last bit of confidence Lexi has that my friends will come around to us being together. She's been optimistic that they will come around and accept our relationship. As much as I wish she was right, I'm not so sure it's going to happen. Especially with the way Hunter is painting her as some crazy obsessed girl desperate for attention.

Then there's the fact that St. Patrick's Day is around the corner. I usually spend it at Fireball if I'm not working. It's a big night at the bar for obvious reasons. I'm already trying to find a way out of it. I can't use the case as an excuse because Hunter won't, and we are working the same damn case. To be honest, I just want a simple night in with Lexi. We can make dinner together, and relax. It might be a way to talk to her about what's going on. That's if I don't have to talk to her about it before then.

Fuck, I hate this. Yeah, I really need to start thinking about other career options. I am in my early thirties. I've been fighting fires for over ten years. I thought moving into fire investigations was the way to go. I thought it was a smart career move, but I'm starting to realize I'm burnt out with being a firefighter. Fire investigations didn't give me the renewal I was looking for. I thought it was my survivors' guilt getting to me. I thought maybe staying out of the action was the answer, but it's looking like it's not. Maybe it's time for something else altogether. Maybe I should get back to my carpentry and construction. I always liked the idea of flipping houses, but never did it. Perhaps it's time to rethink that idea.

Chapter 24
Lexi

It's St. Patrick's Day. I'm currently preparing dinner. I'm doing corn beef and cabbage along with some potatoes and carrots in the crock pot. I add a can of beer to add some flavor to the broth. I'm also making Irish soda bread. Wash said he would pick up more beer and dessert on the way home. Wash is still busy with his case. They haven't caught the arsonist. They are trying, but the guy is making it hard on them. Wash hates talking about the case at this point. It's stressing him out. I hate that he's so stressed, which is why I want to have a nice dinner tonight.

To be honest, I thought we would be going to Fireball considering St. Patrick's Day is literally every bar's most popular night. We haven't gone to Fireball in at least a month.

I don't know if it has to do with Wash's case or that his friends hate me that much. I'm sure the conflict is making things harder on Wash. It's not like I haven't tried to get his friends to like me. I've tried not trying and being indifferent. I've tried to make conversation, and find things in common. Nothing I seem to do makes a difference. They have made up their minds about me before they even got a chance to know me.

It's not like I'm not used to being judged for being poor. As a kid, I would get made fun of for wearing thrift store clothes, having a backpack that was falling apart, not having as good of lunch as others, and so on. I thought it would be better as an adult, but I guess some people never leave high school.

I know how it looks to Wash's friends and family that, after six years, I show up on Wash's door step asking for help. I guess it wasn't such a big deal six years ago when I was fifteen. I was a minor who just lost her brother in an ugly police shooting and had a mom who ended up in rehab. People felt bad for me back then. I guess their pity outweighed their judgements then.

I'm sure Wash and I becoming a couple makes everyone even more skeptical because why would someone as wonderful as Wash be interested in me. I'm sure the eleven year age difference makes people uncomfortable. I know they look at me as some mid-life crisis that Wash is going through. I know I'm not. Don't get me wrong, the thought had crossed my mind. However, I know Wash. He's not the type of guy to date a girl just because she is younger, hot, or any other superficial reason.

Normally, I wouldn't care what people think about me or my relationship. However, it's different with Wash because I don't want to screw things up for him. I want to make his life easier, not harder. Right now, I feel like I'm making it harder. I hate that Wash is avoiding Fireball. A bar which he partly owns, and he's boycotting it for me because I don't know why else he would. Wash hasn't really been talking to me about personal stuff going on with him. I know a lot of things pertaining to his case and how his friends feel about me. I know he doesn't care what his parents think. He never has. Still, I hate creating a rift in his life.

What I'm starting to definitely not like is Wash shutting me out. I know he's trying to protect me from something that will be hard on me, but I'm not a kid anymore. I've survived a lot. I hate what happened to me, but it has made me stronger. It's proven I can survive a lot of shit. Shit that I shouldn't have had to survive, but I did. I survived things that should have broken me. In ways it did break me, but I've got a thick skin because of it. It's time to take the kid gloves off, and confront Wash about what is really going on. No more beating around the bush to protect my feelings. I need Wash to know that I can handle tough things. I love that he protects me, but I don't want him to hold back because of it.

While dinner cooks in the crockpot, I do some stuff around the townhouse before sitting down to work on Wash's birthday project. I don't work on it when he's around because I want it to be a surprise. I even hide it when Wash is around to hopefully keep him from seeing it. I haven't gotten far with it, and I've restarted it more times than I can count already. I'm glad I have time to work on it, and make it perfect for Wash.

Before I know it, it's almost time for Wash to be home. I'm nervous to confront Wash, but it has to be done. After I put away my secret project, I head downstairs to set up for dinner. Part of me was afraid I would get a text from Wash saying he would be home late, and wouldn't be able to make dinner. Thankfully, that wasn't the case because right now I have the confidence to confront Wash about what's going on. I know that I will eventually lose that confidence for one reason or another, and chicken out.

I decide to set up food out on the back porch since it's a nice enough day. It's that time of year where winter shows up at night, but during the day it's nice enough to enjoy time outside without freezing your ass off. Perks of living in the south. I've lived in the north for a short while. My mom moved us up north for a bit. We weren't there long because the guy she was seeing cheated on her or something along those lines. I honestly stopped paying attention to my mom's excuses about why we moved because it was her hiding her addiction or another bad relationship gone wrong. She might have blamed the loser she dated, but I knew it was her because she chose to date the losers.

With the food plated and ready, I wait for Wash to come home. It doesn't take long for his Mustang to roll into the driveway. I wave from the back porch and Wash waves back as he gets out of the car with a twelve pack of our favorite beer, and white box that appears to have some kind of sweet goodness in it. Knowing Wash, it's something delicious and probably pricey. Wash and I are both foodies, and Wash will spend money on good food without hesitation.

"Hey, there, Doll." Wash greets as he walks up the stairs that connect the driveway to the porch.

"Hey, Lieutenant." I greet back before kissing him.

"Everything smells great! I got us some chocolate beer cake that's supposed to be out of this world. I'll set everything down, grab us each a beer, and I'll be out to join you for dinner." Wash says after he breaks our kiss.

Wash walks inside, but I can tell he's weighed down by this case at work. Yeah, it's time to get to the bottom of what is going on. Normally, I wouldn't push. I know how hard it is for first responders and sometimes the horrors they experience. Talking about their work can either be liberating because they are the heroes, or it can be depressing as hell because they lost the people they were trying to save. Jesse described it as being on the razors edge because you never knew what your shift would bring. It could be boring, it could be amazing because you make an epic save, or it can leave you questioning why you even choose the career in the first place.

I take my seat on the patio furniture that Wash had in storage for the winter. Wash does take care of his things, including me. I know I'm not a possession to him, but I wouldn't mind it if he did think of me that way because it's sexy and turns me on.

A few minutes later, Wash comes back out with a beer in each hand. He looks worn out. The dark circles indicate his lack of sleep. Normally, he would have a wide smile on his face. He loves our little dinners together. My anxiety wants to tell me I'm the reason he looks the way he does. That it's my fault he's stressed. I know it's his case, but what if there's more to it. I need to know. I can't take it any longer.

"Wash, we need to talk." I say as he hands me my beer.

"Sure, Doll. What's on your mind?" Wash responds as he sits down opposite of me.

"Look, I know that your job is rough sometimes. I know that you don't always want to talk about what you see or are dealing with on the job. I wouldn't push if I didn't feel you were keeping something from me. I know that you are doing it to protect me, and I appreciate that. However, I'm not a child anymore, Wash. You helped me with my trauma, and so much. I want you to talk to me about what's going on, even if it might be hard for me to hear. I can tell you are stressed, and clearly something is going on with you and your friends because I know for a fact that Fireball has an event tonight for St. Patty's Day. We aren't there, and we haven't been in a while. What is going on?" I probe, stabbing a potato with my fork.

"Well, I certainly didn't think you would call me out on it." Wash sighs. "I am protecting you, Lexi. I'm not telling you because I don't know how to tell you what's going on. This case is not just hard, but it's somehow personal too. Look, I don't know why the arsonist is targeting us, specifically you, but they are. Yes, there is a rift between my friends and me. They are having a hard time accepting our relationship, and I don't why. To make matters worse, Hunter is fucking convinced you are the arsonist because you want my attention or some bullshit like that. He's got some others in the friend group thinking that you are the arsonist too. He's making so much fucking noise about you being the arsonist that the detectives on the case want to interview you. They want your alibi, and shit. I'm defending you, and I'm trying to put out the fire that Hunter is creating around you. However, I don't know how long I can hold it off for." Wash informs. Well, fuck I was not expecting what Wash was holding back was on that level of intensity. I see why he kept back, but now it's time to show him I can handle it.

"Wash, you really are my fucking guardian, aren't you? Thank you for defending me against Hunter's false accusations. I'm sorry your friends are having a hard time accepting our relationship. I'm sorry I'm causing such a mess. That was never my intention when I came to you." My voice cracks trying to hold back my tears. Afterall, this is what I feared.

"You're not the one making a mess. It's everyone else, and this damn arsonist. You are not the problem, Doll. You are the one person in this shit storm that makes me happy. No matter what kind of day I'm having, I always look forward to coming home to you. This is simply a challenge, and we can face it together. I shouldn't have tried holding back the information. I wasn't sure how to tell you what was going on. I don't want you to blame yourself for any of this." Wash reaches across the table and grabs my hand. He rubs it gently.

"I think we should enjoy our dinner, and then curl up on the couch and watch some TV. Maybe we can start that new anime you've been dying to show me." I suggest, not wanting to deal with this heavy conversation anymore. I know I started it, but now I'm over it because while I hear Wash's words, that it's not my fault, my anxiety isn't listening.

"Sounds like a plan, Doll." Wash gives me a sweet smile. I swear he wants to say something more, but doesn't.

We go about our evening with our plans. We eat our food, which is all delicious including the cake. Things are a little silent between us, but we do cuddle a lot. I half expected us to have sex, but with both of us lost in our own thoughts it's not happening tonight. This is all certainly a challenge. I knew Wash and I would face challenges as a couple. I'm glad we are facing them together and not on our own. I know we will talk about things again. I'm not thrilled about having to possibly talk to the detectives and defend myself against something I didn't do. I'm pissed that Hunter is even spreading such bullshit. His friends can't be that desperate to get rid of me, can they? I can't help but wonder if Kate is fucking involved in this bullshit in some sad attempt to get Wash back. I don't think she's that desperate, then again I don't know Kate well, or Wash's friends for that matter. I don't want to believe they hate me so much they would make up lies about me.

 This is crazy. I didn't think this is what Wash was hiding. I don't really know what I thought it was, but this was not it. I'm shocked and hurt they would go this far. I'm concerned about the arsonist targeting me. I kinda got that from all the businesses I touch burning down. I'm almost afraid to go anywhere in case the arsonist is stalking me. How else would the arsonist even know to target those businesses if he wasn't stalking me? The scariest part is that I don't know who the hell would go out of their way to stalk me, let alone set shit on fire for me or to frame me. It's crazy. There is one person crazy enough, but he's dead, so who then? Great, I'm going to be overthinking for who knows how long trying to figure this out. No wonder poor Wash is stressed. I need to do my best to make things easier on him. I need to be strong. I can handle whatever is coming because I have Wash in my corner. I have Dr. Daniels, and I'm getting my life on track. I'm a survivor, and I will survive this too even if it doesn't feel like it at the moment. I snuggle up closer to Wash letting his strong arms comfort me.

Chapter 25
Wash

Lexi surprised me the other night when she confronted me about hiding what was going on from her. I don't know why I was surprised given that I am more than aware that Lexi is not a little kid anymore. She's been proving she's all grown up for years now. Even when Jesse was alive, she was proving she was grown up. Jesse and I both went straight into our training for our careers when we graduated high school. Lexi was nine and stepping up to take over responsibilities so Jesse could do what he had to in order to get his career moving. Six years ago it was clear how mature Lexi was. If I didn't know she was fifteen, I would have thought she was at least eighteen with how mature she acted. Looks can be deceiving. I'm all about judging someone's age off how they act because to me that's their real age.

 I wasn't trying to hide things on purpose, and I'm glad Lexi realized that. I honestly didn't know how to approach it with her. I knew it would be hard for her to hear. I did ask Dr. Daniels for his advice, and he had good suggestions. I guess I was too nervous to bring it up afterall. Delivering bad news to Lexi has always been hard. I was the one who picked her up from school when Jesse was shot. We were on our way to the hospital when he died. I had to tell her the bad news. It was hard. I haven't had to give her bad news since then.

 Lexi's trauma is what made me hesitate. She doesn't need this bullshit while she is trying to heal. She's working hard to overcome her trauma. Lexi is strong, I've never doubted that. I've seen her strength come out over the years. Even as a kid and teen she was strong. She could carry the weight of the world on her shoulders and not a soul would know. I know because I know Lexi, just like she clearly knows me. I hate that I was such a chicken shit with telling her what was going on with the case. I'm not one to back down from things like that, but Lexi is different. She isn't everyone. She's the one. I fucking love her. I almost confessed it the other night too. I had to stop myself. It wasn't the time.

When I tell Lexi I love her, I don't want it to be after I just gave her bad news. I know she is secretly panicking about being a suspect. We both know she doesn't have an alibi for every fire because sometimes she was home when the fires started and I wasn't home to vouch for her. Not that I think that would help because one of the times she was home with me, but that's not enough. I can vouch for her, but I'm not sure that it won't look like I'm covering for her. Hunter is making me look bad right now, and it's pissing me off. I'm defending my girlfriend against a crime I know she didn't commit, but Hunter is making it seem like I'm blind to her antics. I'm angry he would try to ruin my career before it got started in fire investigations. Maybe Hunter didn't truly want me to join fire investigations as he claimed. In all the years I've known Hunter, I've never known him to be so petty. I'm seeing a side to my friend I don't like. A side that reminds me far too much of Jesse.

This is my first big case, I want to make a good impression even if I don't plan on staying after this case is solved. I don't want to leave the fire department with a negative taste in my mouth or theirs. I worked far too hard to have that happen. I've built a decent career and a good life for myself. I don't want everything I did with UCFD to go up in flames because someone who is supposed to be my friend is convinced my girlfriend is a criminal when she's not. I'm not an idiot. I know Hunter is trying to get me kicked off this case because I'm too biased toward a suspect. This whole case makes my want to end my friendship with Hunter and tell him to fuck off with his shitty ass attuide.

    My phone chimes with a text as I'm getting in the car to head into work. It's Stephen. He needs me to come to the bar tonight because he and Kyle have to talk to me about business stuff. I don't want to go, but I have to. That's if this is even about the business. It could be a way to get me down to the bar. They even asked if I could come by myself because that's not suspicious. I wasn't planning on bringing Lexi anyway because I refuse to expose her to their judgmental bullshit anymore. I let it slide when Lexi and I first started dating, but now it's gone too far. I will not expose Lexi to their negative bullshit any longer. I don't plan on bringing her around them until they can get their shit together. I know I have Stephen and Julia's wedding coming up at the end of the summer, and I can't avoid that. I'm part of the wedding party. Lexi is my plus one. So, at this rate we will do the ceremony, stay for a bit during the reception, and then we are gone. I will do my best man duties but that's it. That's if Stephen even wants me in his wedding or as his best man. With how bad things are between me and our friend group, I wouldn't be surprised if they decide it's better that I don't come.

I text Stephen back that I'll be there after work, and then let Lexi know I have to run to the bar after work. Then I toss my phone on the passenger seat, and head to my job that I'm trying to convince myself I love. I think I enjoyed being in the firehouse because of the action. However, I truly needed a break. I need something different. I'm starting to think I've been doing it for too long, and it's time for a complete one eighty degree change. Something that has nothing to do with fires. It's why I've started looking at properties to buy to flip. I want to work with my hands again. I always loved carpentry, and construction stuff. It's why I did it on the side for years. I stopped when I started dating Kate as she was demanding my free time be spent with her. Kate never understood why I did side projects because I didn't need the money, but that's not why I did it. I did it because I enjoyed the work. I also liked being my own boss. Being my own boss had some serious benefits that I enjoyed.

Work is rough. The chief found some bullshit work for me to do. I got stuck reviewing everything that we have on the case to see if there is anything we missed. It's bullshit work to keep me at headquarters while Hunter and the detectives go canvas again. I swear they better not go near Lexi without telling me. She has a therapy appointment, and then doing some errands like food shopping for the week. I text Lexi to keep her eyes open for Hunter and detectives so she isn't caught off guard in case they do corner her to talk. I'd like to think they wouldn't do that, but I don't exactly trust them right now because I don't trust Hunter, and he's leading the witch hunt right to Lexi's door.

    I'm relieved when work ends. At least getting stuck with bullshit work means I'm done on time for once. I wish I was going home to Lexi, but I have to go to the damn bar. I've never regretted helping Stephen and Kyle start up the bar, but right now I'm skeptical of what this whole meeting is about. I'm a silent partner. There isn't much I'm involved in other than tossing money if it's needed, and intervening if they can't decide on something. So, unless they need money or can't decide on something then this meeting is bullshit. It's been awhile since they have needed money or choice made, so I'm going with bullshit.

    Heading to the bar, I'm already over the conversation that hasn't even begun. I park, and head into the bar. The minute I walk in I smell the bullshit in the air. The bar isn't overly crowded at the moment. It's a weekday, so it's not too surprising. There are a few customers spread throughout doing their own thing. I text Stephen and Kyle to let them know I'm here because I don't see them. My phone pings with a text from Stephen letting me know they are in the back office. I head to the back, and to the office. The minute I open the door, I know the whole thing is bullshit. Kevin, Kyle, Stephen, and Hunter are all in the office. The four men I've considered my brothers and best friends for years are about to do something to piss me off.

"Hey, Wash, come in." Stephen says casually as I shut the door behind me.

"I didn't realize Keven and Hunter were partners in the bar as well." I glare at each of them.

"Well, uh. We aren't really here to talk about the business." Stephen confesses.

"No shit. I figured that out. So, what is this really about." I spit back, trying to not let my anger already get the better of me. I'm already defensive which is never a good sign.

"Wash, we are here because we are your friends, your brothers. We care about you, and we want to openly talk to you about some choices you are making." Hunter begins.

"Are you seriously staging some type of intervention as if I'm an addict who has a problem?" I scoff in disbelief while also trying to not be completely insulted.

"Hear us out, Wash, before you go flying off the handle." Stephen pleads.

"You got five minutes to spew your bullshit." I declare, giving them each a dirty ass look because I already know where there is going. I knew exactly where this was going the minute I got Stephen's text.

"Wash, Lexi is not who you think she is. She's using you for your money, and she is a criminal." Hunter starts bluntly as if he hasn't been saying this to me for weeks.

"Come on, Wash. We know her type. We deal with girls like this all the time on the job. They think they are in love with us because we saved them. You may not have pulled Lexi out of a fire, but you are still her savior, her hero. She's in love with the hero you are. It's false love, and you are feeding into it. It's probably why she is starting the fires." Kyle adds. Did he seriously just blame me for Lexi starting the fires? The fires I know she has absolutely nothing to do with.

"Really? Well, maybe I'd take your words at value if you actually got to know Lexi. However, since she's arrived you all have done is judge her. I've kept my mouth shut for as long as

I can. I've dealt with your passive aggressive comments when she is around and the nastier comments she isn't around. I'm done keeping my mouth shut. Look, six years ago before she left, I told her she could always come to me if she needed me." I defend.

"It took her six years to decide she needed your help? You didn't hear from her for years, and then one day she pops up in your Facebook messages asking to meet up." Hunter raises his eyebrow in question. I can see how that might look suspicious without any context behind it. I thought I had done a good job at explaining the context of Lexi's arrival, but either I didn't do as good of a job as I thought, or they simply heard only what they wanted.

"She didn't stop talking to me because she wanted to. Her mom broke her phone and erased my number. You have no idea how manipulative her mom is. I do. Lexi has had a rough life. Her father wanted to abort her, and left when her mom didn't. Then her mom blamed Lexi for the father leaving. Jesse died, her mom ended up in rehab, and then her mom took her where things got worse. She was raped and sexually assaulted by her mom's various loser boyfriends, and abused by her mother. After her mom got sent to prison, Lexi tried to make it on her own, but she couldn't. She came to me as a last resort. You don't know her like I do because I have known her for her entire life. Maybe you would know some of this if any of you took the time to get to know her. You haven't even given her a chance." I boldly defend. The guardian in me is coming out hard right now, and I need to not punch Hunter in the face.

"Wow, she really knows how to paint the sob story. Also, the fact that you have known her for her entire life and are now dating her is weird, man. Seriously, an eleven year age gap is a lot. I get hotter, younger chicks, but they are meant to be for fun. You're not supposed to be serious about them." Hunter retorts. He seems to be the one ready to lead Lexi to the hangman's noose. I simply don't understand why.

"Let me make one thing very clear to you all right now. I love Lexi. I don't care if you think our age gap is creepy or weird. It's not your fucking relationship. It's mine and Lexi's, and we aren't bothered by the age gap. I wasn't expecting to fall in love with her, or even date her. I had no clue what to expect when I saw her after six years. I certainly didn't think I would be attracted to her, but shit, I was. I still very much am. I've never been so hard for someone or so incredibly turned on before, not even with Kate. I don't have to explain my relationship to you, just like I don't need you to explain your relationships to me. All I want is you fucking support, which you can't give. I can't replace Lexi, she's one of a kind, but friends, well, I can replace. Don't make me fucking choose because I will pick Lexi. Oh, look. You're five minutes is up." I say before storming out the door. Assholes.

They have some serious fucking nerve. I'm done. They can keep accusing Lexi all they want, but I will pick her in the end. I don't care. I know Lexi, and she is not who they paint her as. I have no idea why the fuck they think what they do. I'm also annoyed that they think I'm so blind to Lexi's fake motives that I can make good choices with my life. I'm not a foolish person. I have made mistakes as does everyone, but I've never been a fool.

However, their little bullshit did make me think of someone I've not thought about as a potential suspect. Lexi's dad. That asshole is probably still alive. He's a fucking cockaroach, and those fuckers can survive just about anything. I get to my car and take my phone out of my pocket. I text Drake. He was Jesse's partner. Drake and I have stayed in touch over the years, and always text on Jesse's death day. Drake now works in the gang unit. He might be able to help me find out with the fuck Lexi's dad is up to.

Before I make it home, Drake texts me back. When I read his text, hope flurries in my chest. Bingo! Apparently, Lexi's dad is in a gang, and high ranking in it too. Drake can't tell me too much over text, and wants to meet up to be able to tell me more. I ask Drake if he thinks Lexi's dad could be a serial arsonist. Drake thinks it's possible because the gang has been known to start fires for one reason or another. This might just be the break in the case I need. Now, to meet with Drake and get the information I need to bring back to my chief to get Lexi off the damn suspect list.

Chapter 26
Arsonist

I thought for sure the intervention Wash's friends had would have worked, but Lexi has her claws too deep into him. I've bugged this entire place over the years, so I heard the entire argument they had. I was silently cheering Hunter on, but he couldn't convince Wash to let Lexi go. Hunter impressed me when he started accusing Lexi as the arsonist. Lexi wouldn't hurt a fly even I know that, but no one else has to. It's why I started to target spots that Lexi could be tied to. Burning down Cool Beans was more or less to hurt Lexi and stop her from working. Then she found the library, and well, it had to go too. The hibachi place was because I could, and it helped with painting Lexi as the arsonist.

I've debated about burning down her therapist's office along with the grocery store she shops at, but I don't think it will matter. Wash is determined to prove that Lexi is innocent. I like Hunter. He's on a witch hunt for Lexi, one I've tried to aid, but we are getting nowhere. I don't think burning shit down anymore is the answer. Wash is too blinded, and apparently in love. I almost barfed when he said he was in love with her. Fuck, Lexi is a more manipulative than I gave her credit for.

To be honest, I thought Wash would fuck her a few times, and get it out of his system. Hunter had a point. Young chicks are for fucking and dumping. It's what I do, but then again, I just fuck for fun in general. I didn't think Wash and Lexi would turn their weird relationship into something real. Yet, they did.

It's time for last resort measures. It's time to abduct Lexi, and kill her. She should have been killed as an embryo, but Mom couldn't do it. Dad was right to want to keep it the three of us. Lexi ruined our lives just as Dad predicted she would. Now, I'll do us all a favor and kill the little bitch. I'll free Wash, so he can move on with someone worth it. Lexi is ruining his life, and he's too blind to see it. So, I'll take care of it for him. His friends tried, but they are heroes. They won't kill, but I'm not a hero. I never really was. I only pretended to be the hero. I'm the villain. I've always been the villain, and I'm okay with it. Being a villain has paid off more than being the hero ever did.

I have killed before. I've never killed someone I'd consider close to me, but I guess there's a first time for everything. Time to go stalk Lexi, abduct her, torture her, and then kill her. Oh this is going to be so satisfying. I can't wait to make Lexi pay for all her crimes. I bet she will beg me, and claim she was grateful afterall. Maybe she will call me Dad like she should have. This is going to be so much fun making my murder fantasies come true.

Chapter 27
Lexi

I'm trying to work on Wash's birthday project, but my mind is in a million directions since talking with Wash on St. Patrick's Day. It's only been a few days, and I haven't been able to slow my mind down. It got even worse after Wash had a huge fight with his friends. I know it's over me. Wash didn't have to say it. I could tell by how furious he was, and also by how he fucked me like he was proving to the world we are meant to be. I certainly didn't complain about the fucking part of things, it's everything else that has me concerned.

I feel horrible that he had an argument with his friends over me. Wash doesn't seem to care that he's not talking to his friends at the moment. Then there is the fact that Hunter is still pinning the fires on me, and now I have to go talk to the police in a few days. Wash is working on another possible suspect, but he won't tell me who. He said he doesn't want to say anything until he is certain. I trust Wash. I'm sure he's not telling me for a reason, and this time I don't feel the need to push for information.

My anxiety is through the roof with everything. I know I have nothing to hide when I talk to the detectives. I might not have the best of alibis for every fire, but that doesn't mean anything. They have no evidence other than Hunter's accusations. Wash seems to think they are only interviewing me to shut Hunter up, and also so Wash doesn't look biased and get taken off the case. Hunter forgets that Wash is closer to the cops than he is. Wash got to know a lot of cops because of Jesse. I think he might even still talk to Jesse's old partner.

Frustrated, I put my project away. I thought drawing would help me, and normally it does. However, right now, I'm too on edge. I feel like I'm crawling out of my skin. That's how intense my anxiety is. I haven't felt like this in awhile. I know it's a combination of things adding up and tipping the scales to panic land. I decide to go for a walk to attempt to clear my mind. There's a nice park up the road, and the fresh air might be good for me. If the walk doesn't help then I will take one of my emergency anti anxiety pills. I also have an appointment with Dr. Daniels before I talk to the detectives, so that will help.

I grab my phone and keys, and head out. I make sure to lock the door before stuffing my keys in my pocket. The cool spring air wraps around me like a soothing blanket. The warm sunshine hits my face as I take a deep breath before heading in the direction of the park. I text a selfie to Wash that I'm on my walk. I like to let him know when I'm leaving the house. Call it paranoia, but I like it if at least one person knows where I'm at.

The walk to the park takes about five minutes. I try to push my mind from overthinking, but who am I kidding? I've already over thought this entire situation more than once. Part of me feels like I'm ruining Wash's life, and I just want to run away to protect him. However, I know Wash, he's not letting me go this time. If I ran, he would chase me. To be honest, I don't truly want to run from Wash. I'm happy, safe, and totally in love with Wash. I can't deny that I love him now. I have for a long time. My crush actually panned out. I'm with my dream guy. I'm finally happy.

So, why do I feel like shit? I hate that my mom's words play over in my head constantly. I keep trying to burn away the broken lies that I have believed for so long. The lies my mother and even sometimes Jesse told me. I never told Wash that Jesse called me a mistake and a burden more times than I count. Jesse was not a nice drunk. Not a surprise as it runs in the family. I wonder if our dad was also an alcoholic. Neither Jesse or mom talked about him. I never even found out what our dad's name was. Any pictures or anything to do with him were tossed out before I could walk. Any time I would ask about our dad, I would get yelled at and even slapped by both my mom and Jesse. So, I stopped asking. The older I got, the less I cared that my dad wasn't around. I never understood why he left until I was in my teenage years. That was a hard pill to swallow.

    I make it to the park and find a shady spot to sit. I'm surprised the park isn't more crowded given how nice the day is, but it is late afternoon on a weekday. Most people are at work or school around this time. I make myself comfortable in my spot. I sit Indian style. Closing my eyes I decide to do some deep breathing to try and relax. Surprisingly, it works, and I find myself letting go of some of the anxiety plaguing me.

    My relaxed world is jolted when someone's arms wrap around my neck as their other hand goes around my mouth muffling the scream that attempts to escape me. I'm struggling to break free, but whoever is doing this has a good hold on me. Shit, I can already feel myself slipping into unconsciousness. I'm clawing at the attackers arms as my eyes frantically search for someone else around. Unfortunately, there's no one really around, and those that are around are too far to see me struggling. I'm trying to fight closing my eyes as the lighted feeling intensifies.

"Go the fuck to sleep Little Lex Luthor." Someone whispers in my ear. The familiar voice sends an icy chill down my spine. There's only one person who ever called me that. Only one person even knows that nickname. Not even Wash knows that nickname. The only person to call me that was Superman Jesse, and he's dead. My world turns black as my panicked mind quiets, and I give in to darkness.

Chapter 28
Wash

Drake is able to meet for lunch today. That's where I'm headed now. We are meeting a little later because that's what was easiest. My phone pings with a picture of Lexi walking to the park. I smile, happy that she isn't staying shut in at the house. I've been very worried about her. I've been on bullshit desk duty since I had it out with Hunter. I don't know why he's trying to sabotage me. I'm beyond pissed that he's making me look bad in front of our friends and our coworkers. Not to mention how shitty he's making me look to our chief. I don't need anyone questioning my choices. I'm not happy that Lexi has to talk to the detectives. That's why I'm hoping to get information from Drake to bring back to my chief to stop the need for Lexi to talk to the detectives.

At least doing the grunt work allows the time to have a break to even meet with Drake. I enter the sub shop and order my meal while I wait for Drake to come. When Drake arrives he places his order and then we both sit down at a table.

"It's good to see you, Wash." Drake says, unwrapping his sub.

"It's good to see you too, Drake. We really need to meet up more often and under better circumstances." I jest, which has Drake chuckling.

"I agree with that. I'm glad you ended up on the serial arsonist case. I think we can help each other. Plus, it will feel good to tell someone what my unit has discovered. I'm not supposed to tell anyone, but I will make an exception for you and Lexi. Not to mention what I know might actually help you." Drake informs me.

"Why do I have a feeling we both know the arsonist." I comment, sticking a fork in my potato salad before shoveling some in my mouth.

"We do, and so does Lexi. On a side note, I was happy to hear you two are together." At least someone approves of our relationship I think to myself as I work on unwrapping my own sub.

"Yeah, well, Jesse would have shit a brick if he was alive. I know the rest of my friends have." I add trying to hide my annoyance.

"Well, let's be honest, it didn't take much for Jesse to shit a brick over things. I heard Hunter is on a witch hunt for Lexi as the arsonist. Too bad he's got the wrong Martin." Drake pauses. He said the wrong Martin. Anxiety pumps in my veins. Fuck, don't say it, Drake, I think to myself as I anticipate the words that are about to come out of Drake's mouth. "Wash, I don't even know how to tell you this, so I'm just going to blurt it out. Jesse isn't dead." Drake informs me. Well, fuck!

"What? That's not possible. Is it?" I mean I would be lying if the thought of Jesse being alive hadn't crossed my mind. Especially lately, but I wasn't about to bring up my dead best friend as a suspect when everyone already thinks I'm blind to Lexi. If I muttered a word that I thought Jesse was the arsonist they would all think I'd lost my damn mind. Shit, I wouldn't even blame them at that point because without proof it sounds completely bonkers.

"Let me explain. A couple years ago, we started investigating a gang. The NOMADS. They are a small nothing gang, or that's how they want it to appear. They are more like some combination of a secret society and a gang. It's culty and fucked up. When Jerry Martin's name appeared as one of the ranking members, I was shocked. Jesse only talked about his dad once with me when he was really drunk. He kept a picture of Jerry in his wallet so he wouldn't forget what he looked like. Jesse really looked up to Jerry, I think you know that," I nod my head. Jerry was Jesse's lost hero. I never understood it then, and I don't understand now. "Back when Jesse was alive, he used his resources as a cop to find his dad since it was easy for him to confirm he was still alive. I knew Jesse had found his dad, but that was it. So, when Jerry's name came up with NOMADS, I had my suspicions that Jesse knew about his dad's gang ties. Jesse's death wouldn't be the first death they have staged and faked. They have members everywhere. Anyway, over the last couple of years, we discovered Jesse is still alive and a member of the NOMADS. He goes by Pyro in the gang." Drake informs me as I feel my reality shatter. It's one thing to think these things, it's another to have it confirmed.

"Shit, I don't even know how to process this. How do you know for sure Jesse is the arsonist besides his name in the gang?" I inquire.

"We have been keeping tabs on him. He's stalking you and Lexi pretty hard. We can't say anything to anyone because we can't risk bringing our operation down when we are so close to nailing all the members. We want to bring Jesse in and blow his fake death cover, and get him to testify against the leaders. The minute the NOMADS get wind that Jesse has been arrested they will start burning whatever evidence to the ground. It's what they do when one of their members is arrested. They take no chances. So, when we bring Jesse in we have to be able to flip him quickly, but the problem is we don't know how to get him to flip. So, we've been putting off taking Jesse down until we can figure out exactly how to flip him. However, time is running out. The NOMADS are hard to break. We've tried in the past with other members. We've never had one flip. Not once, not even consideration on their part. The answer is always no because they are fiercely loyal to the NOMADS." Drake dumps some more much needed info on my lap.

"Wait, if Jesse is stalking Lexi and me that would explain how he knew what places to burn down. When are you planning on arresting him and do you have proof he started the fires?"

"We do. We have surveillance footage of him starting a couple of the fires, canvassing places, and so on. It's something your team would miss because they don't know the tactics the NOMADS use like my team does. We know what to look for because trust me the NOMADS are almost god like with how they do things. It's how they get away with so much. I don't know when we are going to arrest him. We want to do it as quietly as possible. That's if Jesse doesn't make an erratic move before then." Drake answers.

Drake's phone rings, and he picks it up. I let him conduct his business while I take a few bites of my food. Drake hangs up, and looks at me with an expression that tells me I am not going to like what his phone call was about. "What's wrong?" I inquire.

"Remember that radical move I just mentioned?" I nod my head yes. "We have undercovers keeping tabs on Jesse. Jesse abducted Lexi, and they lost his trail. Do you have any ideas where Jesse might take Lexi?"

My heart clenches as panic ceases me. I quickly pull myself together. I've had to do this a million times on the job. I feel myself mentally shift from panic to rescue mode. "I don't know. I don't know criminal Jesse." I respond.

"Well, if Jesse is going off NOMAD MO then the place he would take her too would be significant, have some meaning to them. I have to tell you, Wash, NOMADS are killers. Jesse taking Lexi means one thing, and one thing only. He wants her dead, but he won't do it right away. That's not how the NOMADS do things. They like to make it a slow, painful death. We have time to get to Lexi, but we have to find her within twenty-four hours because that's when he will have to kill her. That's their rule that their victims can only live for twenty-four hours then they must be killed."

"Maybe their old house." I suggest, trying to keep focused and not let my fear for Lexi take over. I need to tap into my anger because I am pissed at Jesse. I always knew he was a little off, but I chalked it up to his dad leaving him, and Jesse never properly coping with it.

"Alright, it's a start, but I don't know if it would be something so obvious either."

"I'll keep thinking." I reply, trying to think of every place that would mean something to Lexi and Jesse.

All that matters is we find them. I don't want to think of what deranged, criminal Jesse is going to do. I don't know how he could hurt his own sister, but I've always suspected that Jesse resented Lexi because his life didn't turn out the way he thought it should. He never got over their father leaving, which explains why he looked him up. I assumed Jesse would eventually look up his father. I didn't know he had already done it though. He never told me he did, so I assumed he never got to it before he died. Apparently, there was a whole other side of Jesse I never saw, or maybe I did, but ignored it because it was easier than admitting that my best friend might be a little on the mentally insane side. I can't believe he faked his own death. I don't even know how to process that, and right now, I can't process it because finding Lexi is my top priority.

Chapter 29
Lexi

Blinking my eyes open since I can't rub them because my hands are tied behind my back I attempt to take in my surroundings. My head is pounding and vision is slightly fuzzy, but slowly returning to normal. I realize I'm on a tile floor, and my back is resting against cold metal. The room is lit just enough for me to see that I'm in a restaurant kitchen that's clearly been abandoned. Judging by the debris and the black char marks around the industrial sized brick pizza oven in front of me means there was a fire here. I know for a fact there was a fire here because I know this place.

This used to be Mario's Pizzeria before it burned down years ago. Jesse worked here when he was sixteen all the way up until he graduated from the police academy. The owner,

Mario, was a very sweet man. He felt bad about our home situation, and would let Jesse bring me to work. I would sit in the corner and draw pictures. Mario would always make sure we ate while we were here. He passed away a few years ago. His son tried to run the place, but after the fire happened he let the place go.

As my mind clears I try to remember what happened. I was at the park trying to relax. Someone came up behind me and started choking me. They whispered something to me. It was something only Jesse knew, and the person who said it sounded so much like him. I never thought I would hear his voice again. There's no way it was him, right?

"Did you miss me, Little Lex Luthor?" A shiver runs down my spine at the voice. The voice comes out of the shadows until Jesse steps out in front of me.

"Jesse?" I ask in disbelief. He's different. He's shaved his head, and tattoos cover every part of skin I can see including his face. He's wearing all black clothes.

"It's Superman Jesse. I remember you used to draw pictures of us as Superman and Lex Luthor in this very place. Did you ever wonder why I gave you a villain instead of a hero? I could have called you Wonder Woman or anything other than Little Lex Luthor." He taunts coming closer, and that's when something shiny catches my eye. On one hand Jesse is holding a rather large butcher's knife that looks way sharper than it needs to be.

I swallow hard. Of course, I always wondered why he called me Little Lex Luthor. At first, I didn't understand that Lex Luthor was a villain. I was just happy my brother was showing me attention. As I got older, I figured out that Lex Luthor was the bad guy, and I started to hate the nickname because of it. I never asked Jesse to stop calling me by it because I didn't want to lose the bond it had created between us. So, I just accepted it as our thing, and let it be.

"Jesse, how are you alive?" I ask, trying to figure out what the actual fuck is going on because my dead brother isn't actually dead.

"Don't try to distract me. It won't work. I've done this many times before."

"Done what exactly?" I question, knowing very well I do not want the answer. I try to swallow the lump in my throat as panic starts to rise. Justifiable panic, I might add, because my not so dead brother is looking at me like he's going to do unspeakable things to me.

"Kill," A shiver comes over me at his answer. Yeah, I definitely don't like the answer. Jesse slaps me hard across the face, and I have to hold back the yelp that threatens to escape me. "Listen up bitch. It's story time. See once upon a time a little boy lived very happily with his parents until his mom got pregnant. A pregnancy that would ruin the little boy's happy world. It would have been better if you were never conceived or born." Jesse's tone is laced with hatred like I've never heard before. He steps closer to me, the knife still firmly in his hand gleaming in the light threatening pain and danger.

"Jesse, it's not my fault that our dad left." I defend, knowing it's probably going to piss him off even more. Somehow, I don't think I can win in this situation. It's one of those damned if I do, damned if I don't.

"See that's the thing, Lexi," Venom laces his voice as he says my name, leaning down so he's right in my face. "It's not our dad, it's my dad."

"What are you saying?" I ask, completely confused.

"Mom was having an affair on dad with Mario. She got pregnant with another man's kid. That's why dad wanted you aborted. He refused to raise a child that wasn't his, so he left when Mom refused to get rid of you. Rightfully so. I wouldn't want to raise a child that wasn't mine, yet that's what ended up happening. Mario felt so guilty about the situation that's why he offered me a job when I was sixteen, and why he didn't care if you came with me. It was his way of trying to get to know you." Jesse informs me, and I feel my world shatter more than it already has. Isn't it a good thing Jerry Martin isn't my dad?

"How do you know that?" I inquire.

"Are you calling me a liar?" Jesse accuses before taking the sharp butcher knife and planting it deeply in space right under my collarbone and near where it connects to my arm, twisting the blade into the wound to cause more pain. I scream in pain as warm, slick blood oozes from my shoulder. "I didn't know until I found my dad again. About a year or so into being a cop, I used my resources and found him. We reconnected, and he explained why he left. We ended up bonding. He helped me fake my death so I could join his secret society of the NOMADS that operate like a gang in the city." Jesse pushes the blade further into my shoulder making me cry out harder. He has to be cutting the ligaments, even tendons. I can't tell fully because my hands are bound, but I think he's done damage to the point where my shoulder is immobilized.

"Jesse, please. I'm your sister." I beg.

I know it won't do anything, but I have a feeling Jesse wants me to beg for my life. He's deranged, and certainly not the brother I remember. I always assumed he hated me, or at the very least tolerated me. As a kid I was blind to how Jesse really felt about me, and I bought his lies that loved me. The older I got the more aware I was that Jesse wasn't my biggest fan. Still, I chalked it up to stress of having to be the man of the house, and dealing with a drunk mother. I didn't want to believe he hated me because of how much I admired him. He was my hero, my superman. It was easier to believe he loved me than he despised me.

"Half sister," Jesse spits at me. "I raised you like my own fucking kid, and you still look at me as your brother?" He questions with disgust at me as he pushes the blade deeper causing me to scream once more. Blood is leaking from the wound at a decent rate now, and I'm positive he's severed important ligaments given the extreme pain and lack of movement that I know isn't from having my hands bond. Not that I really want to move with a damn knife inside my shoulder. If I didn't know better I'd swear he's slowly trying to cut my arm off.

"I'm sorry, was I supposed to call you Dad?" I ask sarcastically as tears stream down my face. My shoulder is on fire as pain erupts from the area spreading down my arm and perhaps in other places. The pain is all blending together in a sick cocktail that makes me wish I would just pass out already.

The next thing I know Jesse's fist collides with my eye. For a moment all I see is stars. I can feel my eye swelling, and I'm sure it's pretty shades of black and purple already. "You really are an ungrateful bitch. That's okay, I'll make sure you are taught one final lesson before I kill you. My friends are going to come and do whatever the fuck they want to you while I watch. So, hang tight Little Lex Luthor because I'll make sure you beg me to end your life." Jesse rips the blade from my shoulder causing more blood to leak from my wound. I'm bleeding badly now, and my head is pounding. Jesse kicks me hard a few times in the ribs, causing me to curl over in pain, before walking away.

This is bad. Really bad. I don't want to even begin to think about what his friends are going to do to me. I've been raped before, but gang rape that's a whole new level of trauma I don't want. Not to mention that I'm reeling from the fact that Jesse is alive and part of a fucking gang. Oh, and apparently we don't share the same dad. Mario is apparently my dad.

In some ways, it makes sense. Mario did treat me a lot like a daughter. I assumed he was being nice because he felt bad. If he was my dad, I don't understand why he wouldn't have been a part of my life. Although, knowing Judy she would have made sure Mario stayed away in hopes that Jerry would come back. I'm sure she blamed Mario for Jerry leaving as well as me. I don't know if I believe what Jesse is telling me. If I make it out of here alive, I'm going to get to the bottom of who is actually my father. I hope Wash figures out I'm missing. I don't know how long I've been gone for. I can't see outside, so I don't even know what time it is. All I know is I'm in serious danger, and there's a high chance I'm not going to make it out of here alive.

Chapter 30
Wash

It's been a couple of hours since Lexi went missing. They searched their old house, neighborhood, and canvased the neighborhood. No one has seen them. I'm down at the precinct making a list of places that they might be at. I'm on edge as I cross places off the list, and add more.

"Wash." Drake's voice pulls me from my chaotic thoughts.

"Any news?"

"No, but we are working on pulling traffic light footage. We will find her. How's your list coming?"

"I have a few places that they might be at. Drake, we have to find her. I can't lose Lexi."

"I know, man. I do. I don't want anything to happen to Lexi either. I know she's a sweet girl, well, I guess woman now. Either way, we will find her." Drake states, but I'm not believing his confidence in finding Lexi before anything bad can happen. She's already been through so much.

"The question is what state will we find her in?" I reply, not really wanting to think about what horror Lexi is experiencing at the moment.

I looked over the files that Drake gave me while we were waiting for the search party to get back to us if they had found them. The NOMADS are sick. They are some weird cross breed between a gang and a secret society. They participate in torture, gang rape, drug rings, and other bad shit. They aren't good people, and I understand why Drake and his team are determined to take them out. They are smart to operate in a smaller city than Atlanta, NYC, or any other major city. It took a while for them to even draw enough attention to themselves for the UCPD to even care.

My insides twist with worry at what Jesse could be doing to Lexi. The urge to find her is strong. Finding her is my first and only priority at the moment. After we find her, I'm going to process the fact that my best friend, who I thought was dead for the last six plus years, is in fact alive. Not only alive, but part of a gang with his father who he is apparently very close to now. I don't even know how to begin to process this crazy shit. This is the type of shit you see on TV that you tell yourself doesn't happen in real life.

"You can't think about what state we will find her in. If she's alive that's more important than whatever damage Jesse can cause. Now, give me some locations to search, so we can find them sooner rather than later." Drake says, breaking my train of thought.

Looking back down over the list desperate to pick the right location, but nothing currently stands out until I land on the pizza place. Jesse loved working there, or at least that's how he portrayed it. I'm not entirely sure I ever knew Jesse at all. Still, he did like that place, so did Lexi. If I remember the place burnt down years ago, and is abandoned now. It's about fifteen minutes from their old house.

"Hey, I think I have a location they might be at." I inform Drake.

"Where?" Drake questions.

"The old pizza place Jesse used to work out. It burnt down, and as far as I know is abandoned."

"Yeah, that's right. I forgot about that place. Alright, I'll let the search party know where to head next." Drake responds before walking off to relay the information to his sargent.

It feels like hours have gone by since Drake told me the search party was headed to the pizzeria. I hope I picked the right place. I wanted to go, but Drake said it wasn't a good idea. He's right, it's not because I will fucking kill Jesse myself. Drake knows that, and since he needs Jesse alive to attempt to flip him it's best I don't go. I'm on edge, pacing back and forth when Hunter walks into the room with our chief and a few fire investigators. What the fuck are they doing here? I know Jesse is the arsonist we have been looking for, but why do they need to be here. The case should be closed once Jesse is arrested, and they don't need to be here for that.

"Wash." Hunter says walking over to me. Before he can even get another word out I punch him in the face.

"What the fuck are you doing here?" I yell as Drake attempts to hold me back.

"What the hell, Wash?" Hunter questions as he holds his bleeding nose.

"Get him out of my face, Drake, before I do something that will get my ass arrested." I demand as I shake Drake off me.

"What is going on? We came down here because we were told there was a lead on our case." Hunter says, still holding his bleeding nose.

"Take a walk, Wash, I will let you know if we find Lexi." Drake directs.

"What did the little pyro go on the run?" Hunter asks in a snarky tone before I lunge at him as my fist once more collides with Hunter's face. I take a step back before Drake or anyone else jumps on me to pull me back.

"Uh, Hunter, Lexi is actually the victim. She's been abducted by Jesse who plans to kill her if we don't find her." Drake informs Hunter as I'm walking away before I seriously get my ass arrested. The last thing Lexi needs is me to get arrested when she needs me the most.

Outside I bum a cigarette off of one of the cops on a smoke break. I don't make a habit out of smoking. I smoked a bit in my late teens and early twenties. I was more of a social smoker. I stopped fully to help stay in shape and it wasn't really a habit I wanted. I haven't touched a cigarette in years, but right now I need it to stop me from loosing my fucking mind.

I decide to call Dr. Daniels and inform him on what's going on. Lexi is going to need him after this. Hell, I'm going to need several sessions myself after this. This whole situation is insane. I never would have imagined this is what would happen when I took on this arsonist case. Deep down, I think I always knew the arsonist was Jesse, but logically it didn't make sense. He was supposed to be dead; there was no way he could be the arsonist. My gut was contradicting logic. There was no way I was about to tell anyone I thought a dead man was the arsonist we were hunting. I would have been told I was insane. I knew that. So, I kept it to myself, and chalked it up to me missing my best friend. Except, Jesse is actually alive, and my gut was right.

Time passes slowly as I wait for an update. I think I've smoked half a pack at this point. I gave Drake some money to get me a pack when he asked what would help. I don't know who he got to go on the run, and I don't care. The cigarettes are the only thing stopping me from losing my shit. Hunter tried to come out and talk to me, but I told him to get out of my face before I did something I'd regret. He left. Before I knew it I had Stephen, Kevin, and Kyle texting me to see if I was okay. I ignored ever single fucking call and text. They don't get to act like they give a shit about Lexi now.

Finally, Drake comes out. I finish sucking down the cigarette before putting it out in the ashtray. "Any news?"

"Yeah, good news. We found them. Lexi is being taken to the hospital. I can take you over there."

"Yes, let's go. Is she okay?" I inquire as we get into his squad car.

"All I was told is that she has a pretty bad shoulder wound, some bruises and scrapes, but that's all I know. One thing you should know. They found Lexi tied down on one of the tables. There were about five other gang members there. We think the were trying to gang rape Lexi as some initiation or just to torture her. As far as I know the didn't actually get a chance to rape her, but you need to be prepared in case they did." Drake informs as he flips on his lights and sirens, and speeds off in the direction of the hospital.

Anger burns in my veins. I swear if I ever get ahold of Jesse, I will fucking kill him for this. I can't believe he would do this to his fucking sister. He's supposed to protect her, and instead he attempted to kill her. That's okay because I'm her fucking guardian. I always have been, and I will burn this entire fucking city to the ground if it meant she was safe.

Chapter 31
Lexi

I'm not a religious person at all, but I like to believe there is a higher power looking out for us. Right now, I'm thankful to whatever that higher power is because the cops found me just in time before Jesse's so called friends were about to gang rape me. They did manage to touch me. I think one or two of them shoved their fingers up my vagina or a toy. I honestly couldn't tell, and I couldn't see. They also enjoyed touching my breasts. I couldn't believe Jesse let them strip me. They even burned my clothes in front of me to taunt me. I managed to get several more bruises and cuts, but the injury on my shoulder is bad.

The cops covered me with a blanket and let the paramedics take me to the hospital. I'm here now as they look over me and tend to my injuries. The cops and nurse insist I do a rape kit even though I wasn't raped. I guess it's a precaution, or maybe they think I'm in denial about what happened. To be honest, I really don't know what they were shoving inside of my vagina. It could have been one of their dicks, but it didn't feel like it. Maybe I am in denial. It doesn't matter I'm going to do it anyway because if it helps put my brother and his gang in prison for life then they can do what they need. They even take pictures of my injuries for documentation. I know I have to make a statement to the cops, but I'm waiting for Wash to get here. I was told he was on his way with Drake.

I haven't seen Drake in years, but I remember he was nice. He's a detective in the gangs unit, and his team has been investigating Jesse's gang to take down their operation or that's what I've been briefly informed. There's a female patrol officer with me, and she has been filling me in on stuff while the hospital staff takes care of me. I'm only hearing portions of what everyone is saying. I believe the doctor said my shoulder was in bad shape. He said there are damaged ligaments they should heal in 12 weeks but there is a possibility of surgery. Several cuts required stitches. The wound of my shoulder required staples. The memory of Jesse using a butcher knife on me will be something that haunts me in my nightmares forever. After he did damage to my shoulder he sliced me in other areas, mostly on my legs, arms, and stomach. To be honest, I was terrified he would give me a joker smile. Thankfully, he never went near my face or privates with the knife. I've been given meds for the pain, antibiotics, and the morning after pill just in case I was raped along with several other medications that I've lost track of.

I know I'm in shock. I'm numb emotionally as the nurses and doctors do their thing to help me. I know they won't let Wash see me until I'm taken care of, and I'm almost done. A nurse informs me that Dr. Daniels is on his way. I'm sure Wash had someone inform him of what happened. It's wise for Dr. Daniels to come. I know seeing and talking with him will be helpful. Of course, Wash is the person I need to see the most.

Everything is shaken now that we know Jesse is still alive. I can't even wrap my head around him faking his own death. I mean that's the shit you see in movies, soap operas, and stuff like that. That shit is not supposed to happen in real life. I guess the stories are slightly based on real life. Still, it's a lot to digest with everything else in the last twenty four hours.

Then there is the fact that the man I thought was my dad might not actually be my dad. I don't know why Jesse would lie to me about it. I don't think he was because his words were so clear and laced with a hate you can't fake. Plus, Mario was always fatherly to me. I assumed it was because he was a nice guy. He was sweet and caring with many of his customers. I didn't think I was something special to him. In hindsight, I can see it. Back then I was a scared child happy to have anyone show me an ounce of kindness.

"Lexi." Wash's voice pulls me from my wild thoughts.

"Wash?" I question because I'm still not fully convinced I've been saved as I look for him and find he stands in the doorway.

"Yeah, Doll. I'm here." Wash says as he walks fully into the room, and ends up at my side. He takes my hand in his and kisses it.

This is when I realize the doctors and nurses have left except for one nurse typing things into the computer as she scans med bottles. The female cop is now stationed outside of my room. Drake walks in followed by Dr. Daniels. Drake stands next to Wash while Dr. Daniels comes to the other side of me. A nurse whispers something in Dr. Daniels ear as he nods his head.

"Lexi, I know asking if you are okay is a moot point right now. I need a statement from you as soon as you feel ready. I don't want to push, but the sooner the better. Jesse and the other gang members have been arrested. I promise you, they will end up locked up for a very long time if not for life." Drake states, and I believe him.

"Good. They're animals that deserve to be locked in a cage." I angrily declare. "Drake, can I ask you to do something for me?"

"Sure, Lexi. Whatever you want or need." Drake replies.

"Jesse told me that we don't actually share the same father. My mom was apparently having an affair with Mario who used to own the pizza shop you found me in. I don't know Mario's last name. Jesse said that I'm Mario's daughter not Jerry's. Can you help me figure out who my father actually is?"

"Yeah, I can do that. It's fairly simple DNA test stuff. I just need to get in contact with one of Mario's kids and get their DNA since last I heard Mario died a couple of years ago. I can make Jesse give a sample as well and test that way to, at least see if you have the same dad. I'll make it happen, just might need a little bit of time." Drake answers. I nod my head in agreement. I don't care how long it takes, I simply want answers.

"Lexi, I'm glad you were found, and are safe. I know you want to shut down right now, but you can't. It's a lot to process, but there is nothing that needs to be figured out today. You need rest, so you can heal. The nurse has informed me the results of your exam and rape kit have been released. They rushed it for obvious reason with the case. Do you want to know the results?" Dr. Daniels asks.

"No, I don't want to know if they actually raped me or not. I'd rather just keep to my assumptions that it was their fingers inside of me because I couldn't see what they were doing, and my eyes were closed as much as possible." I answer. I don't think I can handle knowing right now.

"I thought you were found before they could?" Wash questions, mostly to Drake. Drake goes to open his mouth but I speak first.

"It doesn't matter, Wash. They found me, that's what truly matters." I interject.

"You're right." Wash says, kissing me on the head.

The rest of the time passes by in a blur. I give my statement to Drake with Wash and Dr. Daniels in the room. Dr. Daniels talks to me for a bit by himself while Drake goes back to work and Wash is getting discharge instructions from the nurses. I want to go home. They wanted to keep me for twenty four hours, but I insisted I go home. Wash is a paramedic. He is more than capable of monitoring me. By the time Wash is helping into the backseat of Drake's unmarked cop car, it's already well into the next day. Relief floods me that I truly am safe. I lay my head on Wash's shoulder completely exhausted. I want a shower, which should be possible, and my bed curled up with Wash. I'm happy I'm going home with my guardian. My guardian that will keep me safe and the one I'm destined to be with.

Chapter 32

Lexi

A week has passed since the entire nightmare happened. Wash has been off since I came home. He's taken a leave of absence to be with me. I appreciate it because I really don't want to be left alone. I've had a couple of panic attacks, and several nightmares. I've been in contact with Dr. Daniels, and I will be going to see him tomorrow.

I haven't fully been able to process how I feel. I'm on some decent pain meds while I heal up. My shoulder is incredibly painful and I'm even in sling until they can determine if I need surgery. The orthopedic wants to do some more scans in a couple of weeks and see where I'm at. I might need physical therapy as well. It's amazing the damage that Jesse did with a super sharp butchers knife. I swear he was trying to chop my arm off in a slow, painful way. Even when he pulled the knife out and started cutting me in other areas, I expected him to go back to my shoulder.

I've only left the house to go to the doctor yesterday to get checked. Most of my bruises and small cuts are fairly healed up. I've spent a good amount of time resting, sleeping, and drawing. Wash has been wonderful tending to me. I know he's trying to process what happened, and the fact that Jesse is alive. It's certainly a lot to handle. I know he was worried sick about me.

Wash walks into the bedroom, and I slowly sit up. He rushes over to my side to help finish sitting up. "I'm okay, Leutinient." I say as I gently swat his hand away. He's been fussing over me, and while it's sweet I don't like feeling broken.

"You are healing, and you need to take it easy. You've been through a lot, Doll." Wash's voice is gentle as he sits on the edge of the bed facing me.

"Thank you for taking good care of me, Wash. You have no idea how all I wanted was to make it back to you. I love you, Wash." I confess.

"Not fair, you beat me to it. I love you too, Lexi. We will get through this together." Wash says as he kisses me gently on the lips before pulling away.

"I know we will. Can you do me a favor right now?" I question.

"Anything you want." Wash answers without skipping a beat.

"I want you to make love to me while you remind me that no matter what I'm yours."

"I would love to do that, but are you sure you feel up to it?" Wash questions as his hand strokes my cheek.

"I can handle it. If it really starts to hurt, I'll let you know. Before paramedic Wash comes out and asks if I can have sex, the answer is yes. I talked to the doctor when I got checked up. She checked me out, and I'm healed up enough that she said we could be gentle." I inform Wash.

In the end, I broke down needing to know what happened. The rape kit was negative. Drake informed us a couple of days later that they found sex toys, like dildos, near where they had me. Drake explained they have gathered from previous investigations that they use a variety of toys first to test how much the girl can take. It's their sick way of deciding exactly how to make the rape worse because they want it to hurt. I didn't ask Drake to go into detail after that, I'd heard enough to fill in the rest.

Wash chuckles. "Okay, you clearly thought this out. It's not just the physical I'm worried about, Lexi. I know you've been having nightmares of what happened. I hear you crying out in your sleep. Emotionally and mentally are you sure you are okay? I'm not going to leave you because you need time to have sex again."

"You are very considerate, and I appreciate it. I promise I'm okay. Honestly, I was in a lot of pain, and fading in and out. I don't remember much." I confess.

"Your body might remember." Wash pauses and I'm afraid he will reject me. "If you want sex, I will happily oblige. If you need to stop, you let me know." Wash says as he gently helps lay down before taking the blankets off.

"Help me get out of my clothes, Sir?" I ask as my free hand goes to my sleep shorts. I'm not wearing panties as it was more comfortable while I was healing.

"As you wish, Doll." Wash replies with his award winning smile.

Wash helps me take my sleep shorts off as well as my tank top and the sling. I don't have to be in it all the time, just most of the time. He's careful as he plants kisses along my wounded shoulder before he gets off the bed briefly to undress. Wash climbs back on the bed, and on top of me. He's careful to make sure he's not hurting me as he sweetly goes back to kissing every inch of my body. It's loving and sweet. Wash is normally a little on the rough side, which I certainly love. However, this time Wash is being careful and gentle. I need him to be, and he knows that. Wash is holding back his intensity level because he cares and that's exactly why I'm comfortable enough to do this.

Wash moves his head between my legs before parting my legs gently. He kisses me down there before his tongue finds my clit. Pleasure spreads through my body as a float to cloud nine with Wash's expert tongue swirling around my clit. Fuck, he is good at this. Wash gently inserts two fingers inside of me as he slowly pumps them in and out. I'm sore, but I know that's why he's doing this. His fingers are making me ready for his cock, and I need it because Wash is certainly not small. He's also making me incredibly wet.

I naturally start moving my hips to the rhythm of Wash's tongue. Whatever soreness I was feeling is replaced by the hazy pleasure Wash is putting me in. My orgasm explodes, slamming me with intense pleasure. Wash positions his cock at my entrance as his lips land on mine. I love tasting myself on him.

Wash slowly enters me, and I love the way he feels. He's the only man I ever want to touch me. Wash erases everything bad that was ever done to me sexually. It doesn't matter what was done because he loves me anyway. Damaged, broken, and stronger for it. Wash moves slowly inside of me as he kisses me. I know that he's holding back his desire to fuck me rough and hard like he normaly does. His movements are slow and precise as if to help maintain control. Wash feels so fucking good as he slowly slides in and out of me.

"You can go faster, I need you to go faster." I beg, breaking our kiss. Yes, he feels amazing moving slowly inside of me. I can feel every inch of him filling me, and it's absolutely delicious. However, I like things faster, harder, and rougher. I know we can't go too rough, but he can go faster.

"You want me to reclaim you as mine, don't you?" Wash whispers in my ear as he slows so much I'm afraid he will stop.

"Yes, but I never stopped being yours."

"I know, but we both need this." He replies as he begins to pick up his pace before his lips come back to mine.

Wash moves faster, still being careful. I'm so lost in pleasure I don't care if I'm in a little pain. It's a nice combination that sends me right to cloud nine. I know I belong to Wash, and I wouldn't have it any other way. I love him so fucking much, and he loves me. I don't know what I would do without him. He's my rock, my guardian, and my love. Wash moves fast chasing his release as I enjoy the feel of Wash inside of me. Wash's body shakes with his orgasm before he rolls next to me. I know he doesn't want to hurt me.

I move myself very carefully to move so I can get into Wash's arm. I'm on my back as my head rests comfortably on his shoulder. "I love you, Lexi." Wash says, kissing me on the top of my forehead as his arm secures me to him.

"I love you too, Wash. How do we even begin to process Jesse being alive, let alone the monster he's become?" I question. It's the elephant in the room, and it's time we face it.

"I know it's a lot, but I think we both always knew Jesse was hiding the monster from us. He was never happy, and forever reached for some repayment for his sacrifices. Looking back, Jesse never did the right thing. He was always walking a fine line that I chose to ignore because it was easier than admitting what he was. There were so many times I wanted to walk away from our friendship because I hated who he was." Wash confess.

"Why didn't you walk away?" I ask even though I think I know the answer.

"You, Doll. I couldn't leave you totally in the hands of monsters even if I ended up doing it anyway."

"Wash, you can't blame yourself for Judy taking me away. You had to let me go because she wouldn't. She was determined to drag me down with her. I think she wanted me to pay for her sins. I don't think Jesse was lying about her affair. Wash, you did what you could, and it was more than enough to help get through the hard parts. I'm just thankful I was able to find my way back to you, and that you were still my guardian."

"We will figure out the truth together. I never stopped being your guardian, and I never will even when we are married."

"Married? I like the sound of that. First, I think we need to put this Jesse stuff behind us." I sensibly suggest.

"I agree, and we will. There's a lot of healing for both of us. Some of it is the same, and some of it is different. We are in it together, and despite Jesse's attempts to separate us, he failed. Fate or whatever is on our side. Now, how about I order us some take out, and we spend the night watching TV and enjoying one another's company. Then tomorrow we both go see Dr. Daniels to talk about Jesse, so we can move forward with our life." Wash suggests.

"Sounds like a very good plan to me. I need to shower though, and I definitely need help with it."

"Oh, I think we can make a shower happen." Wash replies with a chuckle before we both start laughing.

Wash helps me out of bed. I'm so thankful for him and our relationship. I'm glad we are facing this whole Jesse thing together. I'm glad we are talking about our future. I love the idea of being Wash's wife. I've only been picturing it since I was about fourteen. I know we have some things to do to get to that point, but I'm looking forward to it. I'm also looking forward to finding out the truth, and maybe finding a family I didn't know I had while also building one of my own. Despite how dark the past week has been, I'm hopeful for my future. I'm grateful I even have one because the harsh reality is there was a possibility Jesse was successful with his twisted plan that would have ended up with Wash burying my body. I haven't even come to terms with how close to death I could have been. There is a lot to process, and I need to process one horror show at a time. I know now that healing is possible, and I'm grateful to have love with the man of my dreams be a part of it.

Chapter 33
Lexi

It's hard to believe it's already June as the summer heat begins to overtake the entire south. The heat has been taking over since the end of April, but June is when it starts to kick in full force. By July, it's going to be so hot, you'll be able to fry an egg on the sidewalk. Summer and fall are my favorite times of year. I'm ready to sunbathe just like teenage me use to do.

The idea of relaxing on a beach or by a pool sounds nice especially with how crazy things have been. Jesse and his so called friends were sent off to prison. None of them agreed to corporate for a lesser sentence, but that didn't stop Drake and his team from trying. We recently got the news that Jesse's dad was also arrested and sent to prison. The police are slowly taking down factions of the NOMADS throughout the city, which brings me a lot of comfort.

    Turns out Judy really did have an affair on Jerry with Mario. Mario is my biological father. I've been in contact with his son, Luca. Luca has been great with helping me fill in the pieces to some of the crazy questions I have. Luca has yet to let his mom know that Mario was having an affair, but apparently Mario confessed it to Luca before he died. He even told Luca to try and find me, but Luca got distracted with running the pizzeria. After it burned down, he wasn't sure he was ready to find his long lost half sister. I get it. I wasn't sure I wanted to contact him. I didn't want to risk bringing bad news to him and his family. It's a risky choice to reach out to someone and not know if they are going to even hear you out. I was completely anxiety ridden about the whole thing, but after meeting Luca, I'm glad I did.

    I wish Mario was alive today for me to actually talk to him about being my father. I'm glad I had some time with him even if it's not exactly how I would have wanted to spend time with my real father. At least, I had some time with him. I have good memories of Mario. It's still a shock that he's my bio dad. A good shock I might add. It's been a lot to process, along with everything with Jesse.

Wash and I have been seeing Dr. Daniels about Jesse. We have some sessions together, while others are individual. Wash and I have stuck together through this rough time. We have been having a lot of sex, lots of amazing sex. After we confessed our love to one another and had sex, it took a few weeks for us to get back to it. I needed to fully heal up, and I did. As of right now, I don't need surgery but I do need physical therapy. My range of motion with my shoulder isn't great. With me feeling much better physically, we are at it like rabbits.

I do have a not so pretty scar on my left shoulder. I have few other lesser scars that will eventually fade for the most part. Wash suggested I cover up my nasty scar with a tattoo, which I loved. Wash has a tattoo on his right upper arm. It's of a blazing fire with two axes behind a fire helmet with his station number. He got it to honor the brothers he's lost along the way in his career as a firefighter. I haven't decided what I want to do to cover it up. Wash suggested I draw something up. I'll decide eventually. Wash talked about getting a tattoo with me, and he wants me to draw it up if I desire. I like the idea of Wash having ink on his body that I drew. I'll definitely figure out something.

Wash ended up leaving fire investigations and is currently teaching at the academy while buying houses and fixing them up with his impressive carpentry and construction skills. After everything that went down with him and Hunter, and then adding Jesse's whole thing, Wash needed a new change. One that makes him happy. Wash isn't fully ready to let go of being a firefighter, which is why he's teaching at the academy. However, he needed something else. Something that is just his, and I understand that because that's how I feel about my art.

As for Wash and his friends, they have slowly reconciled their differences. They all feel incredibly bad for misjudging me. I haven't been able to bring myself to go back to the bar and reconcile with his friends. I'm not ready for it. I need to work on myself and make sure I'm in a good spot mentally and emotionally before I face Wash's friends. I know they want to apologize and make things right. I want to make things right with them, and I will, when I'm ready. For now, they have to respect that I need time.

I know they are going to feel bad for me, and I just don't want any more pity right now. I get it from a lot of people these days. There was an article about what happened. It's not every day a cop fakes his death to join a gang then six years later, abducts his sister to murder her. Wash and I declined giving any statements to the newspaper, but that didn't stop them from running the article. I know Wash's friends pity me. Also I'm angry that it took something so horrible to get them to give me a chance. Now, I'm just a victim to them, and I don't know if I can face that right now. I know they won't always see me that way, but everything is far too raw and fresh to face whatever pity they might toss my way.

Even for Wash it took him well over a month to talk to any of them. I think they understood he needed space. Wash was furious at them and probably still is. He's been going to Fireball once a week for a couple of hours to see his friends. I also believe Wash needs to repair things with his friends first before I can make peace with them. They fucked up, and they fucked up hard. Some harder than others, but they all gave me a hard time for no reason. I am glad Wash is repairing things with his friends. I never wanted them to be at odds, especially because of me. I'm glad they have come around even if it took an attempted murder to do so.

The library, Cool Beans, and many of the places Jesse burnt down have rebuilt or are in the process of rebuilding. Cool Beans offered me my job back, but I declined since I'm not ready to work after everything that happened. I volunteered at the newly built library. I've been focusing on my art. I've just about finished my anime portrait of Wash and I. I can't wait to give it to him for his birthday next month. I've been pouring so much of my heart and soul into my art. It's been so therapeutic. I've even gotten a few commissions that I've worked on. Volunteering at the library combined with working on my art makes me want to write and illustrate kids books. I might start working on something soon. I just don't know what the story is yet, but I'm confident inspiration will strike.

It feels good moving on from my past, and finding my footing in the present. Moving forward is hard in some ways. It's hard trying to forget about Jesse and our mom. They are both rotting away in prison. They are paying for their poor choices. It's unfortunate that some of us had to suffer in the process, but in the end justice was served.

The best part is I'm moving forward with Wash. I might have been through dark times, but I have Wash as an end result, and that makes it worth it. I'm enjoying watching our love flourish and grow into something wonderful. Sometimes the darkness leads us right where we need to be. I'm thankful I don't have to face the darkness on my own anymore.

Chapter 34
Wash

I can't believe my birthday is around the corner. My birthday is a couple of days after the Fourth of July. My birthday is often celebrated at family BBQs at the beach. My parents own a beach house, and they would have guests for the day at the beach house. There would be a huge bonfire, BBQ food for days, volleyball games going, drinks, and one giant happy birthday cake for me. I haven't been to one of those family celebrations in years. I think the last time I went I was with Kate, so it's been awhile.

    A lot has changed since then. For starters, I'm with Lexi and very much in love with her. I know I'm going to marry her when the time is right. Jesse is alive and in prison, which I still can't fully wrap my head around. I'm not sure I'll ever be able to fully wrap my head around it. Talking with Dr. Daniels certainly helps to process the crazy.

Even though I have reconciled things with Hunter and the rest of the guys, I decided to leave fire investigations. Honestly, after a crazy ass case involving my dead best friend, I was not where I needed to be. I was always questioning if moving to fire investigations was the right move, but Hunter convinced me it was. Hell, I convinced myself it was the right move because I didn't want to admit I was ready to move on from being a firefighter. I still haven't fully given it up. I teach a couple of classes at the academy, but I'm moving on to something else in the process. Something that brings me happiness; fixing up houses that are left in bad condition. I can turn them into something worthy. Who knows maybe I will find a house to fix up for Lexi and I. We aren't going to be able to stay in the townhouse forever. I know eventually we'll move out of the city. I think we both need a fresh start somewhere, but I don't think that will happen until we get married.

I have to admit the thought has been on my mind a lot lately to propose to Lexi. Shit, I went ring shopping the other day. I almost bought something that I thought Lexi would love, but I didn't buy it because it wasn't exactly right. I might have to custom do the ring, but I did only look once. I didn't put this much thought into Kate's engagement ring. I bought the first ring I thought looked nice. I didn't really care if it was special because I didn't truly want to be with her. I caved under the pressure that was put on me to tie the knot, except it was with the wrong person. This time, I'm going to take my time to pick a ring, and plan out something special and romantic for Lexi.

I'm on my way home from teaching a class at the academy. Lexi should also be on her way home from the library. I'm glad she is back to volunteering as she slowly finds her footing in what she wants to do. She's been hard core working on her art, which is great. I have to be honest I was afraid she might shut down after what happened. Not that I would blame her if she did. She lived through a nightmare. However, Lexi is strong and a fighter. She's even gotten a few commissions from friends at the library.

Lexi still hasn't made amends with my friends. I'm not rushing her because I know they did her wrong. To be honest, it was hard for me to forgive them. Hunter took a lot longer. I'm not sure I've totally forgiven him. I'm trying to not blame him for what happened to Lexi because ultimately it's Jesse's fault for what happened. Still, Hunter pushing that Lexi was the arsonist and putting stress on Lexi and me only helped Jesse get away with his shit longer. It's hard to not place some blame, even if it's a little irrational.

One nice thing that has come out of this crazy case is reconnecting with Drake properly. The whole event of Jesse not being dead has bonded us into some strange friendship. Turns out Drake and I have a lot in common. More than we ever realized. Drake also has a girlfriend so the possibility of a double date in the future is likely. Drake has even gotten to know Lexi a bit and they seem to have their own bond now.

As I pull in the driveway to park, my phone rings. I look at it. It's my mom. It's not quite my birthday, so I don't know why she would be calling. I pick up the phone out of curiosity. "Hey, Mom." I greet

"Hey, Son. How are you doing? We read about what happened in the papers. Jesse is alive and in a gang. I mean who would have thought?" My mom immediately word vomits. I shake my head, she has no idea how to talk about serious things at least with me.

"Yeah, it's insane, but we are coping in healthy ways." I answer, surprised my parents would call to check on us. I didn't really think they cared that much, maybe I was wrong.

"That's good to hear. Look, Washington, I know we didn't approve of you dating Lexi before. However, we've had a change of heart about the whole thing. We wanted to invite you and Lexi to the beach house for Fourth of July. Stay the week for your birthday. We can celebrate like old times, and maybe get to know the woman in your life." My mom sincerely offers.

"Uh, wow. Yeah, we can make it. It will be nice to see you guys." I answer. I know I should probably double check with Lexi about going, but even she knows it's not like my parents to offer an olive branch like this. I think she will understand.

"Sounds wonderful. We will see you on the third at the beach house. I will have your room made ready for you two."

"Thanks Mom. See you then." I say before hanging up the phone.

I head inside to tell Lexi the good news because my parents inviting us to the beach house is huge. My parents haven't attempted to celebrate my birthday in years. Usually they call, and send me a fancy gift that I don't need. Typically, it's an expensive bottle of liquor or wine. I can't believe they are willing to get to know Lexi as my girlfriend. It's exciting that they are making this move. It's huge, and I can tell they are sincere. I hate that it took something horrible to happen to get them to change their minds and hearts, but I'll take it.

It's a shame it also took my friends so long to come around, and that something bad had to happen for them to also change their minds. I wish they were more accepting of Lexi in the beginning because it would make it easier for her to make amends with them. I hope she is okay. I agreed to go to the beach house without asking her. I was so excited that my parents asked us both to come, I couldn't help but say yes. I do love my family even if they often make me feel like the black sheep.

Heading inside I don't see Lexi in the kitchen so I head to the living room. I'm excited to tell Lexi the news, I'm actually excited to go to the beach house. However, my excitement dies down a bit when I find Lexi curled up in a ball on the couch looking a little pale. She has saltine crackers and ginger ale on the coffee table.

"Doll? Are you alright?" I ask, kneeling beside the couch.

Lexi groans. "I was feeling fine when I woke up. I was a little nauseous, but I thought I was just hungry or something. I tried to eat but I couldn't keep it down. I never made it to the library because of how icky I feel. I guess I caught some bug."

I can't help the smile that comes to my face. Of course, Lexi would think she caught a bug.

"Lexi, Love, are you sure it's not something else? You turned your nose at the chicken sandwiches we had for lunch yesterday, you've been really tired, and this isn't the first time you've been nauseous in the last week."

"I don't know. Maybe it's the flu," I can't help but laugh. She's not getting what I'm hinting at. I've had my suspicions for a couple of weeks now. I don't even think Lexi realizes she's late. I only picked up on it because I'm a paramedic and firefighter, I have seen my fair share of pregnant women in various stages. I also remember when my sister was pregnant with her first. She was sick, tired, and food aversions were strong. "Why are you laughing at me?" Lexi tries to fake insulted, but she's too sick to make it convincing.

"Doll, you're late by about two weeks." I inform her.

"Wait, you know my period cycle?" Lexi asks in disbelief.

"A good boyfriend does. You never realized how when you're on your period wine, chocolate, ice cream, and salty things appear?" I raise an eyebrow at her.

Lexi giggles before she groans looking like she might puke. "I'm well aware of my cravings when I have my period.

You are sweet for noticing." Lexi pauses as she bites her bottom lip before she asks the question I already know the answer to. "Do you think I'm pregnant?"

"I do, which is why I bought a pregnancy test a couple of days ago. It's upstairs in the bathroom when you are ready to take it." I say, rubbing her arm.

"Wash, do you want a baby?" Lexi questions as fear fills her eyes.

Shit, she must be having some PTSD to Jerry's reaction to wanting to abort her. That was never an easy pill for her to swallow. I remember when Jesse explained to her what an abortion was. She was about twelve. I was there as moral support for both of them because it wasn't an easy conversation to have. I think on some level Lexi understood prior to Jesse's little chat about it with her. Having it confirmed destroyed her on levels only I saw.

My hand cups her check in a caring way. "I promise, I want this baby. Especially, if the baby is with you. We haven't been using protection since we started having sex. It was bound to happen. Look, take the test, and then we will go to the doctor. You aren't alone in this." I kiss her on forehead.

"Okay." She agrees, slowly sitting up.

"Hey, before you take the test, there's something I want to tell you. My parents invited us to the beach house for Fourth of July and to celebrate my birthday. I said yes because they want to get to know you and give you a fair shot as my girlfriend. They saw the news, and they feel bad. It's pretty huge that they asked. They've never offered an olive branch like this before."

"I know. We can go, but you will probably have to help me hide the fact that I can't drink alcohol, and well everything else." We both laugh.

"I will. Okay, let's take this test." I say, helping her off the couch.

Lexi makes it upstairs to pee on the pregnancy test. Sure enough she's pregnant. We both are excited and processing now that it's real. It's definitely making me want to head to the jewelry store and buy a ring. I will do it soon. Lexi needs time to accept that she is going to be a mom while still processing everything else that's happened.

I'm glad she is willing to go to the beach house. We even talked about her coming to Fireball when we get back. I know my friends are going to want to celebrate my birthday. I'm happy Lexi wants to make amends with my friends. We agreed to keep the pregnancy to ourselves until we are out of the first trimester. I will help Lexi keep the pregnancy on the down low until we are ready to officially announce. Life is turning around to a positive rainbow after a dark storm.

Chapter 35
Lexi

I'm packing for our trip to Wash's family's beach house. We are going for a week. We leave the day after Wash's birthday. His sister, her hubby, and two kids will be there, so I will finally get to meet them. We aren't sure if we are going to tell his family about the baby. I still haven't fully wrapped my head around the fact that I'm pregnant. I never even thought about it happening. Wash is right, we didn't use protection. We didn't feel the need to use protection. We have gone several months having hot, passionate sex. I guess it was bound to happen.

To be honest, pregnancy never even crossed my mind. I was enjoying having sex and replacing all the bad shit I've experienced sexually. I was chasing the high of really amazing sex with my dream guy. I love Wash so much, and I am happy to be having his child. Having a family and getting married was something I never really thought about. Occasionally, I would day dream about having a family and marrying Wash, which is now more of a reality than a day dream.

We went to the doctors already. I'm almost two months along. I can't believe I never even noticed I was late. I guess with everything that happened my mind is still lost trying to process. I can't believe Wash realized that I was late, and that he knows my period schedule better than me. Of course he does. He's a firefighter and a paramedic. He's trained to pay attention to these things. Plus, Wash cares enough to know these things. I had realized when I was on my period there were extra goodies for me. I figured it was Wash's subtle way of comforting me, knowing my periods tend to make me emotional, and sometimes horny. We have had sex on my period a couple of times since the first time we did it. I wonder what pregnancy is going to be like. I've already noticed my sex drive is up with the added hormones.

I'm a little nervous for our trip, but I'm going to focus on enjoying myself. It's the beach and what I'm sure is a gorgeous beach house. Wash has promised seriously good food, and maybe a boat ride if my morning sickness allows. I forgot Wash has his boating license and can take out his parents boats. I love the idea of it, I'm just not sure my morning sickness will love it. Wash got me ginger drops that help a lot. My hot firefighter, paramedic is taking very good care of me. I know I'm in very good hands with Wash.

I am happy Wash's parents reached out. I know Wash does love his family, even if he is the black sheep. It will be nice to have this weekend with his family. After that, it's his friends turn to make amends. It's time to clear the air and put shit in the past. I won't be the divide between Wash and his friends or family. I just needed some time to process things, and I'm ready now to face them. Dr. Daniels has been helping me get ready for this. I'm ready. Somehow, I feel even more ready now that I'm pregnant. Still, a shock, but a good shock.

Being a mom is an interesting and appealing thought. I know I'll be good at it because Judy literally taught me everything not to do. Plus, I'll have Wash as a strong person to parents with. I guess I'll eventually have to do an anime drawing of us as parents. I finished Wash's drawing a couple of weeks ago. I'm packing it now. I can't wait to give it to him. It's us drawn as anime characters set in our favorite anime. I think he's going to fucking love it. I got it framed and wrapped it in a box with a bow. I can't wait to see his handsome face light up like a Christmas tree when he opens it.

I finish packing, and then head to make dinner. Wash is teaching a class, and finishing up a construction project before we leave. Wash helped me turn one of the guest rooms into a bigger art studio for me, which I love. It's filled with plenty of art supplies. The other guest room we will eventually turn into the nursery that's if we don't move before then. I think we both are itching to get out of the city after everything that's happened. That's why this beach vacation is a great idea. I'm looking forward to sunshine, sand, the ocean, and relaxing. Relaxing is what this soon to be mama needs. I even brought some art supplies so I could draw while I'm there. The best part is I get to celebrate the man I love with his family. Before we know it we will be celebrating our baby.

Chapter 36
Wash

Lexi and I are heading to my parents' beach house. It's going to be a fun time away, something we both need. I have been reassured by my parents they will be well behaved. Lexi doesn't know but I told them about her being pregnant and that they can not stress her out. We are coming to relax. They were very happy about another grand baby and promised they want nothing more than to welcome Lexi into our family. They know that I will propose to her soon enough. They might think it's because she is pregnant, but I was already thinking about it before we found out.

My family knows to not say anything to Lexi about the baby because I want her to tell them when she is ready. I only told them so they wouldn't stress her out. She needs to relax and take it easy. I don't care if people think I'm babying her. She is mine to protect and now I'm not just protecting her but our baby too. Lexi recently experienced a nightmare. While it was months ago, and her body had healed, her mind and emotions are another thing. Mental and emotional strain can be just as dangerous as physical. I know Lexi is strong, and I know she will keep herself healthy not just for herself but for our baby.

I'm letting Lexi process the baby before I spring an engagement on her too. I don't know when I'll propose. I still need to buy a damn ring. I will find the right one. I'm tempted to let Lexi go ring shopping with me. I can't decide if I should surprise her or let her help me pick it out. I'll have to try to feel her out. Most of her focus has been on the baby since we found out, and I'm okay with that.

My family's beach house comes into view. It's a large beach like mansion with ten bedrooms, eight bathrooms, a large kitchen, living room, a game room, and even a mini movie theater. It's very much like the house I grew up in except that house was a restored old southern manor that my parents turned into their personal project for many years. They added additions and their own touches over the years.

My sister and her family live down the road in a house they built.

I park my car, and we get out just as my family comes out to greet us. They hug us both before we all head inside. I take our stuff to our room while my mom and sister give Lexi a tour. I shake my head as the two of them show Lexi around like she's the newest addition to our family. She is, but only my family can go from being judgmental pricks to sweet, accepting human beings. I'm just happy they are being accepting before the baby comes. It will be nice to share this with them.

After I set our stuff in our room, I head to find Lexi who is sitting comfortably on one of the loungers on the balcony that overlooks the beach and ocean. My mom and sister are talking with Lexi as they sit on the other loungers. My sister's kids are playing on the beach with their dad. My dad is starting up the grill. My dad loves to grill and smoke things. I'm sure there will be smoked brisket and other BBQ goodness over the next week. My father might be a highly respected political campaign manger, but the man loves BBQ and comfort food. His food tastes are so different from what you would think they would be.

Lexi smiles at me, and I notice she has a water in her hand. I've been on her about hydrating in the heat while pregnant. I smile back at her before making my way over to my dad who is sticking some sausage links, clams, and corn on the cob on the grill. I also notice he's got steak cut into cubes marinating nearby with chopped up veggies, so that means kabobs are on the menu.

My dad hands me a beer from the cooler. I pop the cap off and lean against the railing near the grill while my dad cooks. "I'm glad you two came, Washington. It's been far too long since we've had the whole family together like this." My dad prompts with a silly smile. At heart, my dad is a family man, unfortunately, it tends to get buried under the superficial stuff.

"Yeah, it's been a while for sure. I'm happy you guys reached out." I reply, taking a sip of my beer as I enjoy the sea breeze.

"Well, Lexi might not be the one we would have picked for you, Son, but she makes you happy. That's what matters. Lexi is a nice girl, and she's clearly a fighter. I won't lie, your mother and I are very happy to hear you are working your way out of the fire department. We like you alive."

"I know. It's time for a change. I've been working on flipping houses. I'm doing the work myself just like Grandpa Grant taught me." I inform him.

Dad chuckles. "You two had way too much fun building furniture. I think you two furnished his home when he downsized after your grandmother passed away. I never had my father's hands on skills to be a carpenter or even do any remodeling. You two were two peas in a pod. He was also a rebel and didn't want anything to do with politics. I guess everyone can't follow the family tradition of politics. It's good to have some black sheep." Dad says as he nudges me.

"I'm glad you finally see it that way, Dad. I never rebelled against what you wanted for me to be a dick. I simply wanted my own path." I reply.

"I know, Son. As you will soon find out that sometimes being a parent isn't easy. You are going to want what's best for your children, and sometimes you will think they are making mistakes when they aren't because it's not the plan you want for them." I nod my head. Leave it to my dad to be Mr. Understanding now. For all my parents' irrational judging, they can also be understanding. "By the way, I am sorry about Jesse. I know you two were close like brothers. I'm sorry to hear he turned out to be a bad apple. What he did to Lexi was beyond terrible."

"Thanks, Dad. It's been hard, but we are getting through it together. It's certainly something to process." I reply. Some days I don't even know how to process the whole Jesse thing. If anything Jesse led me to Lexi, and for that I will always be grateful to him even if he is psychopath.

My dad and I keep talking while he grills. I get my love of cooking from my dad. He taught me how to grill when I was a teen. It was one of the ways he chose to bond with me. I took it in other directions learning various cooking styles and even baking. I have a feeling Lexi and I will be teaching our kids to cook.

Fourth of July comes and we have a fun time. Lexi is able to get out on the boat. We certainly enjoyed ourselves. We ate way too much BBQ, and at the end of the night we all watched fireworks over the beach. It was probably the best Fourth I've had in years. I have to admit I was hesitant to come, but I'm glad we did. Lexi and I even officially told my family about the baby. Lexi figured they knew, and wasn't mad that I told them. She understood I didn't want her stressed out.

A couple of days later it's my birthday. Lexi and I go back out on the boat for a bit. Jesse and I used to go fishing on my boat. A boat my dad bought me for my twenty-first birthday. There are memories of Jesse everywhere. The memories are bittersweet and sometimes fill me with some serious anger. I'm learning to work through the waves of anger that consume me where Jesse is concerned. I rest easy knowing his ass is rotting in jail.

We end the day with cake before my sister and her family head back home. My parents are leaving in the morning, so Lexi and I will have sometime here by ourselves before we head back. We both are looking forward to it. I'm going to plan a trip somewhere for Lexi and I before the baby comes. I think it's called a babymoon if I remember from when my sister had her kids.

Lexi and I are relaxing in our room getting ready for bed. I'm sitting up in the bed playing some mindless game on my phone when Lexi comes out of the bathroom in a sexy black lace teddy and holding a dark blue box with a silver bow on it.

"Happy Birthday, Mr. Guardian or should I say Lieutenant or Sir?" She says with a seductive grin as she saunters over to the bed.

"Doll, what are you up to, and you did not buy me a gift." I state trying to hide my curiosity.

"Your assumption that I purchased your gift is incorrect, Mr. Guardian." Lexi replies as she hands me the box before hoping on the bed next to me. Her shoulder is pretty much healed at this point and she just finished physical therapy a few weeks ago.

I don't even reply to her comment because she is right, I did make an assumption. Also my dick is already rock hard with her in that black lace teddy. I'm so fucking her after I open her gift. Opening the box I find a drawing Lexi did. It's us as anime characters in our favorite anime. She had it framed. I don't even know what to say because it's incredibly beautiful and thoughtful. I don't think anyone has ever given me such a meaningful gift before.

"This is perfect Lexi. Thank you so much, Doll." I say kissing her on the lips.

"It better be, I spent months working on it." Lexi jokes, breaking our kiss.

"This is going on display somewhere. Seriously, I love it. I don't think anyone has ever given me something so thoughtful and beautiful. You have a serious talent. I'm so glad you are pursuing you dream with your art."

"We are both pursuing what we love. I know slowly taking steps away from the UCFD is hard for you, but you are rekindling your love for something I know you enjoy. Now, do you want to unwrap your other gift?" Lexi asks, gesturing to herself.

"Oh, it's my favorite gift to unwrap." I reply, setting Lexi's gift on the nightstand before I roll on top of her, putting my arms on either side of her head so I can lift my body weight off her.

I stare into Lexi's beautiful eyes as she runs her fingers through my hair. Fuck, I love this woman. My lips fall onto hers ready to devour her. If I wasn't convinced before that this woman is my other half, well, I'm convinced now. I've never felt like this about anyone before in my life. To be honest, I never would have thought I would have met my soulmate the way I did. While I may have never looked at Lexi like my little sister growing up, I didn't imagine she would turn out to be so much more than Jesse's little sister.

"It's your birthday, Sir. I know you like control in the bedroom, and I love giving it to you. However, I want to pleasure you." Lexi says, breaking our kiss.

"Oh, and what did you have in mind?" I question, raising an eyebrow.

"That's for me to know, and for you to find out. Now, can you strip and sit in that chair over there." Lexi directs as she points to the navy blue sitting chair in the corner with a matching foot rest.

"Yes, Doll. Who I am to argue with you when you look sexy as sin." I reply, getting off her and heading over to the chair, but not before I strip my boxers off. Tossing my boxers somewhere on the floor I take a seat in the chair as Lexi saunters over to me before kneeling in front of me.

Lexi gives me a sexy grin before she takes my raging hard dick into her sweet mouth. Shit, this woman knows how to make me hard without even trying, but it certainly increases when she's in something sexy. Lexi licks and sucks my cock the way I taught her I like. She has learned her lesson a little too well because fuck she is sure as shit pleasuring me. Her wicked tongue swirls around my tip before she sucks me into her mouth. My hand threads into her hair guiding her pace. Lexi might be pleasuring me, but I'm always in control even when she thinks I'm not. As much as I want to blow my load, I'm not doing it in Lexi's mouth. No, I want to do it in her fucking pussy. Besides, she can't get more pregnant.

"Alright, Doll. You have pleasured me, but I'm cumming in your pussy tonight." I assert as I pull myself from her mouth.

"As you wish, Sir. How do you want me?" Lexi replies, leaning back slightly on her knees as I let go of her hair.

"You are perfect, have I told you that?" I question as I caress her cheek.

"I don't know about perfect." She attempts to deflect, but I won't let her get away with it.

"You're perfect for me, and that's all that matters. I love you."

I sly grin crosses her beautiful face. "Wash, I have loved you for years. I'm just glad you finally caught up." She firmly states before we both laugh.

"On the bed, hands on the headboard while on your knees, Doll." I command.

Like a good girl Lexi does what she is told. She gets on the bed with her hands gripping the headboard while leaning on her knees. I get up and get behind her on the bed. I slide her teddy up. Lexi was smart to not wear any panties. A lot of these sets come with a thong, but there's never any point because it's coming off. I line my dick up with her pussy that is already wet with anticipation.

Sliding my dick into Lexi's tight pussy is like fucking coming home. I move slowly at first enjoying the way Lexi's tight walls wrap around my dick. One of my hands grips her hips while the other snakes around to her front, sliding between her legs and finding the spot that makes her moan like a goddess. I pick up my speed being careful to not slam too hard into her because she is carrying my child, which makes her that much sexier.

Lexi's moans are music to my ears as I move in and out of her enjoying every fucking feel of her. I move faster chasing my release as Lexi chases hers as her moans increase. Lexi wiggles her ass against me as walls clench around me. Fuck that feels damn good. I pick up my pace as Lexi rides the waves of her orgasm before mine explodes deep inside of her.

We crash onto the bed as we catch our breath. I pull Lexi into my arms as she moves her body so she can nuzzle her head into my chest. "Best birthday ever." I declare.

"How will I top this next year?" Lexi jokes as she snuggles closer to me.

"I believe in you. Plus, now I have to make your birthday beyond fabulous."

"I have the utmost confidence in you." She replies, and we laugh some more.

We talk a little bit about our future before we both are ready to go to sleep. Lexi enjoys sleeping more these days, which is good because she needs her rest. This trip turned out to be a good idea. My family and I seem to have put aside our differences to welcome Lexi into our family. I know they have officially welcomed her into our family because yesterday when my dad and I went out for coffee he did something I never thought he would do, something he most certainly never did for Kate. He handed me my grandmother's engagement ring. It's a rose gold ballerina halo diamond ring. He gave it to me so I could propose to Lexi, and solved my ring issue. It was the ultimate gesture to prove they truly accept her. Now, I have to figure out how to propose.

Chapter 37
Lexi

I can't believe it's October. It's my birthday month. My birthday was a few weeks ago and Halloween is next week. Wash took me on a weekend trip to the mountains where he wined and dined me. Well, non alcoholic wine. I'm about six months pregnant now, and I'm showing so everyone knows.

The news went over well with Wash's friends. We didn't tell them until I reconciled with them, and Wash waited until I felt comfortable to tell them. His friends have accepted me into their little group. It's still sometimes hard for me because of how nasty they were at first, and it's even harder when things come to Hunter because of how he falsely accused me. They all apologized, which was nice. I'm willing to move past it all because life is too short, and I can be the bigger person. I even attended Stephen and Julia's wedding with Wash, which was at the end of August. Wash and I have even become close with Drake and his girlfriend, Colleen. They have hung out at Fireball a few times. Wash and I managed to form our own sort of friend group and I have to admit it's nice.

    Jesse had his trial, which thankfully I did not have to be a witness in. The evidence was damning enough that they didn't need me. That's two family members in prison for life. Not that it matters because they are my past and my family is with Wash as is my future. Besides, I think both Wash and I still like to pretend Jesse died because it's easier to remember him as a hero than the villain in our story. I've gotten to know Luca, who is turning out to be a much better brother than Jesse. We aren't super close, but we talk often through text and we have hung out a few times. As for Wash's family, well, they seem to have fully accepted me into their family as Wash's wife even though we aren't married yet. The proposal is coming, I know it is. However, I know Wash and he will wait for the perfect moment. I honestly thought he was going to do it while we were away, but he didn't. I can be patient. I waited how many years for Wash to finally realize me? I can certainly wait for his proposal.

Wash is still teaching classes and working on his business to buy and flip houses. I'm working on building my own business for art. I'm even working on ideas for kids books. I have a feeling the ideas are going to be abundant once our baby girl is here. We wanted to find out the gender. I couldn't do the whole wait until birth to find out, and neither could Wash. We found out the first chance we got.

Tonight, we are going to a Halloween party at the bar that is also doubling as my birthday party. I told Wash he didn't have to throw me a party, but he insisted. I think it was more his friends wanting to do it to show their acceptance. I'm not going to turn it down because I never really had a party, so I'm actually excited. It's a costume party, but I'm feeling like a whale these days even if I still have three more months to go. So, I wasn't overly enthusiastic about dressing up even though I normally love it. However, Wash took matters into his own hands, and found a cosplayer who makes costumes to make us costumes like our favorite anime characters. Wash wanted to go all out, so I let him. Plus, we can wear the costumes when we go to comic con next year. Mine will need slight adjustments by then because I will not be a whale then.

When I planned on gaining weight, I didn't imagine it would be due to pregnancy. I can feel our little girl move around, and I still can't believe I'm pregnant. It's the little miracle we needed to help us move past the rough time we were having, and to help us push forward toward our future.

The party is tonight, so I'm working on getting ready. Wash will be home soon to pick me up. He's helping decorate and set things up. I was not allowed to come because it's partially my birthday party. I was also told to stay home and rest because I need it, which I do. I never imagined pregnancy would be so exhausting.

Wash comes home and gets ready, and then we head to the party. Wash is oozing confidence tonight, and I begin to wonder if he's planning to propose. Maybe I'm overthinking it, but I know Wash pretty well. The man has got something up his sleeve that's for sure with his cocky grin as we enter the bar.

The entire bar is decorated in Halloween glory, and it looks awesome. Fall is my favorite time of year, and not just because of my birthday. I enjoy summer, but nothing fully compares to fall in my book. I notice it's only Wash's friends and a few other people like Drake and Colleen. I thought the party was going to be bigger than this. Not that I care, but I don't want them to close down the bar just for me.

"The birthday girl has arrived, we can now start the party." Stephen jokes and we all laugh.

"Before we start the party, I have something special for the birthday girl." Wash declares.

"You know my birthday was a couple of weeks ago right?" I teasingly question.

"Doesn't matter, tonight we are celebrating you, but not just your birthday. We are celebrating us too," That's when Wash gets down one knee as he pulls out a ring from his pocket that is stunning. "Lexi, I'm going to keep this short because you know how much I fucking love you. This is my grandmother's ring, and there is no one I would rather give her ring to. Lexi, will you marry me?"

"I think I've waited way too long for you to ask me that question, so yes." I reply

Everyone cheers as Wash gets up, slips the ring on my finger, and then kisses me. That's when Wash walks me over to the table to show me a cake that says 'Congrats Wash and Lexi'. There's also cupcakes that say 'Happy Birthday Lexi'. Wash had his friends help him plan this. They wanted to be a part of it to show they approve and accept me. It's sweet, and

I'm happy they have changed their minds even if it took them a bit too long. Not to mention it took my insane brother abducting me and attempting to murder me, but it's water under the bridge now.

After about forty five minutes more people show up later because Wash wanted some time just for us to celebrate with our friends before others showed up. The party is a lot of fun, and I can't stop staring at the ring on my finger. I've dreamed about Wash putting a ring on my finger for years. I can't believe it actually happened, but I'm so glad it is happening. I'm also shocked when Wash told me his dad gave him his grandmother's ring to give to me. It seems everyone truly has changed their tune about Wash and I being together, which I'm grateful for. I'm happy, truly happy, and I can't wait for what the future holds.

The End

Epilogue
Wash

It's hard to believe Lexi and I are celebrating our daughter Emma's fifth birthday while her little sister Skylar turned three not too long ago. Lexi and I wasted no time getting married. We eloped shortly before Christmas. After Emma was born we had a huge reception celebration with all our friends and family. We even took our honeymoon to Japan while my parents watched Emma for us.

We moved out of the city, and to the mountains. The city was hard to live in after everything that happened with Jesse. Lexi was anxious to leave the townhouse more often than not. She almost never went out by herself because she was far too paranoid since her abduction. So, after Emma was born we moved to the mountains. My parents actually bought us our house as a wedding present. They did something similar with my sister. I still am part owner in Fireball, and we do go to the city to visit as often as we can. I have my own carpentry business that does very well where we live while Lexi takes regular commissions for her art. She also published a few children's books dedicated to our daughters.

We have both healed a lot from what Jesse did. His betrayal will always run a little deep. It's not something someone can really forget. It's one of those things you carry with you even if it's in the past. It's simply something you can't forget. We don't talk about Jesse often. He only comes up on occasion. He's this unspoken topic that almost no one brings up to us. Most people tiptoe around the whole ordeal. The only person who Lexi and I truly talk to about it is Drake. In some weird ways Drake has replaced Jesse in our life. Drake has become what Jesse should have been.

Lexi still keeps in contact with Luca. Luca never told his mom the truth, so Lexi can never really meet the rest of her family. Lexi respects Luca's choice and is happy that she can at least have a relationship with him. We still see Luca, and he is often at family events when he can make it, like today he's here celebrating Emma's birthday along with Drake and his family. Everyone from Fireball is here as well. Our rather large mountain house has become a fun place for people to come, and since it's big they can spend the night. Lexi and I have a great family and friends circle that we are close to. We might have had a rough start with some people, but everyone has moved on in a positive fashion, making for a strong group of friends and family that I wouldn't trade for anything.

Over the years, Lexi and I have managed to run into Kate sometimes when we are in the city visiting. Kate thankfully moved on with a big time lawyer, and has a son of her own. She is still petty when we run into her. She's turned it into some competition of whose life is better. That's just how Kate is. She's competitive and petty because it's a defense to hide her true feelings.

My parents and I have reconciled a lot over the last five years. It was as if something just snapped into place when they finally accepted Lexi was the woman I loved. Surprisingly, Lexi is very close to my sister, and she does things often with my mom and sister. My dad and I spend a lot more time together boating, fishing, and bonding over sports. My brother in law sometimes joins my dad and I, but he's a big time lawyer and even is a partner of one of the top law firms in the southern states. So, he's often busy, but it's nice when he joins. I'm not the black sheep anymore. We have found a rhythm that works for us, and it's been nice being able to make good memories with them.

Looking at my life now, if someone had told me that my best friend's little sister would end up being my beloved wife, I would have said you're crazy. It's not like Lexi and I are exactly close in age. We grew up together, but on different levels. When Lexi came back into my life everything snapped into place for me. She was the missing piece to my happiness. I think somewhere deep down I always knew she would be special to me. I didn't realize how special at the time. I can't picture my life without her. The family and life we have built together is the dream I never knew I wanted. I always had a version of the dream, but I never saw the entire picture until Lexi.

Of course, life has it's not so great moments, but Lexi and I face everything together, the good and the bad. We still go to Dr. Daniels when we need to. We try to do things with level heads. Even when we bicker, we don't go to bed angry. We have a beautiful and healthy relationship that we both thrive from.

Our sex life is has hot as it ever was. I don't think I'll ever grow tired of fucking her. We have had fun experimenting over the years, and exploring new things sexually. We try new things outside of the bedroom too. We enjoy doing new things with our girls. Sometimes life works out just the way it's supposed to, and when it does it's beautiful.

Printed in Great Britain
by Amazon